"Tha
he sa
shou

She be~~nds to check Gil's~~ coat as if it were simply a casual motion instead of an attempt to keep herself from stepping even closer to him.

"As I have said time and again," she said aloud, "it is wonderful to have tasks to fill my time. I will also ask the Cothaire servants to spread the word that you are looking to fill positions here. I have no doubts we will have many suitable candidates within days."

"At least until they see the sorry state Warrick Hall is in."

"Have faith, Jacob. By the time your family arrives, the house will be ready."

"Are you sure of that?"

"Absolutely," she said, even though she was not. However, she knew he needed to have faith… as she did that all would resolve itself as it should. A half sob caught in her throat, because she knew everything resolving itself as it should would mean some other woman relishing his sweet caresses.

Jo Ann Brown has always loved stories with happy-ever-after endings. A former military officer, she is thrilled to have the chance to write stories about people falling in love. She is also a photographer, and she travels with her husband of more than thirty years to places where she can snap pictures. They live in Nevada with three children and a spoiled cat. Drop her a note at joannbrownbooks.com.

Books by Jo Ann Brown

Love Inspired Historical

Matchmaking Babies

Promise of a Family
Family in the Making
Her Longed-For Family

Sanctuary Bay

The Dutiful Daughter
A Hero for Christmas
A Bride for the Baron

Visit the Author Profile page at Harlequin.com.

JO ANN BROWN

Her Longed-For Family

HARLEQUIN® LOVE INSPIRED® HISTORICAL

Recycling programs
for this product may
not exist in your area.

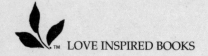 LOVE INSPIRED BOOKS

ISBN-13: 978-0-373-28341-5

Her Longed-For Family

Hearken to me, ye that follow after righteousness,
ye that seek the Lord:
look unto the rock whence ye are hewn,
and to the hole of the pit whence ye are dug.
—*Isaiah* 51:1

For Greg and Marcia Rose

Thanks for making us feel so at home in your home.
It's always a special treat.

Chapter One

Porthlowen, North Cornwall
November 1812

Jacob Warrick pushed his spectacles up on his nose as he followed a footman and wished he could be anywhere else. Not that his surroundings were not pleasant. In Cothaire, the great house overlooking Porthlowen Cove, elegant furniture and artwork filled the hallway. The walls were not pocked with chipped paint. No dust or wet stains created strange scents in the corridor. Servants moved in an easy, efficient rhythm through the home, doing tasks needed to keep the Trelawney family in comfort.

Everything was exactly as the manor belonging to the Earl of Launceston should be.

Everything was the complete opposite of Warrick Hall, his estate.

Until last night, he had not been bothered by the sorry condition of the house he had inherited from his uncle, along with the title of Lord Warrick. He had easily looked past the peeling wall coverings and the definite stench of mildew. Instead, he had focused on safety at the estate's mines. His uncle had apparently paid as little attention to maintenance at the mines as he had at his house.

Jacob had intended to repair the ancient manor house someday…until the letter arrived from Beverly Warrick, his stepmother, announcing she and his brother, Emery, and Emery's wife, Helen, would be arriving at Warrick Hall to spend Christmas with him. It was not until the final line of her excited note that she had mentioned Helen's sister, Miss Faye Bolton—in his stepmother's opinion, a well-polished young woman—would be traveling with them.

He knew exactly what those few words meant. His stepmother was not satisfied with having arranged the marriage of her niece Helen to his brother. She intended to wed her other niece to him.

Understanding that had set him to pacing his bedchamber all night. One of the great advantages of moving to Cornwall, far from the rest of his family, was he could escape his stepmother's meddling. Ignoring her was impossible, and resisting her plans created an uproar. He should have guessed his new title would attract her interference in his life like a hound to the fox's scent. And she would be as persistent as a dog on the trail of its prey.

He had no time for courting. In his few spare moments, he had begun the arduous task of writing a textbook on engineering for mine operators. He had considered himself a skilled engineer after years of study and teaching, but many aspects of tin mining surprised him. Once he completed the manuscript, he would have the book printed. The profits from its sales would allow him to continue updating the mines. That would save lives, for conditions at the estate's mines when he had arrived in Cornwall last year had been deplorable. Two years ago, a half dozen miners had died. He prayed every night the miners would emerge from underground alive the next day. So far, his prayers had been answered, but he was determined to make the mines as safe as possible.

Finding a wife was a task everyone expected he must put his mind to at some point. The title, along with its obligation of assuring that it continued in their family, coming to him was like a cruel joke. How could he risk suffering that grief another time? After Virginia Greene had died, he had vowed never to fall in love again.

Yet, even if he wanted to marry, his concentration now must be fully on replacing the out-of-date equipment at the mines. Since he had started updating the machinery, fewer men had been hurt and none had died in the depths of the Warrick mines. He did not want anyone else to die because of his negligence.

That had been his plan, but now everything had changed. One look at Warrick Hall would confirm his stepmother's belief he was in desperate need of a wife.

Immediately.

Even a single breach of etiquette would provide the proof his stepmother needed to show he was unprepared to find a proper baroness on his own. Without a doubt, she was already convinced, which was why she was providing him with the "well-polished" Miss Faye Bolton. The description made him think of a glossy table rather than a wife. A wife who could die as Virginia had because of his carelessness.

He had tried to tell his stepmother the truth about that horrible night. Or at least what he knew of it, because his memories were unreliable in the wake of the injury he had sustained. She refused to listen. She insisted on calling it an unfortunate accident. She was wrong, and he would not endanger another young woman who was foolish enough to fall in love with him and believe his promise she was always safe with him.

There was only one solution. Jacob needed to have Warrick Hall—or, at the very least, the parts of it any guests might see—meet his stepmother's exacting standards by the time of her arrival. That way, he could show he did not need a wife straightaway.

He could scrape together funds for repairs, but where to begin and what to do? Those questions had kept him awake, and he hoped he would find the answer at Cothaire.

The footman stopped by a closed door Jacob recognized. The room beyond it overlooked the back garden and was small enough to be cozy. He had been in the informal parlor the last time he had called at Cothaire. Then he had come seeking the Trelawneys' assistance in finding a child he believed had been abducted from his estate. The missing child had been found unharmed and returned to her family. All had ended well.

His mouth tightened as the footman placed a knock on the door and waited for an answer. He forced himself to relax. He could not greet the earl's older daughter, Lady Caroline, with such a grumpy expression. Most especially when he was about to ask her to grant him a very large favor. He was not accustomed to asking others to help solve his problems.

The footman opened the door, stepped aside to let

Jacob enter, then followed him in. Puzzled why the servant was shadowing him and clearing his throat quietly, Jacob glanced across the room to where Lady Caroline waited by the hearth. The light from the flames danced with blue lights off her sleek, black hair. Her neat bun accented her high cheekbones and crystal-blue eyes. She wore a simple yellow gown beneath a fringed paisley shawl draped over her shoulders. As nearly every time he had seen her, a baby girl was not far away. The infant and a little boy were on the rug in front of the fireplace.

"Good morning, my lady," Jacob said, pushing his spectacles up his nose again after bowing his head toward her. "I appreciate you receiving me when I arrived without an invitation."

The footman cleared his throat again, this time a bit louder.

Had Jacob said something wrong? Already? He hoped the heat rising from his collar did not turn his face crimson. He seldom blushed, but when he did, there was no hiding it.

That was why he preferred speaking plainly as he had while teaching math and science at Cambridge. Unlike Lady Caroline, who was poised and never seemed to say the wrong word, he had the manners of a man who had spent most of his life with his nose in a book and his fingers upon some piece of machinery.

Another deficiency his stepmother had put on her litany of the faults that would keep him a bachelor unless she stepped in to provide him with a bride.

"By this time, you should know our neighbors are always welcome at Cothaire, my lord." Lady Caroline smiled, and the room lit up as if it were the sunniest summer afternoon instead of a chilly November morn. She walked gracefully to a chair near where the baby slept while the little boy played with wooden blocks. Sitting, she asked, "Will you join us here by the fire?"

"Thank you." He took a single step, then halted when the footman cleared his throat again.

When Jacob glanced back, the liveried man repeated too quietly for Lady Caroline to hear, "Ahem!" Did the man have something stuck in his throat?

"My father will be sorry he is not here to speak with you himself," Lady Caroline said.

"If this is not a good time—"

"Nonsense. As I said, you should always consider our door open, my lord." Again she motioned for him to join her by the fire, then reached down to check the little girl. The baby had opened her eyes and stared at him sleepily. Lustrous curls topped her head.

"She has grown so big!" he said.

That brought an even warmer smile from Lady Caroline. "Yes, Joy is thriving at last. Just as Gil is." She stretched to ruffle the little boy's brown hair. "All six of the children have settled in well, whether here or at the parsonage with my brother or with my sister on the other side of the cove."

The Trelawneys, from the earl to his four children, had taken six abandoned waifs into their hearts after the children were discovered floating in a rickety boat in the cove. The family had never stopped looking for the children's parents, even though he guessed it would be a sad day when the Trelawneys had to return the children.

The footman cleared his throat yet again.

About to ask the man to stop making the annoying

sound or take his leave, Jacob realized he still wore his greatcoat and carried his hat. Even he was familiar enough with propriety to know the footman had expected to take them upon Jacob's arrival. He hastily shrugged off his coat and handed it and his hat to the servant, who had the decency not to smile.

He turned his gaze to Lady Caroline. He needed to obtain her help. She was the perfect choice, and not only because she had taken on the task of overseeing Cothaire after her mother's death five or six years ago. From what he had heard, she had no interest in remarrying since her husband's death around the same time, though he suspected such a lovely, gentle-hearted woman had many offers. She treated Jacob with respect but had not flirted with him during their previous conversations. Because of that, he was willing to ask her this favor. Another woman might see his request as a prelude to a courtship.

Stepping carefully around the children, Jacob went to where she sat primly. He lifted her slender hand from the chair's arm and bowed over it before sitting across from her. His hope that he had handled the greeting correctly withered when he adjusted his spectacles and saw astonishment on her face. What faux pas had he made now?

He bit back the question as the little boy grinned at him, then pointed to the baby girl as he announced, "My baby!"

"Gil is very protective of Joy." Lady Caroline smiled when the baby smacked the little boy on the arm and giggled. "Though some days, I feel I should be protecting *him* from her." Her voice was soft and soothing as she bent toward the baby and said, "Do not hit Gil, Joy. You don't want to hurt him, do you?"

"Gil is a big boy," Jacob said with a smile Gil returned brightly. "He can take care of himself."

"Gil big boy." He tapped his chest proudly, then turned to Lady Caroline and repeated the words. Standing, he leaned on Jacob's knee. "Big, big boy."

"That you are, young man."

When the little boy laughed, Jacob could not help doing the same. He could not recall the last time he had a conversation with a child as young as Gil. He had been more accustomed to talking to his students at the university, and now most of his discussions were with the miners who worked on his estate.

The baby girl picked up a shiny stick from the rug and stuck it in her mouth, holding it by one end that appeared to be made of silver.

Jacob's bafflement must have been visible because Lady Caroline said, "Joy is getting her first tooth."

"And the stick helps?" he asked.

"It appears so. She chews on the coral. Because it is hard, the coral seems to give her relief from the pressure of the tooth on her gum."

"Do you have another teething stick?"

Her light blue eyes narrowed. "Yes, but why do you ask?"

"I would be interested in examining such a helpful device, but I dare not ask Joy to relinquish hers. She seems to be enjoying it far too much."

She rose and walked past him without a word. He jumped to his feet belatedly. Was she going to the nursery now? He glanced at the children playing on the floor. She was leaving him with two babies? If she knew the truth of how untrustworthy he could be when his thoughts were elsewhere...

No! He was not going to blurt out the truth. Nobody in Porthlowen knew of his past, and he intended to keep it that way. He had no worries about his family discussing the tragedy that had left his darling Virginia dead the night he proposed to her; they preferred to act as if the accident had never happened.

"My lady—"

"Yes?"

Too late, he realized Lady Caroline held a bell to call for someone to fetch the teething stick. He should have guessed, but he was too unaccustomed to having servants ready to answer any summons.

Somehow, he managed to say, "If it is an inconvenience..."

"None." She rang the bell, and the door opened in response.

While she spoke to a maid, Jacob tried to regain his composure. How she would want to laugh at him for being unsettled at the idea of being left alone with a two-year-old boy and a baby! Not that she would laugh. She was far too polite.

The maid returned moments later with another smooth stick. Lady Caroline took it, then handed it to Jacob before thanking the maid, who curtsied before leaving. As Lady Caroline went to sit by the children, Jacob examined the coral stick. The flat sides resembled a table knife.

"Fascinating concept," he said, glad to concentrate on something other than his disquiet. He ran a single finger along the smooth, cool coral. The silver handle, which was connected to a ribbon, was embossed with images of the sun and flowers and birds.

"The ribbon can be tied to a child's waist to keep the teething stick from getting lost, but my mother stopped doing that after I almost knocked an eye out with mine when I was a baby. Apparently, my cheek bore black bruises for a week."

Jacob tried to envision Lady Caroline as an infant with a black eye. The image banished his dark thoughts temporarily, and he laughed. "It sounds as if your mother was a wise woman."

"She was."

The sorrow in her voice subdued his laughter. What a fool he was! Speaking of her mother's death would remind her as well of her husband's. He knew how impossible it was to forget someone loved and lost forever. Unsure what to say, he fell back on the clichéd. "You must miss her."

"Yes." She squared her shoulders and looked at him directly. "Now tell me what has brought you to Cothaire this morning, Lord Warrick. I know you are a busy man, and I doubt this is a social call."

"I would like to ask you if… That is…" He was making a muddle of what should be a simple request. Taking a deep breath, he sat once more facing Lady Caroline and placed the teething stick on a table by his chair. He kept his voice even as he said, "I need your help."

"My help? With what?"

"Please hear me out before you give me an answer, my lady." When she nodded, words spewed from his lips before he lost the courage to say them. "My family is coming to Warrick Hall for the Christmas holiday."

"How wonderful!"

He kept his smile in place. Wonderful was not the way he would describe the visit, because his stepmother loved drama and excitement while he preferred quiet for his writing and other long hours of work. "It would be wonderful if Warrick Hall was in any condition to receive guests."

"That does present a problem, but we would be glad to have your guests stay here with us. We have plenty of room, and it is a short drive from here to Warrick Hall."

"Thank you, but my family will expect to stay at Warrick Hall."

"Of course." She paused when the baby chirped. Lifting Joy, she set the squirming baby in her lap. "Forgive me, my lord, but I am confused. Will you explain how I can help you?"

He appreciated her getting right to the point. He would do the same. "I need help in redoing Warrick Hall so it is ready for my family. I suspect there is enough furniture in the attics, but I have no idea what pieces to use or how to arrange it. Nor do I have any idea which colors to use to repaint. Will you help me?" He jabbed at his spectacles, pushing them up his nose, and held his breath.

If Lady Caroline did not agree to assist him, he had no idea where to turn next to keep his stepmother from interfering in his life with disastrous results…again.

Caroline Trelawney Dowling struggled not to grin at Jacob Warrick. The baron was not as tall as her brothers, but of above-average height. His hair was ruddy-brown, his jaw firm and his face well-sculpted. However, the first thing she always noticed was his brass spectacles slipping down his nose. When she had been told he was calling, she had never guessed he would make a request that could gratify a craving in her heart. She had been struggling in recent months not to be envious when her younger brothers and sister began creating homes of their own. She had not realized how much she wanted to do the same. Cothaire had been her responsibility for the past five years, but that changed when her brother Arthur, Lord Trelawney, had married.

Even though she would always have a place to live at Cothaire, Caroline had been shunted from her position as the great house's chatelaine. Not that Arthur's wife, Maris, was anything but the epitome of kindness. She sought Caroline's advice regularly. However, the household now looked to Maris for direction, not Caroline. It was as it should be; still, Caroline longed for a house to make into a home.

Now Lord Warrick was here with an offer for her to help him do exactly that with dilapidated Warrick Hall. Assisting him to make the old manor house comfortable for his family would show her father she should be allowed to renovate a house in the village for her, Gil and Joy. At last, she would have the snug cottage she had hoped to share with her late husband John and their children.

That dream had died along with John when his ship sank. Even before then, because she had been told by the local midwife the chances of her becoming pregnant diminished as each month passed and she did not conceive. She had continued to pray for as long as John was alive that she would someday hold their baby in her arms. Others wondered why she had not remarried in the years since his death, but how could she wed when she might never be able to give her husband a child? She had sensed John's disappointment each month, and she did not want ever to hurt someone she loved like that again. It was better she remained unmarried and found a small home of her own in the village.

She looked at Joy who took a block from Gil, then let it fall to the floor as she giggled. God had heard her prayer and brought children into her life in a way she could not have imagined. And now He was answering another prayer from deep within her heart by giving her the chance to help Lord Warrick with renovating Warrick Hall.

"I would be glad to do what I can," she said, proud how serene her voice sounded when her thoughts were whirling like a tempest.

Lord Warrick's hazel eyes widened behind his brass spectacles. "Really?"

She smiled. "Yes, really."

A flush rose from his collar. "My lady, I didn't mean to suggest you would speak anything but the truth. I admit I expected you to demur because you would be busy with holiday preparations at Cothaire."

"Our New Year's Eve gathering has been held for so many years, everyone knows what to do in preparation." She did not add that many of the tasks she had done in previous years would now be assumed by the new Lady Trelawney.

Joy cried and raised her hands. Caroline picked up the baby, who was growing rapidly and getting plump. She had guessed the baby was little more than a newborn when Joy was rescued along with five other children at the end of summer. In the past few weeks, Joy had begun to act a couple of months older than anyone had assumed. She pulled herself up on anything and anyone, and she made jabbering sounds, which had earned her the nickname of "little monkey" from Father. Soon she would start saying real words. Caroline wondered what Joy's first word would be. She secretly hoped it would be "Mama."

"When does your family arrive?" Caroline asked the baron.

"In about a month. Will that be enough time?"

"It must be, because it is all we have." She stood as the baby gave a sharp cry. Reaching for the teething stick on the table next to Lord Warrick's chair, she nearly bumped her nose into his as he came to his feet. He leaned away, and she snatched the teething stick from the table. She handed it to Joy, not looking at the baron. She hoped her face was not as red as his had been a moment ago.

Caroline froze at a distant rumble. The glass in the garden doors rattled sharply.

"What was that?" she asked as Gil jumped to his feet and ran to hide his face in her skirt.

"It sounded like thunder," Lord Warrick said, lines of bafflement threading across his forehead. "But the sky is clear."

"Storms can come up quickly at this time of year." She did not add more as Joy cried out in pain. She put the baby to her shoulder and patted Joy's back. The little girl flung aside the teething stick and began chewing on a seam along Caroline's shawl.

"One more thing, my lady," he said, clearly trying not to look at the widening spot of damp from the baby's drool on her shawl. "I have no doubts my family will wish to entertain while they are here. Because of that, I must ask another favor. Will you help me learn the niceties and duties of a host so I can avoid any mistakes that might embarrass my family?"

Caroline blinked once, then twice, then a third time. "You want *me* to teach *you* the proper graces of Society?"

"Yes, if you are willing." His unsteady smile warned her how important this request was.

Why? She wanted to ask that question but swallowed it unspoken. Lord Warrick's explanation did not ring true for her. Other than his late uncle, no member of his family was of the *ton*, so why would they expect him to know the complex intricacies of the Beau Monde when, as far as she knew, he had never been to London or even attended many gatherings in Cornwall? There must be some other, more important reason he was not sharing with her, but asking that would prove her own manners were beneath reproach.

She could think of many reasons to say no. She needed to discover the truth about the children. She needed to spend time with Joy and Gil and her family, both its longtime members and its newest ones. That was very important, because she had no idea how much longer the children would be in her life.

Withhold not good from them to whom it is due, when it is in the power of thine hand to do it. The verse from Proverbs, one of John's favorites, burst out of her memory. She had the time and ability to help Lord Warrick with both of his requests, and, to own the truth, she was thrilled to have the chance to see inside ancient Warrick Hall.

Gil took advantage of her silence to go to Lord Warrick and, grinning, hand him a wooden horse.

"Thank you, young man," the baron said.

"You welcome." Running to the other toys, Gil began piling blocks one on top of the other.

"You have taught him well," Lord Warrick said, drawing her gaze to him. "Would it be any different to teach me?"

"Of course, it would be different. He is a child."

"And I am as a child when it comes to etiquette. You have seen that yourself." He held up his hand. "You need not be polite and try to deny it, my lady. I saw the truth on your face when I made blunders upon my arrival today."

"If I made you feel uncomfortable or appeared judgmental, I am sorry."

He crowed, "There!"

"There what?" she asked, confused.

"What you said." He set the toy horse on the floor near Gil, and the little boy pretended it was galloping along a road of blocks. "Gracious and kind. I want to learn how to be as eloquent and cordial in social situations. Will you help me?"

"I will try." She did not hesitate before she went on, "May I ask you for a favor in return?"

"Whatever you wish." His words were casual, but she sensed an undertone of tension in them. What was he hiding?

"You know we are searching for the children's families and are desperate to discover why they were left in a wobbly boat."

"And by whom, so you know who was heartless," Lord Warrick said, his voice as serious as a magistrate handing down justice. "I will be happy to do whatever I can to help in the search."

She nodded, glad he understood. She could not imagine leaving six small, very active children in a tiny boat. Any of them could have tipped it over, and they would have drowned.

"Thank you." She was happy to have someone else involved in the search that had been fruitless for more than four months.

"So?"

Caroline was startled by Lord Warrick's abrupt question. "Pardon me?"

"Which lesson shall you give me first?"

"You want to start now?"

"Why not?" He gave her a grin that reminded her of Gil when the little boy was trying to wheedle her into reading him another story before bed. "Perhaps you can begin with what I should have done when I came into the room today."

"As you wish." She bent to put Joy down, but halted when the floor rocked under her feet.

Thunder erupted around her. So loud she could not hear the baby cry, even though the little girl's open mouth was close to her ear. Gil threw himself against her. His small hands grasped her skirt again, holding on as if for his very life.

Broader hands tugged her to the floor that spasmed beneath her. Lord Warrick! He gripped the chair beside her with both hands. His arms surrounded her and the children.

The cacophony receded enough to let her hear the children's frightened shrieks. She gathered them both closer to her, wanting to shield them from whatever was happening.

A warm breath brushed her ear. She started to turn her head, but a firm hand clasped her chin, holding her in place as Lord Warrick warned, "Wait. It may not be over."

Was he shouting or whispering? She could not tell.

"What may not be over?" she asked.

His answer vanished beneath another swell of chaotic noise. The glass in the garden doors exploded inward into sharp splinters. She ducked, pulling the children and him toward the floor with her.

What was going on?

Chapter Two

The din rolled away, fading like distant thunder. Beside Caroline, a lamp slid off the table, cracking and spreading oil into the rug. A pair of painted porcelain spaniels bounced across the mantel. One shattered as it hit the hearth, the other remained, hanging precariously, on the very edge of the mantel. Books crashed to the floor.

Joy shrieked in her arms, and Gil babbled in terror. She cuddled them close. Their heartbeats were as rapid as her own.

"Lady Caroline?" asked a taut voice.

She raised her head slowly and looked around. Every book had tumbled off the shelves along the far wall. Ornaments set on shelves or hanging on the walls were now on the floor. Most were broken. Paintings had fallen, too, and frames were chipped and awry. Glass from the garden doors lay splintered on the floor or glittering on the furniture.

"Lord Warrick, please take Gil," she said.

"Where?" He lowered his arms from around them and drew back.

"Pick him up and keep him away from the glass."

The little boy yelped when he was tugged away from her, but Lord Warrick said, "Come and help me save that dog on the mantel, young man."

Caroline rose as far as her knees while the baron went with Gil to push the porcelain spaniel from the edge of the mantel. The room was a mess. What about the rest of the house? Had anyone been hurt?

As if she had asked aloud, Lord Warrick asked, "Are you unharmed, my lady?"

"Yes. You?"

"Relatively."

She faced him and gasped when she saw blood trickling down his left cheek.

"Lady Caroline, what is wrong?" he asked as he rushed to her side. "Are *you* injured?"

"No, but you are!"

"Ouchie," Gil said, poking at the baron's face.

Lord Warrick gently took the little boy's finger and moved it away from his cut cheek. Pulling out a handkerchief, he ripped off a piece and pressed it to the laceration where drying blood would hold it in place. "I was nicked by flying glass. Nothing to worry about."

The door flew open, and her older brother, Arthur, burst in, shouting, "Carrie, are you in here?"

"Over here." She stood, careful not to put her hand out to steady herself when her knees wobbled beneath her. Broken glass covered every surface. She felt the oddest need to weep as her brother used the nickname he had given her when he was unable to say her name as a youngster. She had not realized how fearful she was for her family's safety. "Are we under attack again?"

It was not a frivolous question. Cornwall was in a precarious position in the midst of a war being fought on two fronts, Napoleon to the east and the Americans to the west. Most of the French fleet had been destroyed or captured at Trafalgar seven years before, but pirates flying the French flag haunted the Cornish coast. There were rampant rumors of Americans harassing shipping, as well.

"No ships have been sighted in the cove." Her brother's black brows lowered when he glanced toward their neighbor. "Warrick, you are bleeding."

"I know. It is nothing." Lord Warrick dismissed Arthur's concern as he had Caroline's. He took a step toward them but paused when glass cracked beneath his boots. "Anyone badly hurt?"

"Our butler, Baricoat, was going upstairs when the biggest blast hit the house. He twisted his wrist badly when he tried to grab the banister." He grinned swiftly. "As you can guess, he is not letting that slow him down." His smile faded as he added, "The house has suffered the most. Windows facing the moor have been shattered throughout Cothaire. Any that are seaward are intact."

"The village?" Caroline whispered, her voice trembling as much as her knees.

"I sent a few men from the stables as well as the footmen to check on the villagers. They have instructions to visit the parsonage and Susanna's house, as well."

"Thank you." Again she could not speak very loud. Their younger brother, Raymond, was the local parson and lived in the parsonage with his wife and a child who had been on the same rickety boat as Gil and Joy.

She prayed they, along with Susanna, the youngest of the Trelawney family, and her husband and everyone at her house around the curve of the cove were safe and unhurt.

"Maris is working with Mrs. Hitchens to check that we have enough medical supplies." Arthur's gaze cut to Lord Warrick. "Mrs. Hitchens is our housekeeper. What of your people? Do you think you will need help? I was told several people saw a bright flash up on the moor."

Lord Warrick handed Gil to her startled brother. The baron muttered what sounded like a curse under his breath, then added a hasty apology with a glance in her direction.

"You know what happened." Caroline did not make it a question, because, in spite of his unpolished manners, Lord Warrick must have been furious to allow such a phrase to slip out when she and the children were nearby.

"Not for sure yet." He ground out the words past clenched teeth. "But I intend to discover as quickly as humanly possible. If you will excuse me…"

"No."

"No?" he repeated at the same time as Arthur asked, "Carrie?"

"I'm coming with you," she said.

The baron frowned. "My lady, though I understand your need to ease your curiosity about what has occurred, under these circumstances, the mines are no place for a woman."

"You said you don't know for sure what the explosion was." She held up her hand before he could retort.

"There must be anxious families at the mine. Allow me to see to them while you investigate the explosions."

"Arguing will gain you nothing with my stubborn sister," Arthur said, shifting Gil to hold the wiggling boy more securely.

Lord Warrick opened his mouth to reply, then nodded. "You must promise me, my lady, you will not allow your fervor to entice you to enter the mines."

"There is nothing in the world that would compel me to go even a step into the mines." She shuddered at the thought of creeping into the deep shafts, leaving light and fresh air behind as the fear of rising water stalked every breathing moment.

"Good."

She looked at Joy, who clung to her shawl. For a moment, she considered remaining at Cothaire to soothe the children. Irene, the nursery maid, loved them, and they returned her affection. She would ease the children's fears.

"I will be only a few minutes," she said. "If you don't mind waiting, my lord, so I may ride in your carriage…"

"I came here by horseback." He took a step toward the door, clearly anxious to be gone.

"I will not slow you once I have a horse saddled."

Her brother said, "I will arrange for horses, Carrie, and get the supplies gathered while you settle the children. Give me a hand, Warrick?"

She followed them out of the damaged room. In the hallway, where paintings were askew on the walls, Arthur put Gil down. She took the little boy's hand and went as quickly as his short legs could manage toward the stairs. She glanced back to see her brother and Lord Warrick hurrying in the other direction.

She wondered what they would find when they reached the mine high on the moor. *Please, God, watch over us especially closely today.*

Halting his horse in the shadow of the beam engine house, Jacob looked at the scene in front of him. The three-story tall building with its brick chimney was not silent, a good sign, because the pumps worked to lift water from the mine shafts deep below the ground. The rhythmic thud of the beam engine was unbroken. If a shaft had collapsed, the area would have been filled with desperate relatives and others trying to make a rescue.

The miners' wives and daughters swept glass in front of the terrace houses where they lived. He had repaired rotten roofs and cracked foundations, then had both the exteriors and the interiors whitewashed. New floors had been put in where needed, along with strengthening unsteady staircases. Now, every window he had replaced after his arrival at Warrick Hall was probably broken.

When he frowned, it felt as if a hot poker pressed to his skin. He ignored it. What could have gone wrong? Had he made another mistake that had led to the explosion? He pushed that thought away, not wanting to imagine someone else dying from his failure to pay attention to what was going on around him, as Virginia Greene had because he did not notice the road was icy.

A child shrieked.

Lady Caroline jumped down from her horse. She reached up to her brother for the bag of medical supplies he carried. He handed it to her. She called to a nearby lad to take her horse's reins.

The boy, his eyes wide, scurried to obey.

"Can you keep my horse from wandering away?" she asked with a gentle smile. "I don't want it to get injured."

He nodded, then squared his narrow shoulders when she thanked him as if he were the answer to her dearest prayer. Pride and purpose battled on the lad's face as he raised his chin, clearly ready to do his duty for her.

Jacob watched a miner step forward to take the heavy bag she carried. The man grinned broadly when she asked him to follow as she hurried to where the women had gathered around a crying child. Every request Jacob made to these stubborn Cornishmen and their women was met with reluctance and often outright defiance. A single smile from Lady Caroline, and they were as docile and eager as a litter of puppies.

"It is a gift she has always had," Lord Trelawney said as he moved his horse closer to Jacob's. "She cares so much about others they cannot help but care about her."

"How did you know what I was thinking?"

"You are not the first to stare in disbelief." He arched a brow. "I admit I envy her that ability, especially when a couple of tenant farmers are about to come to blows over a matter that could be handled by cooperation."

"You should take her with you to ease the anger."

Lord Trelawney smiled. "Trust me. There have been a few times when her help saved the day." Glancing around, the viscount became serious again. "It does not look as if the explosion occurred here."

He turned his horse past the engine house and away from the village. "I hope I am wrong, but I suspect the explosion came from this direction."

"Why?"

"Come with me, and you will see." He did not want to make any accusations until he had facts.

They did not have to ride more than a quarter of a mile. Across the open moor where even the gorse had lost its bright blossoms with the coming of winter, soot marked where a fire had flared. A few men stood at one side of the blackened earth, beating out low flames.

A tall, thickset man rushed toward them. As he looked at Jacob, he wore his usual sneer. He started to speak, then glanced at Lord Trelawney. Whatever he had intended to say ended in a sharp gulp.

"Yelland," Jacob asked as he swung off his horse, Shadow, which shied nervously at the strong odors from the smoke, "what happened?" He knew, too well, from what he could see in front of him, but he wanted to hear the mine captain's explanation.

Paul Yelland had held that prestigious title and the duties of overseeing the men and the mines since before Jacob's arrival. Jacob let him continue, but was growing more disillusioned with the man's character and abilities. Yelland preferred evading work. As well, he had made no secret of his lack of respect for the new baron, though Yelland was intimidated by Lord Trelawney.

"It went off," Yelland said, staring at his feet.

"What went off?" asked Lord Trelawney as he dismounted.

"Gunpowder, my lord," Yelland replied with an obsequiousness he never showed Jacob.

Lord Trelawney rounded on Jacob. "You are making gunpowder this close to your mines and village? Are you mad, Warrick?"

Jacob kept his voice even. "We are not making gunpowder here. I would never put the miners and their families in such danger."

"Then what—?"

Knowing he was being rude but determined to deal with the matter himself, Jacob looked at Yelland as he said, "If you will excuse us, Trelawney…"

"Yes, certainly." Curiosity burned in the younger man's eyes, but he nodded. Patting his coat as if making sure something important was beneath it, he added, "I need to check the nearby farms and Porthlowen. I trust you will share what you discover with Carrie before she returns to Cothaire, so she may inform Father."

"Yes, certainly," he said, using the viscount's own words. "I will see she arrives safely home."

Trelawney startled him by laughing. "She has been riding along this moor and the seaside since she could walk." He glanced toward Yelland and the other men who had gathered to listen. "However, I appreciate you escorting her to Cothaire."

Wondering what the viscount had sensed from the miners, Jacob nodded as Trelawney mounted and rode across the moor in the direction of the ancient farm foundations. Nobody in the area could be unaware of the multitude of troubles with the mines. His attempts to update them had brought more problems. The beam engine required constant vigilance and failed time after time. Whenever it stopped, water had to be pumped out of the shafts before the miners could return to work. Was it simply the new beam engine had inherent faults, or was there a more sinister scheme behind its many problems?

Jacob shook that thought from his head along with

his curiosity as to why Trelawney was riding in the opposite direction of his closest farms. He had enough to deal with right now. Being distracted was something he could not afford again, not after a young woman had lost her life because of his inattention.

"Tell me what happened, Yelland," he said with the stern tone he imagined Trelawney would use. "Now and quickly."

The mine captain stiffened but replied without his usual, self-important tone, "We decided to test the gunpowder to see how useful it would be when we next need to cut new shafts."

"Without alerting anyone?"

"We figured we were far enough away."

"You blew out windows at Cothaire."

Faces paled on the men behind Yelland, but the mine captain stood with his chin jutted toward Jacob, as if asking for a punch to knock him off his feet.

One of the men, a miner named Andrews, whispered, "The old earl? Was he hurt?"

"As far as I know, no." Jacob knew the miners esteemed the Earl of Launceston, who had provided for the miners and their families when his own uncle had failed to in the months leading up to Uncle Maban's death. "The house was damaged, and the family and their servants were terrified."

Yelland folded his arms over his chest. "A few broken windows seems to be the worst of it."

Jacob was irritated by the man's attitude. Remembering the horror on Lady Caroline's face and the children's fearful cries, he fought his rising temper.

"How much did you detonate?" he asked.

"All of it."

Shock stole every word from Jacob. He was tempted to ask Yelland if he had lost *his* mind, but the answer was obvious. "Was anyone hurt here?"

"We took shelter in the old stone circle." Yelland fired a glance at the men behind him. A warning, no doubt, not to complain of any injuries.

One man was cradling his left arm in his right hand. Another was trying to staunch a bloody nose. Several pressed a hand against their ears, and he suspected they rung from the explosion's concussion. The fools who had assisted Yelland could have easily been killed, and he could see they knew it.

"Clean up this mess. Make sure the remaining fires are put out. Once you are done here, come to the village. There are a lot of windows to be boarded up as well as plenty of shattered nerves to be soothed." He glanced around at the scorched moor. "And don't forget to thank God you are alive. He has been merciful today."

The men behind Yelland nodded, knowing what Jacob said was true. They hurried to follow his orders. After glaring at Jacob another moment, even the mine captain walked away.

Remounting, Jacob did not have to urge Shadow toward the village. The horse was eager to put the stench of fire and destruction behind him. The fine-boned Arab, a gift from Jacob's brother to commemorate him becoming a baron, could challenge the ever-present wind from the sea. It had been too long since Jacob had found time to ride neck-or-nothing on Shadow, but he could not give the horse his head now. He must return to the village to examine the damage more closely.

He sighed as he drew in Shadow near the engine

house. Before he had come to Cornwall, he had envisioned his life at Warrick Hall would be one of ease, where he could enjoy racing his powerful horse any time he wished. What a witless air-dreamer he had been!

Jacob scanned the crowd. In its center, Lady Caroline was tending a little boy's hand while a long line of others waited for her attention. She spoke softly to the child, too softly for Jacob to hear her exact words as he dismounted again and lashed the reins to the building's railing. Her tone was clear, however. She was offering comfort as well as trying to win a smile from the child. She succeeded before a woman took the little boy's uninjured hand and drew him aside so another hurt child could take his place.

As he walked toward the crowd, no one paid him any attention. Every eye was focused on the earl's daughter.

Even his. Lady Caroline's round face was alight with caring. Strands of her ebony hair curled along her cheeks and accented her gentle smile. She wore a patched apron she must have borrowed from a miner's wife, but it could not detract from her elegance. Somehow, she combined grace with a warmth that made the villagers feel comfortable around her.

As he did.

He had not expected ever to be at ease in the company of a woman after the terrible night that changed his life. However, from the first time he had met Lady Caroline, she had treated him with kindness.

"What happened to you, sweetheart?" Lady Caroline asked the little girl standing in front of her.

The child, who could not be much more than six,

held up her right hand. Tears washed down her cheeks, and her lips trembled as she spoke. "Hurt my finger."

"I see." Dipping a cloth into a bucket, she dabbed gently at a small cut on the girl's finger. She spoke in a soothing tone while she bandaged the finger. Again, by the time she was finished, the child was smiling.

Lady Caroline noticed him and straightened. Asking a woman to bring more boiled water, she assured those waiting for attention she would return in a moment. Only then did she walk toward him.

"How do they fare?" he asked above the noise from the beam engine.

"There are no serious problems. Mostly small lacerations. The worst injuries are twisted ankles or wrists when someone was knocked to the floor." She glanced toward the terrace houses. "With your permission, I would like to ask Mr. Hockbridge to pay a visit here to confirm there are no broken bones."

"Thank you."

She looked past him. "Where is Arthur?"

"He decided to check on some of your tenants."

"Have you discovered what caused the explosion?"

"Gunpowder." He explained what Yelland had admitted to before adding, "They were overeager to discover if they could use it in the mines."

Her brows lowered in concentration, as her brother's had, and she folded her arms in front of her. "They had gunpowder without you knowing?"

"I knew, but I intended they test only a small amount under my supervision. Before I allowed even that, I would have informed your father."

"But such explosions are dangerous."

"Rest assured, my lady, I have experience with detonating chemicals."

"I thought you were at Oxford before you came here."

He smiled for only a second as pain sliced his cheek. "Actually I was at Cambridge. I taught mathematics and physical sciences. I supervised many experiments with my students." He clamped his lips closed, wondering why he was babbling about matters that probably were of no interest to an earl's daughter.

"I should have known you would be cautious, even if your mine captain was not."

He appreciated her faith in his good sense. He wished he could trust it, as well. Once, he had been sure he would make the right decision in any situation. No longer. If his brother had not come upon the broken carriage the night of the accident as Jacob fought to hold on to his consciousness, Virginia might not have been the only one to die.

Jacob realized Lady Caroline had gone on speaking and was giving him an overview of the damage inside the terrace houses. He almost groaned, because it was more extensive than he had guessed. The ones closest to the explosion were unsafe, and he would need to find temporary homes for those who lived there.

"If they do not mind," she was saying when he focused on her words again, "we have some empty buildings about a mile from here. Not cottages exactly, but they have roofs and doors." A grin eased the tension on her face. "Best of all, they have no windows."

He could not keep from returning her grin, though the expression tugged at his sore cheek once more. "If those in Porthlowen who have lost windows wish to present me with a bill for the replacement glass, I will reimburse them."

Lady Caroline unfolded her arms and nodded. "That is generous of you. I will ask Raymond to take an accounting in the village, and then we will send the list to you."

"Thank you." He hoped the parson would be as forgiving. "And you should include any windows damaged at Cothaire."

"That will not be necessary."

"It is. I—" His frown sent a heated pulse of agony across his face, and his fingers went to his cheek. Foolish! Another wave of pain rushed over him as new wetness rushed beneath his fingertips.

Shock riveted him when Lady Caroline grasped his shoulders. She steered him to sit on the engine house steps. She bent and gripped his chin, shocking him again. Tilting his head, she said, "You are bleeding."

"It is barely more than a scratch," he asserted, even though every change of expression seared his cheek.

"Those explosions happened an hour ago, and your face is still bleeding. It is more than a scratch. Take a deep breath."

That was his only warning before she yanked the piece of his handkerchief off his face. He yelped but bit his lip to silence any further reaction as she called for someone to bring her medical supplies to her.

She leaned toward him, one foot on the first step. "That cut is as long as your forefinger, and it runs from below your spectacles to the top of your lip. Your glasses may have saved your eye."

A woman rushed over to them. She dipped in a

quick curtsy as she handed a small basket and a pail to Lady Caroline.

Thanking her, Lady Caroline dipped a rag in the bucket of steaming water. "This will sting," she warned.

That was an understatement. The soft fabric brushed his face with liquid fire. He clamped his teeth together and stared straight ahead as she cleaned the wound. He winced when she dabbed the skin closest to the cut. When she started to apologize, he waved aside her words and lifted off his glasses, holding them on his knee. "Do what you must, my lady."

He drew in a deep breath of some sweet scent he could not identify. It came from her gentle fingers. He sat as still as he could while her fingers flitted about him as quick and soft as butterfly wings. Strands of her ebony hair fell forward and brushed his ear in a tantalizing caress as she spread a cooling salve on his cheek.

When she drew away to get fabric to wrap over his head and under his chin to secure a clean bandage on top of the salve, he watched her easy motions. She fit perfectly in her world. Would he ever be as confident in the role thrust upon with Uncle Maban's death?

The door behind him opened at the same moment he realized the beam engine had stopped. Jumping to his feet, he caught Lady Caroline's arms to keep her from being knocked to the ground. Her eyes widened, but he did not care if his actions were overly familiar. He did not intend to let someone else, especially this kind woman, be hurt because of him.

Not releasing her, he shouted, "Get the men out of the mine. Now!"

Lady Caroline wrested herself from his hold and asked him to excuse her.

"My lady—"

His name was yelled from the engine house. Turning to Lady Caroline, he took her hand and offered his very best bow. He saw her astonishment when he straightened, and he knew he had made another etiquette mistake.

"I—I—I must go," he said, stumbling over the few words.

She held out the salve she had put on his face. "Take this jar and use the salve liberally when you change the bandage tonight."

"Thank you." He took the jar. Something very pleasant surged up his arm as his fingers brushed hers. If she had a similar reaction, he saw no sign of it in her polite smile.

Bidding her farewell, he ran up the steps and into the engine house. He was unable to shake the feeling he had made another, even bigger mistake.

Chapter Three

Wiping his hand on an oily cloth, Jacob watched the steady motion of the beam engine that had taken him and his assistant two days to repair. The great beam rocked in and out of the opening high in the front of the three-story building. With every motion of the wooden beam, that was thicker than he was and twice as tall, water was pumped out of the mine and sluiced away.

"Seems to be working now, my lord," his assistant, Pym, said.

Treeve Pym resembled a well-fed cat. Short and round, he was topped by thick brown hair. As always, he smelled of oil, sweat and too many days without a bath.

Jacob had grown accustomed to Pym's reek. The man was a genius when it came to figuring out what was wrong with the beam engine and fixing it. Maybe he would be better described as a foxhound. He had the ability to sniff out a problem before Jacob could discover the cause.

"It does." Jacob ran his fingers through his hair as he watched the pendulum motion of the beam. "Any idea what caused the trouble?"

"One of the screws connecting the bob to the rod outside the building loosened."

Jacob picked up the beef pasty he had brought with him at dawn when word was delivered to Warrick Hall that the beam engine had halted again. He had been fortunate his cook rose earlier than the sun. He unwrapped the pasty as he climbed the stairs so he could look out and watch the great beam which Pym called a bob.

He leaned his elbow on the thick sill of the window that gave him the best view of the beam. As he watched, he could not determine how a screw holding it to one of the cylinders could have come loose.

Taking a bite of the beef and potato pasty, he smiled. He appreciated the efficiency of a Cornish pasty, which the miners carried underground with them. Because it had a thick edge almost two inches wide, they did not have to remove poisonous tin from their hands before they ate. The crimped edge allowed a miner to hold the pasty while eating the inner crescent-shaped dough and filling. Once he was finished, the miner tossed the outer edge away. It was, Jacob had decided, a brilliant idea, and he had asked Mrs. Trannock to prepare the same fare for him when he worked at the mines.

He wondered if Lady Caroline ever dined on something as commonplace as a pasty. Now, where had *that* thought come from? The lady had slipped into his thoughts often while he should have been concentrating on fixing the beam engine, and not only when he inadvertently touched his sore cheek.

Pym asked from behind him, "See anything to tell you what went wrong?"

"Nothing but a properly working beam engine." Jacob pushed himself away from the window and started down the stairs after Pym. "If you see something that gives you an idea of what happened, let me know."

"I can't say now why it stopped, my lord, but I will try to find out."

Thanking him, Jacob took his greatcoat from a peg and shrugged it on. He pulled on his gloves and set his hat on his head. Outside, his horse Shadow waited patiently for him. While the beam engine had been converted to steam, Shadow had stood outside the building the whole night on several occasions. He knew there were those in Cambridge who would call him a fool for spending time and money updating the mines. However, he was determined to make a success where his uncle had failed, leaving the mines in intolerable condition and the mining families on the precipice of starvation. Only the generosity of the Trelawneys and the Porthlowen church had kept them from slipping over the edge.

It was not as if the miners' families had other opportunities to make a living. The poor, thin soil of the moor did not allow for farming. Jacob knew the best and perhaps only way to provide for the people on the estate was to keep the mines open. They had been neglected by Maban Warrick. Some miners had turned to thievery and other crimes. Those caught had been hanged or transported, leaving their families in an even worse state.

The thump of the beam's motion was a comforting sound as Jacob rode to Warrick Hall almost two miles higher on the desolate moor. He did not look toward the scorched ground, but the wind coming off the land blew the odors of burnt brush and gunpowder to him.

Yelland had made himself scarce since that debacle. Pym had asked several times if Jacob intended to dismiss the mine captain. Jacob wished he could. He knew Yelland had intimidated the miners. Firing the man for his insolence and outright stupidity would cause trouble in the mines. The miners would be forced to join a protest against his dismissal.

To own the truth, Yelland did an excellent job... when he worked. The men willingly followed him, and after almost a year, they still did not trust Jacob. The sorry truth was Jacob needed the mine captain to keep order in the mines and production moving smoothly. With the beam engine claiming too much of Jacob's time, he had few opportunities to show the miners he respected their skills and hard work.

Now, somehow, he had to find time to repair Warrick Hall enough to make it suitable for his family's visit. Also, he had to arrange to take lessons in etiquette with Lady Caroline so, if anyone from neighboring estates called, he would not shame his family with his unrefined manners.

The chilly wind crept past his collar, and he shivered. Last winter had been one of the worst anyone could remember. Signs pointed to another cold and snowy one.

Coming over a ridge, Jacob saw Warrick Hall in front of him. It was a dark, hulking building. Oddly enough, Warrick Hall had not sustained any damage from the gunpowder explosion. The contour of the moor had protected the ancient house from the concussion. That was good, because the shock from the detonation could have done far more damage to the run-down structure than break a few windows. He was grateful the roof did not leak or had fallen in as ones had on some of the outbuildings.

The house had only two servants indoors as well as the lad who tended the horses and cleaned the stable. The two servants were both so elderly, Jacob felt as if he should serve them. Mrs. Trannock, the cook, oversaw the kitchens, which were as out of date as the mines had been. Wherry was butler and footman, and he would have been Jacob's valet if Jacob had allowed it. The wizened man could barely climb the stairs, but insisted on answering the door and attending the table during meals.

As Warrick Hall seldom had visitors, Jacob did not have to worry about them being left out in the rain or cold while Wherry shuffled his way slowly to the door. He had solved the other issue by telling both the cook and the butler he preferred to collect a tray from the kitchen and eat in his room while he read reports or toiled over the paperwork that never seemed to end. He should hire an estate manager as well as someone to handle the mine's accounts, but he did not have time to interview anyone.

The wind grew stronger as he rode toward the house. He would order a cup of something warm from the kitchen and sip it while he handled the week's correspondence. Actually, the correspondence was almost a month old, and there was no more room on his desk for another piece of paper.

He was relieved when he saw Howell standing in the stable's doorway, ready to take Shadow. Thanking the lad, Jacob rushed to the house. There were closer doors than the front one, but they opened into sections of Warrick Hall where the floors could not be trusted. Something he had learned shortly after his arrival. He had been exploring the vast house. The floor had broken beneath him, and he had nearly fallen into the cellar.

"Good afternoon, my lord," said Wherry when he opened the door to usher Jacob in. His white hair was brushed back from his face, and not a speck of lint ruined the perfection of his black livery. "*She* is waiting for you in the gold parlor."

"She?"

"Lady Caroline. She said you were expecting her."

Was he? He could not recall setting a date or time for Lady Caroline to visit Warrick Hall. His heart had begun a cheery dance in his chest at the mention of her name, and his lips wanted to turn up in a silly smile.

"I trust having her wait in the gold parlor was what you would have wanted, my lord," Wherry continued.

He was astonished how excited the butler sounded that Lady Caroline was calling. Again it was as if Lady Caroline made everyone's life brighter simply by being a part of it…as she did his. He swallowed his chuckle as he imagined how she would laugh at his frivolous thoughts.

His urge to smile vanished as he glanced around the entrance hall. The heavy wood on the walls had been painted a deep black that consumed every bit of light. For some reason, his uncle had had wood installed over the windows, so no sunshine could enter. The rest of the house was as dark and dreary. The gold parlor, called that because of a hideous gilt frame around a mirror on the chimneypiece, was one of the least grim rooms. It did reek, however, of the tobacco his uncle had used, an odor so overwhelming that Jacob avoided the room whenever possible. He could not leave Lady Caroline sitting in the stench.

"Thank you, Wherry. I trust a fire was laid and lit in the room."

"Most certainly." The butler acted offended that Jacob had asked such a question. "Shall I have a tea prepared for you and the lady?"

"Thank you."

Wherry bowed his head, then walked away at the best pace his bowed legs could make.

Jacob went to the gold parlor. He took a bolstering breath before he walked through the parlor's open door. He must not make another faux pas while greeting Lady Caroline, though that might be difficult when he did not know what he had done wrong before.

He almost groaned when he saw the state of the room. It was in no condition for a lady. Canvas was draped over the furniture. Pictures were wrapped in linen and leaning against walls beneath the lighter rectangles where they once had hung. Even the mirror that gave the room its name was draped. The rug had not been unrolled. It remained beneath the bay windows on the far side of the room. A fire burned merrily on the hearth. At least someone had opened the draft, because the smoke rushed up the chimney.

If Lady Caroline was bothered by the disarray, he saw no sign of it as she rose gracefully from the only chair not covered with dusty canvas. Her dark red velvet coat matched the ribbons at the bodice of her gown. A cut velvet bonnet the same color perched on her black hair. The shade accented the deep rose brushing her cheeks and complemented the sparkle in her blue eyes. When she walked toward him as if they stood in the gallery of a fine palace instead of a run-down house, she did not offer her hand.

He was relieved because he obviously had done something wrong when he bowed over her fingers at Cothaire. Now he did not have to chance repeating the error.

"This is a pleasant surprise," Jacob said as he stepped around the mound of canvas that had been swept off her chair and left on the floor. He hoped Wherry had handled that task rather than expecting the lady to do it herself.

She faltered. "Surprise? I thought you wished my help with preparing your house for your family's visit."

"I do need your help, and I am delighted you are here." There. That sounded like something a titled gentleman would say. Emboldened by the thought, he said, "I am glad you are here. Do you think Warrick Hall can be made presentable in a month's time?"

Caroline wondered if the air had been sucked out of the room. She could not draw in a breath. When she had been shown into the parlor, she had guessed it was because the room was ready for guests. What a shock to discover its abandoned state! She clasped her hands in front of her, wondering if the parlor truly was the best available space to receive people. Certainly the entry hall offered no welcome.

"A month…" Caroline repeated while she tried to determine how best to answer without insulting Lord Warrick and his home. To own the truth, she doubted the house could be repaired to the point of welcoming guests in anything less than a year.

"It is a herculean task, I realize," he said, and she guessed her thoughts had been on her face.

She walked to where the door hung from one hinge. She fought the urge to push it straighter, because she had the irrational thought that moving a single item could bring the whole structure down on their heads. Looking into the corridor, she stared at the peeling wall coverings and damp stains. The reek of mildew filled every breath she took. She wondered how Lord Warrick managed to live amidst the ruin of what had once been a grand house.

"It is impossible," she said, then wished she had not been blunt when his face fell.

His fingers folded into frustrated fists at his sides. "If it is impossible for you, then…" Turning away, he picked up the canvas and tossed it atop another chair. "Thank you for calling, my lady. I am sorry to waste your time."

"Wait a moment!" she called as he took a step toward the door. "I didn't say I would be unwilling to try."

Hope flared in his dark eyes. "Really?"

"Yes." She drawled the word out, searching his face. His relief was so strong. "May I ask you a question which is truly none of my bread-and-butter?"

He chuckled. "You cannot ask any question that I would take the wrong way."

"You may not think so when you hear my question."

"Fire away."

For a second, Caroline considered saying something other than what had been on her mind from the moment he first beseeched her assistance; then she asked, "Why is having both this house and yourself make such a good first impression with your family so important to you?"

"A fair and honest question, and I shall give it a fair and honest answer." He folded his arms in front of him. "My stepmother is bringing a young woman who she believes would make me the perfect bride."

His tone was bleak. When she could not restrain her laugh, he regarded her with bafflement.

"I thought you might have empathy for me, my lady," he said.

"Forgive me, but you sounded as if you were about to be marched off the plank by a band of rapacious pirates. Surely you are accustomed to matchmaking. An unmarried man with a title often finds himself the target of eager mamas."

"I am not accustomed to it. Perhaps if I had spent time in London, where matchmaking has been raised to an art form, I would be. My brother is very happy with his wife, who was introduced to him by our stepmother. Do not mistake my words. I don't mean to cast aspersions on the young lady. May I be blunt?"

"Please do," she said, even though she wondered how much more straightforward he could be.

"It is the not the young woman herself I object to, for I have met her on occasion, and she seems quite pleasant."

"Faint praise is no praise."

"That was not my intention. I don't object to the young woman in particular. I am not like you, my lady. I cannot balance children and a household and the needs of my family at the same time. Certainly not with the ease you display." He smiled wanly. "I know I must marry one day because the family's title requires an heir, but my focus at present is on keeping the mines operating and safe. I have no time now for courting or a family of my own."

"I understand."

His smile became more genuine. "I am glad. No one else seems to."

"There are expectations on every member of the *ton*, especially…" She halted herself before she could say something untoward. To discuss her inability to conceive was sure to embarrass both of them. After all, she did not discuss such an intimate subject with her own family.

"Ah," he said, nodding. "I see you have been the target of matchmaking, as well." He did not give her a chance to respond before he went on. "I came to Cornwall as soon as I received my title because I had reports of the sorry situation with the mines."

She nodded. "You have made many improvements, and I know people are grateful."

"Doing that takes the majority of my time. I have not been able to convince my stepmother of that. If she sees the pitiful condition of the house, she will be even more determined I need a wife."

"What you need are a carpenter and a maid with a dusting rag," she said drily.

A roar of mirth burst from him. He laughed hard and had to lean forward to put his hands on his thighs while he struggled to regain control of himself.

Caroline smiled. Since she had first met him months ago, she had never heard such lighthearted laughter from him. Usually he was serious about the obligations that weighed upon him.

Raising his head, he wiped tears from the corners

of his eyes. "I thought one had to be less blunt within the strictures of Society."

"Yes, but beyond the polite and prim conversation at formal events, you will find people speak plainly. The goal is never to hurt another's feelings." She smiled. "I did not think you would be insulted by my comment."

"Quite to the contrary." He motioned for her to lead the way into the passage. "You must have known the situation was dire when I came begging for assistance. Maybe you did not realize how dire."

Caroline decided silence was the best answer. The house was a disaster. As they walked along the corridor, she kept up a steady patter about cleaning and airing the draperies and rugs and the need to get *all* the cobwebs out of the corners of the intricate crown molding. She had no idea how many servants worked at Warrick Hall. As they toured the ground floor, she saw a butler and a cook, but two old retainers would not be enough to bring the house to a suitable state to receive guests. She was about to say that when she heard a skittering as she and Lord Warrick entered another room.

"You will need to do something about the mice," she said. "Many women are frightened of rodents, no matter how small."

"They don't seem to bother you."

"Not during the daylight. I would not appreciate waking up to the sight of one of them crossing my room, but that will not happen if their numbers are lowered. The best way is to bring cats from your outbuildings into the house. A good mouser will rid a home of vermin very quickly, especially if you make sure there is a fresh bowl of milk available as a treat."

"A dandy idea." He halted, putting his hand on a

table hidden beneath a cloth. When a cloud of dust rose from the spot he had touched, he shook his hand clean. "I assume there are cats around, because I have not seen many mice in the stable. However, I have not seen any cats, either."

"Your uncle used to complain there were more of them here than fish in the sea. I am sure we can find a couple to bring into the house."

"Shall we look now?"

Caroline was about to say she needed to return to Cothaire, but halted when chiming came from a short-case clock hanging on the wall. In spite of the dust, Lord Warrick's butler must have kept it wound.

"I can stay a bit longer," she said, more pleased than she expected to be that she could help Lord Warrick with this small task. "I want to be at Cothaire when Joy wakes from her nap. She is peevish with teething."

"It should not take too long to recruit a cat for mousing duty."

Lord Warrick showed her the way to the stable. It was, she noticed, one of the few outbuildings with a door. The stable was in better condition than the house, but only slightly.

When they entered, the three horses inside stirred and regarded them with curiosity before returning to munching their oats. The space was surprisingly large and had as many cobwebs as Warrick Hall. Faint sunlight came from windows in the hayloft overhead.

A lad rushed out of a room beyond the stalls. "My lord, what may I do for you?" He put his fingers to his forelock as if tipping a cap as he glanced from Lord Warrick to her. "Shall I have the carriage readied?"

The baron stiffened. What an odd reaction to a commonplace question!

Then she wondered if she had seen something that was not there. Lord Warrick's voice was unchanged. "That is not necessary, Howell. Have you seen any cats about?"

"Cats?" The lad nodded, eager to please. "There are always some about. Do you want me to try to find some and bring them to you?"

"No, just point us in the right direction."

He looked toward steps at the far end of the stable. "They seem to gather in the lower haymow."

"Thank you." Lord Warrick offered his arm to Caroline, surprising her.

When she put her gloved hand on his coat sleeve, her fingers sparked as if she had grabbed a bolt of lightning. She almost jerked her hand away. Somehow, she kept her fingers on his sleeve, so she did not call attention to her reaction. If he felt it as well, she saw no sign, because his smile did not waver.

Bits of hay crunched beneath Caroline's boots, releasing the aroma of dried grass to mix with the ancient dust dancing in the sunlight. She wondered how long it would be before the new stable at Cothaire smelled like this instead of freshly cut wood and paint.

Comparing this stable with Cothaire's kept her from thinking about how Lord Warrick's greatcoat brushed against her legs on each step. She could not ignore his masculine scent. She told herself she found that fragrance intoxicating because she had not stood close to a man other than her father or brothers since John's death.

When the baron withdrew his arm to allow her to

precede him up a trio of stone steps, regret flooded
her. She chided herself. A lack of sleep after trying
to soothe Joy most of last night was no reason to act
witless today. Lord Warrick was a gentleman to offer
his arm, and he was being polite stepping aside to let
her go first.

But, for those few moments, it had been pleasant to
be on the arm of a man again.

Stop it! She turned the scold into a prayer for good
sense. She was no longer a young miss who blushed
and tittered whenever a man stood beside her.

Caroline looked around the haymow, which was almost full. When she saw a bright ray of sunlight aimed
at the stone floor to her right, she headed in that direction. Cats, whether they lived in a barn or in a house,
always sought out a sunny spot for a nap. She smiled
when she saw a half dozen felines stretched out in the
warmth.

As she approached, they scattered except for one,
which arched and hissed. She smiled and squatted an
arm's length from the calico. She held out her hand as
she murmured, "Don't be afraid, Miss Cat."

The animal snarled again, her white, black and
brown hair standing on edge.

Behind her, Caroline heard Lord Warrick say, "Be
careful. She will scratch you. Step aside, and give her
a chance to escape."

"She would have fled before if that was her choice.
She must have a litter hidden in the hay behind her."
She rose and edged forward, then around the hissing
cat. It raced away only a few feet before turning to
glare at Caroline, who had not given chase as the cat

had hoped. Bending, she shifted the hay and smiled as she heard small mews.

A pair of heads popped up, curious about the noise. One was black with a white blaze on its nose. The other was a gray tiger. They bounced out, ready for battle, though they could not be more than two months old.

"This one seems bold enough." Lord Warrick picked up the black-and-white kitten. As he balanced it on his hands, the kitten batted tiny paws at him and gave a warning growl.

She scooped up the other kitten who began to purr as loudly as a cat twice her size. "A mother cat and two kittens will be perfect, assuming the mother cat can be caught. These kittens are the right age for her to teach them to catch prey. While they learn, they will be ridding your house of vermin and insects."

"I will have Howell bring the mother cat to the house, but will she stay?"

"You may have to keep them in a box for a few days, but if you provide food and water and milk, she will realize quickly she is better off in the house. Cats are smart that way." She stroked the satiny fur on the kitten's head. "What are you going to name them?"

"Name them? Do they need names?"

"How will they know to come when you call for them?" Smiling, she asked, "Did you never have a cat or dog?"

He shook his head. "My mother said cats made her sneeze, and dogs eat too much."

Caroline turned away to pat the tiger kitten, not wanting him to see her shock. It was easy to forget Lord Warrick's upbringing had been different from her own. She thought of the rumors she had heard. How could Maban Warrick hoard his fortune at Warrick Hall and allow his brother's family to struggle in poverty?

"What name would you suggest?" he asked.

"Something simple." She saw the mother cat skulking toward them and her kittens. "*Mam* is the Cornish word for mother. How about that for the calico?"

"Good. What about this bold black-and-white kitten?"

"He appears ready to chase the mice already, so *Helhwur* would be a good name. It means hunter."

"And the tiger? What is the Cornish word for tiger?" She laughed. "Tiger."

"I think we can do something better than that."

"*Tegen* would be a good name for her, because the word means pretty thing."

He rubbed the kitten's head. "Would you like that name, Tegen?" A tiny pink tongue brushed his wrist, and he chuckled. "I will take that as a yes."

She watched as he continued talking to the kittens as if they could comprehend every word he spoke. His hands, calloused from his work at the mine, were gentle on the kittens. Exactly as they had been with the children. Lord Warrick would be a caring and loving father. A twinge of envy twisted her heart at the thought of him holding his own son and teasing him as he had Gil.

Envy was an ugly emotion, but she could not pretend she did not feel it. She was envious of Lord Warrick and his future wife and their children. How many nights had she silently cried herself to sleep, knowing she had failed—*again*!—to give John a child? He had tried to act as if being childless did not bother him, but she could not forget how often he spoke, in the months after they were first wed, of the family they would have together.

She had to leave before the tears burning her throat reached her eyes. Telling Lord Warrick she needed to hurry to Cothaire, she handed him the tiger kitten. She rushed through the stable, even though she knew she could never escape her greatest failure.

Chapter Four

On Sunday morning, Caroline looked up from adjusting Gil's shirt and smiled as she heard hurried footsteps on the main staircase. Arthur's wife, Maris, chased Bertie, another little boy rescued from the boat.

"Slower, Bertie!" Maris called, putting up her hand to resettle the bonnet perched on her golden hair. Caroline's new sister-in-law was lovely, both inside and out, and Arthur had been unable to resist falling in love with her.

Catching the little boy as he tried to stop beside Gil and skidded past instead, Caroline chuckled. "You need a strong set of reins on this colt, Maris."

"I agree." She picked up Bertie and hugged him. "That might help me keep track of him."

"Look for Arthur, and you will find Bertie." The child spent every possible moment with her brother. "Oh! I almost forgot. Baricoat told me a letter arrived for Arthur this morning. I suggested he wait to deliver it until you two were ready for church. I know Arthur arrived home late last night. I thought he might want to sleep a bit later this morning."

Maris looked up, her face taut. "How do you know he came in late?"

"Joy is teething." She adjusted the sleeping baby in her arms. "I was up most of the night walking the floor with her, and I happened to be by the window when Arthur rode in. Is everything well?"

"Yes. Why do you ask?"

Caroline hesitated, not wanting to state the obvious about how Maris had tensed at the mention of Arthur being out late. The Trelawneys were accustomed to Arthur, in his role as their father's eyes and ears, being out at all hours as he traveled from one tenant farm to another. Perhaps it was a sore point between the new-lyweds, but that made no sense. Maris had been as aware as the rest of them of the long hours Arthur kept.

Rather than ask the question taunting her, Caroline said, "I wanted to remind you that any help you need from me, you have only to ask."

"Thank you." Maris's smile returned, and the conversation turned to the children, who discussed who would sit on which seat in the family's carriage.

Arthur came down the steps, looking refreshed. He greeted Caroline with a kiss on the cheek and teased the boys, so the children were giggling as they went out to the waiting carriage. Swinging the boys inside, he gave his new wife a loving smile before he handed her into the vehicle.

Nothing seemed amiss, but Caroline could not shake the feeling something was.

"May I?"

Caroline put down the prayer book she had been helping Gil hold and smiled at Lord Warrick's flushed face. From the cold or his obvious rushing, or was he blushing as every eye in the sanctuary was aimed at him? His greatcoat had fallen open, and she noticed his waistcoat was covered with dust and grime. Had he come from the mines?

From the pew across the aisle, Charity Thorburn scowled in their direction. The woman seldom smiled, and she seemed happiest when she was finding fault with others. Caroline had learned to ignore her petty comments. Mrs. Thorburn had always been prickly, but since her husband's death, her bad temper had taken a turn for the worse.

"When they are late, most people remain at the back of the church," Caroline could not resist saying to Lord Warrick with a smile.

"I thought, by now, you would have known I don't do things the proper way. Besides, there was not any room there." He gestured toward the pew where she sat with the children and asked again, "May I?"

"Of course." She edged aside, continuing to bounce Joy on her knee.

Letting the prayer book drop with a thump on to the wooden pew, Gil scrambled over her lap and sat between her and the baron. He began to tell Lord Warrick about everything that had happened that morning, his voice rising with his excitement.

Caroline put her finger to her lips and whispered, "Remember? As quiet as a church mouse, Gil. Parson Raymond is about to begin the service."

The little boy nestled against her side, and she put her other arm around him. It was easier to cuddle him now that Joy was able to sit up on her own. She thanked God as she had every day since the children were brought ashore. There had been an emptiness in the Trelawney family since the deaths of her mother and her husband. Six small children helped fill that void.

Toby, the boy they guessed was the oldest, was perched on her sister-in-law Elisabeth's lap. He had recently begun to call Elisabeth mama and announced he wanted to be a parson like his "papa." The twin girls who sat on either side of her sister, Susanna, were about a year younger, and they were blossoming in the care of Susanna and her husband. The irrepressible Bertie was close to Toby's age, and the only time Caroline ever saw him sit still was in church.

Lord, I know I should not ask for You to let the children remain with us because there must be families missing them. You have a plan for them as You do for each of us. I cannot help hoping that plan includes the children staying with us a while longer.

She murmured a silent, "Amen," before turning her attention to the verse Raymond had chosen for the service.

He read from the eighteenth Psalm: *"For who is God save the Lord? Or who is a rock save our God? It is God that girdeth me with strength, and maketh my way perfect."*

Bending her head to hide her smile, she knew her brother could not have chosen a more apt verse that morning. Her heart felt more at ease by the time they stood to sing a final hymn at the end of the service.

"Talk now?" asked Gil before her brother had time to step from the raised pulpit.

"Yes," she said with a chuckle. "But talk while you put on your coat."

Gil picked it up and frowned when it was upside

down. He tried turning it, but now he had it inside out and upside down.

"Let me help you, young man." Lord Warrick winked over Gil's head at her.

"Thank you," she said.

Neither Lord Warrick nor Gil heard her reply because they were chatting again. Gil was very anxious about whether it would snow soon or not. As the baron answered him, explaining about wind currents and storm clouds, the little boy listened in fascination. Somehow, Lord Warrick made the information simple enough for a child but did not sound as if he were talking condescendingly to Gil.

Putting Gil's hat in place, the baron said, "Now it is Lady Caroline's turn." He lifted her coat from the pew and held it up for her to put her arms through the sleeves. As she did, he said more softly, "I do have a few manners."

"More than a few." She hoped he had not felt her quiver as his warm breath caressed her nape. "Thank you." She edged away as far as she could in the narrow space between the pews.

"And thank you for letting me sit with you and the children." He stepped into the aisle, which was emptying quickly as the parishioners went out the door. "I was late because I foolishly decided to go into the attic to see what might be available for making the house ready for my family."

"What did you find?" she asked as she halted Joy from tearing a page from the prayer book and stuffing it in her mouth as she did with everything.

"A jumble extraordinaire. Crates and furniture and luggage and trash in no visible order. The truth is I have no idea where to begin. I moved dozens of boxes and trunks, but didn't make a dent in what has been tossed any which way into the attic. I wonder how many generations have left their castoffs up there and forgot about them."

She laughed as she put Joy's new light blue coat on the baby. "Mother insisted every year that we go through the attic and discard anything with no further use. We despised being up there in the heat, because it was hot even in the spring. Did you find anything you can use?"

"Not yet, but I found stacks of wool blankets. I counted more than a score of boxes of woolen blankets before I stopped. Even if I had two beds set up in every bedroom, there would be enough to put five on each bed. Most had moth holes, but a good number of the blankets are still thick." He hesitated, then said, "I need your opinion about what might be a contentious issue. You know the stubborn Cornish better than I do."

"Because I am one of them."

"I meant no offense."

"None taken." She smiled as she finished tying the ribbons on Joy's tiny hat.

"See? I already am making a bumble-bath of this."

She picked up the baby. "Say what you need to, my lord."

"When I saw those blankets, I thought about the children at the mining village. Do they have coats for the coming winter? As a child, mine was sewn from scraps my mother salvaged from old blankets or one of my father's coats. I would gladly give the blankets to the miners' families, but they are very proud people."

"So you are wondering if they would accept them?"

"Yes, and if they will, how can I be certain the blankets will be distributed fairly?"

Drawing Joy's little fingers away from the silk flower on her bonnet, Caroline said, "I suggest you speak to Raymond. As our parson, he knows which families are in need."

"Good. I knew you would have a solution for me."

"By passing you along to my brother. That is hardly a solution."

"Nonsense." He took Gil by the hand and led the way down the aisle. "You set me on the right track." As they stepped outside, he turned up his collar and said, "Confound it, it is cold today. Feels more like mid-January than the end of November."

"I hope this winter is not as unforgivingly cold as last year." She moved around the church to get out of the wind.

He followed, but looked around the churchyard. "I recognize some of these people from my estate. I assumed they were attending church at that parish."

"Recently they have been coming here because your parson has been ill. Raymond offered to go there to lead the services, but it was decided they come here so your parish church doesn't have to be heated." She let Joy kick her feet against the ground as if walking. "And you are here today, as well."

"As I told you, I wanted your advice."

She lowered her eyes from his steady gaze. How could she have failed to notice the amber flecks in his hazel eyes before now? They seemed to change intensity with his emotions, glowing like melted gold.

"Lady Caroline!" called a familiar voice.

Caroline turned to see the Winwood sisters coming toward them at a pace that belied their many years. Their hair was white, and their faces lined with matching wrinkles. Miss Hyacinth was dressed, as always, in a subdued shade of purple, while Miss Ivy wore her favorite dark green coat. Otherwise, the elderly spinsters were identical. They were the first set of twins ever born in Porthlowen and lived together in the small cottage where they had been born.

"Boat," Gil shouted, jumping and jerking on Lord Warrick's arm.

"Not now, Gil." Caroline smiled as the twins neared. "Good morning." Their eyes were, she realized, focused on the man beside her. "Lord Warrick, have you met Miss Hyacinth Winwood and Miss Ivy Winwood?"

"Yes." He bowed his head politely. "However, it is always a pleasure to have the opportunity to be introduced anew to two charming ladies."

Miss Hyacinth giggled like a young girl. "He has a silver tongue, doesn't he?"

"As the Bible says, 'The tongue of the just is as choice silver,'" quoted Miss Ivy, "'the heart of the wicked is little worth.'"

"Proverbs," Miss Hyacinth said.

"Chapter 10."

"Verse 20." Miss Hyacinth clearly did not intend for her sister to have the final word. "One of our mother's favorite verses." Without a pause to take a breath, she asked, "Are you just, my lord?"

Miss Ivy frowned at her sister. "Are you suggesting he might be wicked?"

"Most certainly not."

"But you asked him if he were just."

"A jest, Ivy."

Caroline decided the sisters, who could bounce a conversation between them endlessly, had said enough on the subject. "Lord Warrick is looking forward to having his family join him for Christmastide."

"How wonderful!" Miss Hyacinth said. "Warrick Hall has been too empty too long. Your uncle seemed to prefer his own company to anyone else's, which was a pity."

"Filling a house with family is always wondrous." Miss Ivy's smile returned.

"The more, the merrier. Don't I always say that, sister?"

"Indeed you do."

"Lady Caroline, you must be looking forward to Christmas as you have not for such a long time." Miss Hyacinth smiled, as well.

"With the children," confirmed her sister as if Caroline might have misconstrued Miss Hyacinth's meaning.

"What a blessing! They must be excited about Christmas."

Caroline jumped in when the sisters paused to draw a breath. "I would say we adults are more excited. For the children, a year is an impossibly long time, so they have forgotten last Christmas."

"And this is Miss Joy's very first Christmas," Lord Warrick added.

"The older children will get caught up in the celebrations of Advent once they begin." She ruffled Gil's hair.

"Boat," he chirped.

The sisters glanced at one another quickly, then turned to Caroline with the same puzzled expressions. "Does he want a boat as a Christmas gift?"

"Maybe, but I think it is more likely he wishes to sail his boat in the cove. It has been several weeks since the weather was clement enough to allow the children near the water."

"Boat!" Gil insisted, stamping his foot with impatience.

She handed Joy's fingers off to Lord Warrick, then embraced Gil as the twins moved away to talk to others. The hug seemed to satisfy the little boy because he flung his short arms around her neck and squeezed her breath from her. She reached up to loosen his grip, but her hands brushed rough ones. Raising her eyes to meet Lord Warrick's, she knew she could not have drawn a breath at that moment, even if Gil was not holding her tightly.

"You need to let Lady Caroline breathe," the baron said with a laugh as he lifted Gil's arms from her neck.

His skin, which was as coarse as a plowman's, brushed hers above her collar. Closing her eyes, she savored the sensation that banished the day's chill. The contact was inadvertent, she knew, and she should pay it no mind. Easily thought, impossible to do.

Coming to her feet, Caroline shook herself. She needed to be sensible. Featherbrained flirting and stolen touches were for young misses looking for husbands. She was neither a young miss, nor did she want to remarry. Too bad she could not convince her nerves that danced with delight. She needed to get them under control again.

Immediately.

Jacob kept his eyes on Joy, who was trying hard to walk, wobbling even while he held her hands. Gil marched like a small soldier in front of the baby, encouraging her to follow him.

"Should I thank you, my lady, for rescuing my ears from the Winwood sisters?" he asked.

"I seldom talk of someone else's business," Lady Caroline replied, "but nothing can change the subject for the Winwood twins more quickly than a tidbit of information they have not heard before."

"I saw the results with my own eyes." He chuckled as he raised his gaze to the uncertainty on her face. "And heard it with my own ears."

"They mean well. They were among the first to welcome the children to Porthlowen."

"After you and your family did."

"Actually, I believe they were on the sand when the children were rescued, so they saw them before I did. Many of the villagers went to see what the commotion was."

"But none of them saw who shoved the boat into the water?"

"No."

He frowned. "That means someone or maybe multiple someones are lying."

"Or not telling the whole truth."

"What is the difference?"

"In this case, nothing." She smiled. "I should know better than to discuss matters of logic with someone who taught at a university."

Gil yelled with excitement as snow began to fall around them.

"Try this." Jacob stuck out his tongue to capture a snowflake.

The little boy had a difficult time keeping his tongue

stuck out because he giggled every few seconds. He ran around, bumping into people, until Lady Caroline called him to her side. He obeyed and kept his mouth open in case a snowflake fell into it.

When Lady Caroline frowned, Jacob said, "Don't scold him for copying what I did."

"I should scold you instead?"

"Nobody should be scolded. Every boy needs a few bad habits," he said with a laugh. "It is only as we grow older that we have to become civilized and require tuition in how to become so. Speaking of lessons, when would you like me to come to Cothaire for our first one?"

She picked up Joy and cuddled her close. He liked how her face softened with love as she looked at the baby. A twinge cut through him as he thought of his promise to help discover the whereabouts of the children's families. It was painful to imagine her happiness becoming grief when she had to return the children.

"That is your choice, my lord," she said, drawing him from the uncertain future to the present. "You have many tasks while I am at loose ends. If it is more convenient, I can come to Warrick Hall."

"Go Warrick!" Gil forgot about snow as he tugged on Jacob's coat. "Cuddle kitties."

Jacob arched his brows. "News does travel fast in Porthlowen."

"He asked about the cat hair on me the other day." She smiled an apology before looking at the little boy. "Lord Warrick is a busy man, so you need to wait for him to ask you to visit."

Gil nodded.

"How are the cats doing?" she inquired.

"Well. Since we brought them into the house, the mother cat and her kittens have left dozens of dead mice at the kitchen door. The cats prowl the corridors, the closets and the corners."

"It sounds as if they are making themselves right at home."

"I would say so. They show no interest in returning to the stable. Mrs. Trannock is pleased the cat has already killed or scared away the mice that chewed on boxes and bags in the pantries. Though I wonder how long the cats will hunt."

"Why?"

"I have no doubts the mother cat is being fed treats, because she often follows Wherry around the house like a shadow. Actually three shadows, because her kittens go wherever she does."

"Go see kitty now?" asked Gil.

He laughed when Lady Caroline rolled her eyes at the little boy's idea of patience being quiet for barely a minute. "That is Lady Caroline's decision. You are welcome any time you wish."

"Now?" Gil whirled to Lady Caroline.

Over the little boy's head, she met Jacob's eyes evenly. "I would not mind examining those blankets you found. Will your carriage hold all of us?"

Carriage!

How could he have forgotten Howell had had the carriage waiting when he came out of Warrick Hall? The carriage horse needed exercising, and Shadow, his Arab, was reluctant to come out of his cozy stall on such a cold morning.

Jacob had considered returning the horse and carriage to the stable and having his horse saddled, but he had been late already. He decided he would take the carriage because no one else would be in it. He need not worry about another tragedy.

His stomach ached as if someone had punched him. Take them in his carriage? For the past three years, he had been successful in devising excuses to avoid having passengers with him. So successful he had let his guard down today.

Lady Caroline's simple question brought forth his unreliable memories. Many were bits and pieces of sights and sensations. His stepmother believed it was because he had struck his head hard against the road. He recalled a fragment of something Virginia Greene had said to him earlier that evening, but only a few words. Something about being vexed with him. Because he had not asked her to marry sooner? He had hesitated to propose because she could be fickle in her moods, but he had promised Beverly he would make Virginia an offer of marriage that night. He could not recall getting on one knee to propose, but he must have. He could remember a splinter of agony when he woke by the broken carriage. It was as if every bone in his body had broken, though only his arm and two ribs had. He would never be able to forget the unsteady image of Virginia lying on the ground, not moving. The next thing he knew, his brother was leaning over him, calling his name. A haze of pain; then nothing until he awoke in his bed.

If he could only remember what had happened before Emery arrived… Those memories were gone, along with everything before he and Virginia had stepped into the carriage. He recalled Virginia pleading with him to let her drive, but was unsure if her words came from that day or another. Why would he have agreed to let her drive if the roads were not safe? But he clearly had, and she had died.

"Is something wrong?" Lady Caroline asked as her gaze searched his face.

How he wished her eyes were not keen! Then again, sweat beaded on his forehead, and he had frozen in midstep. Even the most opaque person would notice something was amiss.

Hoping no sign of his thoughts emerged into his voice, he said, "Nothing important." Guilt surged through him anew at his lie, so he amended, "Nothing that is important right now."

"If you are worried about traveling in an open carriage with the children, I assure you that Gil has no intentions of letting go of your coat." A smile drifted through her words. If it was on her face, he could not tell because he stared at the ground. "He does not plan to let you out of his sight until he is able to pet your kittens."

Perspiration cascaded along his back, even though the air was cold. How could he explain to her that just the idea of having her and the children as his passengers during the short drive from the church had revived the disgust and guilt and anguish he felt in the wake of the accident?

"Are you unwell?" she asked, concern filling her voice, when he did not answer.

It was the excuse that would free him from taking her and the children to Warrick Hall. And it was the truth. He felt as if he would spew everything in his stomach at any moment.

"Yes."

"Are you well enough to drive to Warrick Hall? I can take you there if you wish."

No! Worse than having someone riding with him would be having someone driving him as Virginia had the night of the accident.

"I can manage," he said, forcing his feet toward his carriage. He felt like a bounder leaving her and the children to walk to Cothaire on such a chilly day.

"Cuddle kitties!" Gil's excited voice drove another dagger into his heart.

She shook her head with a gentle smile. "Not today. Lord Warrick is not feeling well."

"Ouchie?"

"Yes, ouchie." She held out her hand to the little boy. "If there is anything we can do to help, please, send word to Cothaire." She took a step, then paused. "Why not come Tuesday afternoon for our lesson? If you feel well enough by then."

"I am sure I shall."

She gave him a scintillating smile before walking away with the children. They ducked their heads into the wind as they began the climb to the grand house overlooking the cove.

A renewed surge of guilt almost drowned him as he went to his carriage. He knew, no matter how fast he drove to Warrick Hall, he would never escape it.

Chapter Five

It was silent in the beam engine house, save for the clatter of tools against metal. Pym was crouched near the steam engine as he checked every bolt and connection. Above him, Jacob was doing the same.

Nothing!

He could not see a single thing wrong. He rubbed his hands on an already filthy cloth, then pushed his spectacles back into place. What could have stopped the beam engine? It had been working well last night. Even when he had left Warrick Hall intending to ride to Porthlowen to talk with the parson about the donation of blankets, its rhythm had been regular. He had not gone more than a half mile, though, before he was turning his horse away from the sea and onto a narrow track across the moor.

The door opened, and he peered over the railing to see who was entering.

"Lady Caroline!" he gasped.

Pym popped up from beneath the engine, bumping his head into a pipe. He rubbed his skull and started to curse, then stopped, turning the color of the lady's dark red coat.

"I guessed," said Lady Caroline as if both he and Pym had greeted her politely, "you might be hungry." She held up a large basket with a piece of fabric over the top.

Jacob took the steps two at a time. He knew he was grinning like Gil with a new toy, but he did not care. After they had spent three frustrating hours of trying to fix the engine and getting nowhere, her arrival was like a second wind.

"That was a very good guess, my lady," he said as he cleared the last step.

He admired the warm flush on her cheeks. The interior of the building was only slightly warmer than the air outside. When the steam engine was functioning, the open space at the front of the engine house, where the beam rocked in and out, offered a way for the sometimes overwhelming heat to escape. Now cold air was flooding in.

"I thought it was a safe assumption." Her light blue eyes twinkled with merriment as her lips tilted in a smile.

Her oh-so-kissable lips.

Looking away, he wished he could erase that thought from his head. A man who had seen the last woman he loved die in front of his eyes should never let another woman slip past the defenses he had raised.

"Why would you say that?" He hated the gruff sound of his voice but hoped the clank from Pym's direction would smooth the roughness from it.

"We are accustomed to the sound of the beam engine, and when it stops, we take notice. How are you feeling? Better than yesterday, I would say, by the color in your face."

"Much better. Thank you." He would not tell her that his nausea had vanished by the time he returned to Warrick Hall.

Looking at the wooden floor, she asked, "Do you have a blanket, by any chance?"

Jacob was about to say no, then remembered the old woolen blankets he had intended to show the parson. "If you are not averse to a few moth holes, I have the thing."

"Sounds lovely."

Collecting two of the blankets he had tossed in a corner, he spread them on the floor. She sat gracefully and set the basket beside her. He could not tear his gaze from her delicate profile with the dark curls tumbling along her cheeks.

"Go ahead," she said as she looked from him to his assistant. "I don't want to interrupt your work. I will serve the food while you do what you must to get that device moving again."

"You?" He exchanged a glance with Pym, who was as shocked by her offer as he was. "My lady, you don't have to serve us."

She gave him a scowl he knew was false because her eyes sparkled even more brightly. "Lord Warrick, as you may recall, you have designated me as the judge of proper etiquette. Do you wish to gainsay me on an aspect of it?"

Laughing, Jacob raised his hands in a pose of surrender. "Far be it for me to dispute such a matter with an expert."

"Now you understand." She waved her hands at him.

"Go and do what you must. I will call you when your meals are ready."

Jacob did try to concentrate on finding why the beam engine had failed again, but his mind focused on Lady Caroline, who was humming a cheerful tune as she prepared something that smelled delicious. His stomach growled, the sound echoing through the building. When she and Pym laughed, he did, too.

"It will be ready soon," she called up to him.

"I can be patient," he said, leaning over the rail, "but I cannot vouch for my stomach."

When she called them to come and eat, Jacob realized he had spent the whole time staring at a single bolt while he listened to her motions below and her happy tune. Pym was already by the blanket, accepting a plate of steaming food by the time Jacob reached the main floor again.

His assistant thanked her, then turned to walk away.

"You are welcome to join us, Mr. Pym," Lady Caroline said with a smile. "There is plenty of room."

"Thank you, my lady, but I need to finish testing a part of the engine. I can watch it while I eat."

"As you wish."

Jacob saw the broad grin and wink his assistant aimed at him before Pym dropped beside the lower section of the beam engine again. The man was wasting his time matchmaking. No matter how attractive Jacob found Lady Caroline, there would be no banns read for them. He intended to keep his heart under firm control.

But that did not mean he could not enjoy Lady Caroline's company. When she handed him a plate topped with hearty portions of meat and bread and vegetables, he sat beside her. He listened to her stories about how

Gil had persuaded her to get a kitten from the Cothaire stables. The kitten had a mind of its own, which Gil had learned when he squeezed it too tightly and received a scratch.

"Now he knows he cannot treat it like a toy," she said. "Would you like more?"

Jacob was startled to see his plate was empty. He had been hungrier than he thought. Even though he would have liked to remain sitting beside her and having a second helping, he needed to return to his work.

When he told her that, she nodded and reached for the basket. He began to help her repack it, but she told him his time would be better spent fixing the beam engine. He contented himself with collecting Pym's plate and spoon. Handing them to her, he thanked her for her kindness.

She picked up the basket and stood. "I am glad to help. If you need supper—"

"Thank you for your kind offer, but Mrs. Trannock will send food for our evening meal, though I do hope we will be done before then. Besides, it is too dangerous for you to ride along the steep moor roads after dark."

She laughed, the sound swirling within him like the sweetest melody he had ever heard. "I have been riding these roads since I was first in the saddle. I was determined no boy, especially one younger than me, was going to out-ride me. If our parents had had any idea of the risks we took, we would have been confined within the walls of Cothaire. However, those reckless rides taught me to respect the hills and the moors and the cliffs along the shore."

"Even so, there is no need to risk yourself tonight."

With the basket between them, he could do no more than look into her gentle eyes. He had heard tales of highwaymen and lights on the moor where there should be none. She must have heard them as well, but he saw no fear in her eyes.

"I hope you discover what is amiss," she said.

"So do I!"

She took a single step back, but he could not compel himself to turn away. Holding her gaze with his own, he wished he could close the distance between them. He did not, aware Pym was a witness to everything they said and did.

When a smile curved along her expressive mouth, he grinned, too. He was unsure how long they might have stood there if the door had not opened.

A miner named Nance poked his head in and snarled a single word before he saw Lady Caroline standing between him and Jacob. Instantly the man's face altered from rage to deference.

"Excuse me, m'lady," he said so fast his words tumbled over one another. "I did not realize you were here. I can return later."

Lady Caroline motioned for him to enter, then bid them farewell as she went to the door Nance held open for her. She thanked the dirt-crusted miner as prettily as if he were the Prince Regent. The miner put his fingers to his forehead in a sign of respect.

Jacob felt the light fade from the building when Lady Caroline took her leave. He girded himself for Nance's complaints. When the miner asked only when the pumps would be working again, Jacob had to hide his shock at how the lady's kindness had dissolved the man's rage.

He gave Nance his best guess that it would be close to dark before the engine was pumping water from the mine again. The miner accepted the answer, then left.

Jacob had hoped his estimation was correct, but twenty-four hours later, he and Pym were still trying to get the pumps working, with no success. Jacob's eyes burned with fatigue, and his reflexes were slow. That accounted for the new scrapes he had on his face when he had not ducked quickly enough as Pym checked one arm on the pumps. His fingers had been pinched and rammed and struck while he used various tools to test different parts of the engine.

Everything seemed to be in working order, but the engine refused to keep running. They had gotten it started shortly after midnight and again before dawn, but both times, the engine had sputtered and died.

When he heard the door open, Jacob was startled. He had locked the door after too many miners came to ask questions and distract them from their work. Only one man other than him and Pym had a key.

"Yelland!" he called from the top floor. "Up here."

The mine captain wore a sore expression as he climbed the stairs.

"If you came here to find out when the pumps would be working again," said Jacob testily, "the only answer I can give you is: I don't know."

"The men aren't happy."

"Neither are we!" He took a deep breath, then said in a calmer tone, "We are examining the beam engine as quickly as we can. If we start it when there are problems we have overlooked, then we may do further damage to it."

Yelland clearly had no interest in being placated

with facts because he growled, "The men are saying the beam was stopped on purpose."

"Nonsense."

"They say you would rather have them working at Warrick Hall pulling off old wallpaper and paint."

"You know that is absurd."

"Aye, I do, but they don't. They know if they fail to meet the deadlines set in their bids, you won't have to pay them a farthing."

That was true, because, like most mines in Cornwall, the Warrick Hall ones ran on the tutwork system. Groups of miners bid against each other for a section of work. The one with the lowest bid and the most favorable deadline was the one chosen. If the work was not finished as bid, they did not get paid.

Jacob had tried to change that system when he first arrived because he believed it was unfair. The miners refused to change, not wanting to listen to his suggestion of replacing it with a daily wage. They feared they would end up with fewer coins in their pockets and were angry at the idea that those who worked the hardest would be paid the same as those who shirked.

Knowing it was a battle he would never win, Jacob had given up. It would be useless to mention that now. The men felt as thwarted as he did in their work.

He came to his feet and looked over his shoulder through the opening cut for the beam. The sun was past its zenith and heading toward the western horizon.

How could he have let time get away from him? He had been expected at Cothaire this afternoon for his first lesson with Lady Caroline. Looking at the motionless beam, he sighed. That lesson must be postponed.

"Tell the men we are proceeding as quickly as we

dare," Jacob said, wondering if Lady Caroline would have the same effect on Yelland she had on the miner yesterday. Foolish thought. "As well, I need you to have someone take a message to Cothaire. To Lady Caroline."

"What do you want the messenger to say?" Yelland's forehead furrowed as his eyes narrowed.

"He should express my apologies for not calling as I promised." He was not going to say anything about lessons in Yelland's hearing. The mine captain would spread the word far and wide that the new baron needed etiquette lessons.

"Anything else?"

"No. That covers it. Send someone immediately. If—"

His name was shouted by Pym. Urging Yelland again to have the messenger leave without delay, he ran to where Pym held a broken bolt in one hand and a wrench in the other.

"I found the problem," his assistant said. "This bolt failed, though I am not sure why."

With a sigh, he slid down to stand beside Pym. "Now, let's see if we can devise a solution so this doesn't break again."

As they bent to the task, Jacob knew the repairs would take all afternoon and longer. He doubted he would return to Warrick Hall before dawn.

Other than her footfalls, the upper gallery was silent. Caroline paced from the large window to the top of the front staircase. At first, she had been walking Joy in an effort to get the baby to sleep. She had made the journey back and forth so many times, it was a wonder her shoes had not worn out.

Where was Lord Warrick? He was more than tardy. He was late.

She paused by the window and looked out. She had a clear view of the road to the gate. It was empty. Holding her breath, she listened for the sound of the beam engine. A storm last night had roiled the waves in the cove, and they crashed on the shore. She could not hear over them to determine if the beam engine was running or not.

Lord Warrick had seemed pleased to see her when she brought a midday meal to the engine house yesterday. Only now did she realize how much she had looked forward to spending time with him again. Teaching him gave her a purpose that helping with Warrick Hall did not. She was not sure why, and it might be immaterial if he had decided to forego the lessons.

"Staring out the window is silly," she said aloud. She wished she had not spoken when her words echoed hollowly along the gallery. The baby stirred but did not wake up.

Suddenly, being with only Joy seemed too much like being alone. Gathering up her skirt, she went to the stairs and descended them.

Baricoat met her at the bottom. He mentioned that her sister, Susanna, and her sister-in-law Elisabeth had arrived for a call, and Maris had returned from the village where she had been delivering a basket to a sick family. She sent up silent thanks to God, who had heard her prayer for company.

Caroline's steps were lighter when she went to the room they called the solar. Its big windows offered a view of the gray-and-brown landscape. Even the sea was dull beneath dark clouds that hung from one horizon to the other. Inside the room, bright conversation mixed with the children's cheerful voices. The little ones were playing on the floor. Joy wiggled eagerly in her arms, so she put the baby down.

"Look at her go!" crowed Susanna as Joy scrambled on hands and knees to the other children.

"She wants to walk." Caroline took a seat next to Maris and smiled at the circle of women. Picking up a cup, she reached for the teapot. "Or rather, I should say she wants to walk desperately. See?"

The littlest girl crawled to Bertie, then up him in an effort to lever herself to her feet. Gibberish burst from her once she was standing like a miniature mountaineer who had reached the peak.

Her victory was short-lived. They laughed when Bertie shook his head, and Joy dropped to sit on the floor with a soft plop. That did not deter her. She made a beeline for a nearby chair and began to pull herself to her feet again.

"Persistent, isn't she?" Maris asked with a smile.

"You have no idea how stubborn she can be. She refused to nap this afternoon, but I had hoped she would before Lord Warrick arrived for his etiquette lesson."

The other women stared at her. Elisabeth found her voice first to ask, "Etiquette lesson?"

"Yes, I agreed to tutor him on what a gentleman needs to know to be a part of the *ton*." She could not contain a chuckle at her family's astonishment.

Her sister exchanged a glance with their sisters-in-law before Susanna said, "I know you are advising him on preparing that old mausoleum for his family's visit, but I had not heard you were giving him etiquette lessons. Why would you do that?"

"In part because it is the season for giving." She smiled as Joy used her leg to pull herself to a standing position. Stroking the little girl's silken curls, she raised her eyes and looked at each of the other women, one by one. "I have been given much this year. It is only right I give something in return."

Elisabeth said quietly, "You are right, Caroline. A gift is a blessing, especially the gift of time and knowledge."

"I cannot argue with that," Susanna replied, "but Lord Warrick is more than a bit eccentric."

"You have said that before." Caroline laughed. "If he is not willing to learn, I will put an end to the lessons. However, if he is as eager as he says to refine his manners, then I will be more than willing to help."

Maris stretched to make sure each boy had an equal number of blocks. She looked at Caroline steadily as she asked, "What is the other reason?"

"I am not sure what you mean."

"You said you were helping him in part because it is Advent. What is the other reason you agreed?" Maris winked at the other women. "Have you set your cap on our neighbor? He is a fine-looking man, especially when he is not covered with oil and dirt. Say the word, and we will play matchmaker for you."

Caroline shook her head. "No, thank you. If I do set my cap on another man, it will be because he moves my heart as John did. I suspect there is a different sort of being alone if one marries someone they do not love."

She hoped they would accept that as the truth. Speaking of her infertility was too intimate a subject, even with her sister and sisters-in-law. She had told no one but John and her mother about the midwife's opinion that Caroline would never conceive a child, and she had sworn them to keep the sad truth a secret. Sometimes she thought her mother might have told Father, because unlike her siblings, he never brought up the topic of her remarrying. It could be he had remained a widower for as long as she had been a widow, so he respected her decision not to marry again.

It was a choice she must not ever reconsider. She did not want to disappoint another man as she had John when she could not give him the child they both had wanted.

The beam engine had been repaired, because Caroline heard it when she awoke after a night where nothing seemed to assuage Joy's pain. She hoped the baby's tooth would break through soon. Until then, the baby was ill-natured day and night.

Her own temper was not much better. She was annoyed at Lord Warrick for not coming to Cothaire yesterday. She was equally irritated with herself for caring.

Deciding an outing might cool her head and also keep Joy awake during the afternoon so she would sleep that night, Caroline collected the baby and Gil, as well as the wagon she put Joy in when they went for a walk. Gil asked to go to the village store Elisabeth had inherited from her parents. The children liked to choose a sweet from the ones available there.

Maybe one of the hard candies on a stick would be the way to free Joy's tooth.

With that thought, she sent for her coat and the children's wraps. She checked Gil's feet to make sure his shoes were securely on while she explained his kitten would not be allowed to go with them because it would not walk on a leash.

"Lady Caroline," called the familiar voice belonging to the Porthlowen doctor.

Mr. Hockbridge had followed in his father's footsteps as the area's only doctor when the elder man's struggling heart had forced him to retire. His hair, that was such a pale blond it looked almost white, thinned at his crown. Fatigue had worn lines into his face, even though he could not be more than a year or two older than she was.

"May I speak with you, Lady Caroline?" he asked.

She looked at Gil, who gave her an anxious glance. She wanted to reassure him they would have their outing this afternoon, and she gave him a quick smile before saying, "Of course, Mr. Hockbridge. I did not realize you had been called to Cothaire."

"I like to stop in and see how the earl fares between attacks of gout. He seems to be doing much better."

"He has not had a bout in almost a month. Previously they seemed to come one right after another." She clasped Gil's hand, so the little boy did not scurry away.

"That is excellent news. I assume he is following the food restrictions I have suggested."

"With reluctance." She smiled. "Mrs. Ford has been very creative with our meals, but Father misses meat and fish. He complains each time a course is served without either. However, I believe he finds that easier to understand than why he should not use tincture of willow bark to fight the pain."

"It seems to make gout worse. Winter is coming,

so it should be easier for you to obtain ice to ease his discomfort."

"Our ice house has provided what he needs. With a late spring and early winter, we should be able to replenish what has been used."

"I am glad to hear that." He hesitated, glanced at the tip of his boots, then asked, "Would you like to walk with me along the cove?"

"To discuss Father's care further?"

"No."

"Oh." Caroline knew hesitating on her answer might suggest she was not pleased at the idea of spending time with him. "As you can see, I had planned to take the children on an outing. Gil has been teasing to go to the shop in the village where he can get a treat."

"Excellent," he said, even though his expression discounted his answer. "I will walk with you, if you don't mind."

"Certainly not."

Pulling Joy in the wagon behind her and holding Gil's hand, Caroline went with Mr. Hockbridge through the gate and on to the narrow road leading to the village on the cove. Already candles were visible in windows, because dark came early in the weeks leading up to Christmas.

Caroline asked his advice for easing Joy's difficulties with her first tooth, and he thought her idea for a piece of hard candy on a stick might be the very thing to help the tooth come out. More than once, he seemed to be on the edge of changing the subject, but he did not. She wondered what he had on his mind.

The collection of cottages flanked the streets in the village set on the cove's inner curve. Two lengths of

ragged cliffs curled around, one inside the other to protect the beach from storms. Drying seaweed and other
debris marked the high tide on the sand and stones. The
fishermen's boats were drawn up beyond that dark line.

Caroline slowed as they reached the street where
the doctor lived. Bidding him a good day, she thought
once more, he had something else he wished to say.
Again he said only he hoped she would have the same.
He began to walk away, and she raised her hand to
wave farewell. He turned on his heel, came back and
took her hand, bowing over it with perfect manners.
His fingers caressed her palm, but she was unsure if
he did so on purpose, or it was nothing more than him
releasing her hand.

"I hope I shall see you again soon, my lady," he said.

"You are always welcome at Cothaire."

With a flicker of something that looked like vexation, he nodded and bid her a good day.

How odd! Usually Mr. Hockbridge was straightforward and said what he meant.

Caroline walked to her sister-in-law's small shop,
which provided items the villagers could not make or
trade for themselves. Gil threw open the door and ran
in. The shelves ringing the interior were filled with
items, from glass jars to sugar and flour, but Gil had
eyes only for the collection of candy in a basket on the
wood counter.

He pulled up a stool so he could see over the top of
the counter. Peggy Smith, Elisabeth's young assistant,
came over to discuss the important issue of which piece
he would select. Dark-haired Peggy had been on the
sand the day the children were rescued and brought

ashore. A shy girl, she delighted in talking with the youngsters.

After Caroline lifted Joy from her wagon, she followed Gil across the shop. She had no chance to say as much as a greeting before Elisabeth came around the counter.

"I saw the doctor with you. Is everyone well at Cothaire?" she asked.

"Yes. He came to check on Father." Caroline frowned. "Though I must say he acted oddly."

"I agree. I saw him bowing over your hand before he took his leave. And in public!" Elisabeth laughed lightly. "By nightfall, everyone in Porthlowen will be prattling about how you and the doctor are courting."

"I cannot halt silly tongues from wagging. Let them think what they wish."

"'Tis not the gossips I worry about. 'Tis Mr. Hockbridge. Does *he* think you are courting?"

"Of course not."

"Are you sure?"

Caroline wanted to reply she was, but the truth was that Mr. Hockbridge's words and actions today could be explained easily if he believed he was beginning a courtship with her. She must find a way to let him know as quickly and as gently as possible that she was the wrong woman to woo. Even a doctor would want a son to inherit his business.

This was a complication she did not need, and she had no idea how to put an end to his courtship without putting an end to their friendship.

Chapter Six

"You made a complete jumble of your chances with the earl's daughter." Yelland chuckled as he leaned one shoulder on the doorjamb at the entrance to the engine house. He wore a superior smile, revealing several missing teeth.

"Is that so?" Jacob gave one more tug with the wrench, then stood as the beam engine started moving again. "I think that is it, Pym."

From a floor above where he knelt, he heard Pym's faint reply. He leaned back, watching the beam engine in its steady dance through the building, the metal arm catching the light from the rising sun.

Refusing to be ignored, the mine captain said, "While you were fixing this machine, she was out walking with the village doctor. Arm in arm, all cozy-like."

"And you saw this with your own two eyes?"

Yelland faltered, then mumbled, "Well, no." He rallied, crossing his arms over his chest. "I heard it from someone who saw them with his own eyes."

"Therefore, you have no idea what the circumstances truly were." Jacob did not want to discuss Lady Caroline with Yelland.

"But she was with the doctor."

Jacob sighed. Yelland clearly did not intend to give up on the subject. "That is not unusual. Lady Caroline cares for the people of Porthlowen. She might have been going to visit someone who was ill."

"With a babe and a boy in tow?"

Keeping his expression bland, he said, "You are asking me to speculate on gossip, and I will not, especially as neither you nor I witnessed the events."

"Thought you would want to know, seeing as how you have been visiting Cothaire and the lady." He shrugged. "If you don't care, then why should anyone else?"

"Exactly."

His terse answer cracked Yelland's arrogance. The mine captain had not expected Jacob to agree with him. It was a skill Jacob had learned when dealing with recalcitrant students and his family. During their youth, his brother, Emery, had often refused to give up on an argument even when it clearly should have been over. As soon as he could, Jacob would concur with one of Emery's less outrageous statements, and the quarrel would have to end.

Yelland opened his mouth once, then twice and a third time before he stamped out. The door slammed so hard in his wake the wood panel vibrated.

Jacob paid it no mind. Yelland was becoming more troublesome with each passing day, always looking for the opportunity to incite a brangle with Jacob or to cause foment among the miners. Why? Jacob had no answer.

As he turned to see the beam rocking overhead, he frowned. The many breakdowns raised his suspicions. He looked past the rail. The pumps brought up water from the mine shaft again. The system was simple. To have it fail over and over was infeasible.

Unless someone was damaging it intentionally to create trouble.

A troublemaker like Yelland, perhaps.

Pushing away from the rail, he turned to his assistant. "We did it again, Pym. You have a real nose for finding what ails this engine."

The shorter man preened. "Glad to be of help."

"Nobody knows this engine as well as you and I do." He clapped Pym on the shoulder.

"Not Yelland, that is for sure." Pym's mouth contorted as he spat out the mine captain's name. "No matter how much he loiters around here, he will never be able to learn everything about this beam engine."

"I agree, but I also want you to start training someone else in keeping the beam engine going." When his assistant's face blanched, he added, "Not Yelland. Find someone with an interest in machinery."

Did Pym suspect the mine captain was involved in the engine's failures, too? Jacob wanted to ask, but, until he had more information, he needed to keep his suspicions to himself.

"But I can handle her as well as anyone else," Pym argued. "Better!"

Jacob did not smile at how Pym always called the engine "her." Instead, he nodded as he picked up a discarded cloth and wiped his hands on it. He threw the rag in the barrel with the other trash. It was tempting to think of doing the same with Yelland.

"Let me know if there are any more problems," he said, grabbing his greatcoat.

"Are you returning to Warrick Hall?"

He was about to say yes, then shook his head. "I need to stop at Cothaire first." He owed Lady Caroline an apology for missing his lesson yesterday.

Pym nodded before turning to watch the beam engine.

As he pulled on his coat, Jacob realized he needed to change out of his clothes that were covered with stains from his long hours of work. He could not appear before an earl's daughter covered with oil and sweat.

He knew better, even before his first lesson in deportment. Yes, that was the reason he wanted to look his best when he appeared at Cothaire. He wanted to believe it, but could not ignore how something gnawed at him each time he imagined Lady Caroline and the doctor strolling with only a toddler and an infant for chaperones. Not that they would have a chance to do anything untoward, because they were on the oft-traveled path between Cothaire and the village.

He was being absurd. Lady Caroline was a diamond of birth, and she would not do something to risk her and her family's reputations. He must not allow Yelland's words to poison his mind.

The house was busy with its usual routine when Caroline reached the ground floor after leaving Gil in the nursery to have breakfast with Bertie. When Irene had offered to look after Joy as well, Caroline had agreed. Trying to eat while keeping small fingers off her plate was a futile exercise. Aromas of breakfast urged her to hurry to the breakfast-parlor, and she gave into temptation. Something to eat and a steaming cup of coffee would fortify her for the day ahead of her.

No one else was in the breakfast-parlor. She was glad to see the windows now had glass in them. The room had been dark with wood put over the windows in an attempt to keep out the cold November air. Food waited on the sideboard, steaming and smelling delicious. As she entered, a footman appeared to fill a cup with coffee and place it where she usually sat each morning.

She selected what she wanted from the covered servers. Eggs, sausage and some toast. Perhaps a bit of jam, as well. As a young woman, she had starved herself in order to look like the illustrations in pattern books. She had given up before she met her husband, and John had never complained she was not as thin as a stick. To own the truth, her clothes would soon need to be taken in if she kept losing weight. Chasing after a baby who could crawl unbelievably fast and a little boy who was even quicker had melted inches off her.

She had seated herself at the table when Baricoat opened the door and walked in. He no longer carried his left arm at a stiff angle, and she was glad it had healed despite his insistence he would not take any time away from his duties. After one attempt to suggest he rest, the household had given up, knowing he found the very idea he could not fulfill his duties while he had breath in his body inconceivable.

"Lord Warrick wishes to speak with you, my lady," he said.

Caroline hid her shock. "Show him in."

If the baron had come to apologize, she would remind him the lessons had been *his* idea. He was welcome to change his mind, but she expected him to let her know. Her whole afternoon had been planned around his visit.

And if he had been here, I would not be the source of speculation about Mr. Hockbridge courting me.

She silenced the thought. She could not blame Lord Warrick for others' misconceptions...or even her own. Had Mr. Hockbridge intended his escorting her and the children to the village to be the first step in a courtship? No matter how many times she replayed the events in her mind, she could not be certain. If he truly thought she was interested in him, she must let him know immediately he was mistaken. To speak of it before she was certain, however, could lead to embarrassment for both of them.

The doctor vanished from her mind when Lord Warrick appeared in the doorway. Her breath caught as she took in the sight of him. His navy blue coat was so dark it appeared black. The yellow waistcoat he wore beneath it was embroidered with white and green in an intricate pattern. Pale cream nankeen breeches ended in the brightly polished boots that rose to his knees. From his well-tied cravat to the tips of his toes, he looked every inch the peer he was.

The very handsome peer he was.

Realizing she held a piece of toast partway between her plate and her mouth, she lowered it. She looked away, aghast. She should not be staring at him like some awestruck miss gawping at her first soirée.

"May I come in?" he asked.

"Of course. Would you like some coffee?"

"Yes, thank you."

Rising, as a footman poured a cup and set it in front

of Lord Warrick, she went to the sideboard and spooned a generous portion of food on to a plate. She let the steam from the serving pieces wash up over her face. If she appeared as flushed as she felt, she could blame the food's heat.

She returned to the table and handed him the plate. After he thanked her, she sat again. "Please, sit." She smiled her appreciation to a footman who replaced her cup of coffee with a fresh one. "Go ahead and eat, my lord. I suspect you have not broken your fast yet this morning."

He bowed his head for a moment to say grace, then reached for a fork and pushed a generous portion of the eggs on to a piece of toast. Taking a large bite, he repeated the motions twice more in rapid succession. He closed his eyes in obvious appreciation. Opening them, he hesitated as he was about to take another bite.

"Do not let me keep you from eating," Caroline said with a smile. "With two brothers, I am accustomed to hearty appetites."

"I did not come here to eat but to apologize for failing to arrive for my first lesson yesterday. I hope you understood why from the message I sent."

"Message? I received no message from you."

He set his fork beside his plate. "You didn't? I asked for a messenger to come here and explain why I would not be able to call as we had planned. I should have checked and made sure the messenger was sent. My only excuse is the same as the reason you were supposed to hear from the messenger—the beam engine continues to fail."

"*More* problems with your new steam engine?"

"Both Pym, my assistant, and I have plenty of

knowledge of such engines, but neither of us have been able to ascertain why it fails to run as it should. We fix each problem after we find it. I am thankful that Pym has a real ability to pinpoint the trouble."

She heard his frustration in every word. Lord Warrick was not averse to hard work. He could have left the day-to-day running of the mines to the miners, as his uncle had, but instead, he spent long hours, week after week, ensuring their safety.

"Do you think you have solved the problem now?" she asked.

"One disruption does not seem related to another. Random failures, but nothing bad enough for me to make the decision to replace the unit." He sighed. "That would be a last resort, requiring me to close the mine for at least a month while a new steam engine is shipped here and installed. I find…" Emotions flashed through his eyes so quickly she could not gauge them.

"You find what?"

"That I am prattling as if I had enough tongue for two sets of teeth." He shook his head. "I despise silly clichés, but it fits me today."

"But what did you find, my lord?" she asked again.

"If this is a lesson in manners, you can change the subject as you did with the Winwood twins at church. I know I am obsessed with machines and how they function or don't. I find most people fall asleep if I talk too long about my work."

"But you should talk about it. Father taught us it did not matter which topics interested us. Whatever they are, we should pursue learning more about them, no matter what."

A sincere smile edged across his expressive face. "You are very kind, my lady."

"Not simply kind. I am being honest. Who knows what I might learn if I listen to you? The teacher can be a student, as well."

"True." He began eating again, then looked up. "I hope your father is well."

"Why do you ask? Oh, you heard about Mr. Hockbridge walking the children and me to the village." She shook her head with a wry smile. "Even though I have lived my whole life in Porthlowen, I am amazed at the speed of gossip. Mr. Hockbridge was here to check on Father, who is doing well, and—"

"You do not owe me an explanation."

"My words were not intended as an explanation, but a recital of the facts. Repetition can wring any truth out of gossip."

He flinched, even though she had answered him in her gentlest voice. In many ways, this intelligent man was naïve. Living in his academic world had meant him failing to learn about how other people acted.

As if she had spoken her thoughts aloud, Lord Warrick said, "Thank you for reminding me of what I have learned too well. A small town has nothing on a university where young men can spread gossip more swiftly than they do an ague."

"That is fast." She laughed.

When he chuckled, too, he changed the subject to the work underway at Warrick Hall. He planned to hire artisans to do the final work, but some of the miners and their families were glad to do the necessary demolition in exchange for a fair wage.

At last, he pushed aside his empty plate. "Shall we start?"

"On what?"

"My lessons." He gave her a teasing smile. "I have not given up on the idea of bettering myself."

Caroline nodded. "If you have time after our lesson, I know the children would be pleased to see you. Gil has drawn a picture he wants to give you. He tells me it is a kitten, so, please, act as if you can see exactly that."

"I appreciate knowing ahead of time. I would not want to hurt his feelings."

"So, which aspect of etiquette do you wish to start with?"

"Paying calls. I made a muddle of it, I could see, when I came here the day of the explosion."

She stood, and he came to his feet, too.

"Don't look startled, my lady," he said. "I do have basic manners."

"I know that, of course. If I appeared surprised, it is because my thoughts were already moving ahead."

When he nodded and motioned for her to continue, she was relieved he had failed to see that she was not being completely honest. Her thoughts were moving forward, but not to the lesson. As she had seen him standing across from her on the other side of the breakfast table, she had—for the length of a single heartbeat—imagined how it would be to have a handsome, intelligent, witty man like him sitting across from her each morning. No, not like him. *Him.*

Not that it ever could come to pass, but for a brief moment, she had savored the idea.

Caroline pushed the foolish fantasies aside and instructed Lord Warrick to pretend the breakfast-parlor door was the entrance to a London townhouse. As he stood in the corridor, she drew a chair away from the table and sat. She was, she explained, sitting in her front parlor and ready to receive guests.

He grinned uncomfortably as he knocked on the molding. "Like this?"

"Yes. The door opens. When you come into a house, a servant should greet you."

"A footman?"

"Yes," she repeated. "If we were in London, the footman would expect you to present a calling card."

Lord Warrick's gaze rose toward the ceiling as if seeking heavenly help, and, grinning, he shook his head. "A calling card? Why can't I tell the footman my name, the name of the person I am visiting, and find out if he or she is in?"

She laughed, but halted when he frowned. Did he think she was laughing at him? In a way, she was, she realized. She swallowed the rest of her laughter. "I am sorry, my lord, but you shall find the logic of a mathematician you hold dear has little bearing on the rules governing behavior among the *ton*."

"Then I am doomed."

"Do you always give up easily?"

His eyes narrowed. "I do not give up, Lady Caroline. Neither easily or any other way. Don't my efforts to keep the beam engine running prove that?"

Holding her hands up in a pose of surrender, Caroline said, "I retract the question." She began to outline how he should present his card. "We will discuss more complex aspects of calling card etiquette later."

"More complex?"

"You have no idea."

With a terse chuckle, he said, "That is what I want you to teach me. It seems as if there is more to learn than I imagined."

Caroline continued to walk him through what he should do. She explained how a person could be in the house when one called, but was said not to be at home if not receiving guests. She told him the days someone was at home were general knowledge during the Season. Some peers intentionally chose a time that overlapped a rival's.

"I had no idea people were so competitive in Town," he said, shaking his head in puzzlement.

"The Season is a race, and prizes go to those who compete the hardest. The best matches, the largest marriage settlements, the greatest prestige, the most political clout at Whitehall and beyond." Her smile returned. "Which is the reason why I chose not to return after my first Season there."

"And you had found a match here."

"Yes."

"It must have been a shock to the *ton* when an earl's daughter married a sailor."

She knew he did not mean to be cruel as some had when her banns were announced. There had been whispers she had anticipated her vows and was pregnant with John's child. Others suggested the child belonged to someone else, and her father had bribed John to marry her to give her baby a name. Knowing those were the people who always sought the worst in any situation in order to make themselves look better, she had tried to pay the comments no mind. Still, they had hurt.

"It was." She added nothing more.

He came into the breakfast-parlor and over to where

she sat. Dismay lengthened his face. "Forgive me. I should not have reminded you of your greatest grief. I know how painful it is to lose someone you love."

The urge swept through her to throw her arms around him and hug him as another stone fell from the wall she had built around her heart. What a kind man he was! He thought her silence was because of sorrow at John's death.

"Thank you." She flicked her fingers toward the door before she could no longer fight the yearning to have his arms around her. "Let us continue."

"As you wish."

Watching him return to the door, she wondered if he had spoken of the loss of his parents or someone else. She could not ask. Having him tell her might dismantle the protective walls they both kept around their hearts.

Caroline forced such thoughts aside as she began the lesson anew. She spoke of what he could expect upon being invited into a house. When she mentioned a footman would take his hat, gloves and coat, he grinned.

"Now I understand," Lord Warrick said, "why your footman sounded as if he were trying to loosen a clog from his throat when he followed me that day. He had expected me to surrender my outerwear upon my arrival."

"Yes. Now…" She gestured for him to step into the room. "Let's assume you have been brought to a lady who lives in the house. You might be calling on her, or she is receiving you if the person to whom you wish to speak is delayed. What do you do?"

He walked to her. When she laced her fingers together, making it impossible for him to take her hand, he asked, "What am I doing wrong now? I thought I was supposed to bow over the lady's hand upon greeting her."

"You are, but only after she offers her hand to you."

"Oh." His face lengthened and paled, making the healing cut on his cheek more obvious.

She patted his arm. "Don't look crestfallen. Surely you have had students who make errors, and you helped them learn not to do so again."

"Yes, but on paper." He gave her a wry smile. "I dare say I cannot recall the last time a piece of paper was offended."

"True." Holding out her hand, she said, "Once a lady has extended her hand, you may take it and bow over it, raising it slightly if you wish. Do not lift it too high, because you don't want to pull her up off her chair or her feet."

He did not take her hand. "What of kissing a woman's hand? When is it appropriate or expected?"

"You would if you were very familiar with the lady and knew that was her preference. Otherwise, you are wiser simply to bow over her hand." She nodded toward her hand. "Why don't you give it a try?"

He reached out, and she noticed the many scars on his knuckles and his hands. They were hands belonging to a man who used them for hard labor. For the first time, she wondered how he managed to keep fixing the steam engine at the same time he must oversee the rest of his estate. No wonder he had not turned his attention to Warrick Hall until he learned of his family's upcoming visit.

When he took her hand in his, thoughts of his family, the beam engine or anything else vanished from her mind. She seemed surrounded by him, even though he stood an arm's length from her. His eyes caught hers as he bent toward her, and everything else in the room faded into oblivion while sweet sizzles spread outward from his hand. He touched only her fingers, but she was as aware of every breath he took as her own.

Lowering her eyes, she drew her hand out of his. That broke the connection between them. She came to her feet and laced her fingers together in front of her.

"How did I do?" he asked, pushing up his spectacles.

"Do?" Her voice was unsteady, and she wondered if he had even felt the sensations she had.

"Did I bow over your hand properly?"

"Yes. Yes, you did fine." She forced a smile, but it refused to stay on her lips. Glancing in his direction, she added, "I must ask you to excuse me. The children expect me."

"I thought you wanted me to go with you to see them."

"Yes, I did say that, didn't I?" She was babbling, but she could not halt herself. "I forgot which day it is. We are supposed to go to Susanna's house, so Gil and Joy can play with the twins. Forgive me for not seeing you out."

"When should I return?"

"What?" Her brain seemed incapable of a single thought. How had an ordinary touch unnerved her so deeply?

"For my next lesson. When do you wish me to return?"

Knowing she should not answer when she had her back to him, she faced him. He wore an easy smile. He saw her as his teacher, someone to explain the intricacies of etiquette. Nothing more. She was the one whose mind had sent her spiraling out of control when he bowed over her fingers.

"It probably would be best if I talk to my brothers about what you should learn. I don't want to make any mistakes." *As I did when I let you take my hand.*

"As you wish." Disappointment filled his voice.

She felt awful. She could not blame him for her silly reaction to his touch. "Why don't you give me a day or two to talk to my brothers? Does that make sense?"

"Yes," he said, though with reluctance.

Thanking him for coming to Cothaire and asking him to have any questions on etiquette ready for the next time they met, she hurried from the breakfast-parlor. A day or two? Would that be enough time to get her emotions under control? She wondered it was even possible, even if she had a lifetime.

Chapter Seven

Caroline took a steadying breath as she stepped into the entry hall of Warrick Hall. This time, she was prepared for the deterioration she would see. She had prayed on the trip from Cothaire that she could keep her reactions to the baron under control. The best ways, she knew, were to avoid letting him touch her or looking too deeply into his eyes.

Wherry, the butler who looked as ancient as the house, greeted her warmly. If he was surprised to see she had brought Gil and Joy with her, as well as two footmen from Cothaire, he gave no sign.

"I will tell Lord Warrick of your arrival, my lady," he said with a bow of his head.

"No need." The baron walked into the entry hall.

Caroline's good intentions came to naught as she stared at him again. Unlike the last time she had seen him, he did not wear a coat. The cut of his waistcoat emphasized the breadth of his shoulders, which gainsaid his former academic life. His hair was tousled, and a streak of dirt underlined his left cheekbone.

Giving her a beguiling smile, he said, "I can see

from the astonishment on your face that our next lesson needs to be about properly receiving guests. I have been working alongside the men I hired in an effort to get the project finished on time. I think it has gone from impossible to improbable that we will be done before my family arrives."

She held the baby close like a shield between her and Lord Warrick's ineffable charm. "I hope you don't mind I brought the children. Gil pleaded with me to let him come." She looked at the little boy who was staring wide-eyed around them.

Lord Warrick bent so his face was even with the child's and held out his hand. When Gil put his on it, the baron solemnly shook the little boy's hand.

"Master Gil, you are always welcome at Warrick Hall," he said.

"Really?" Gil's eyes crinkled in a grin.

"A man says what he means. That requires him to tell the truth and not make up any stories."

Gil nodded, as serious as Lord Warrick acted. "Tell truth." He paused, then asked with sudden dismay, "No stories?" He gave Caroline a horrified glance.

"We will have stories before bed," she said quickly. "That is not what Lord Warrick means. He means we should always be honest. The stories in books are just that. Stories."

"Stories go in books. Gil tell the truth." He repeated the sentences a couple of times, then asked, "Kitties?"

"We may see them in the house," she said to the little boy. "If not, you may ask Lord Warrick if you can go into the stable to see the cats there."

"Go?" he asked the baron.

"First," Caroline said, "we have to see the kitties here."

"Cuddle kitties here." Gil's eyes widened again as he pointed at a strip of torn wallpaper and said, "Kite."

Lord Warrick ripped it from the wall. "I don't think it will make a very good kite, but you can try."

Gil ran around the entry hall, letting the paper flutter behind him.

"As you can see, my lord," she said, "his attention jumps from one subject to another with the speed of a shooting star crossing the sky. It is a challenge to keep up with him." She smiled at Joy, who was kicking at the blanket wrapped around her. Loosening it, she went on, "Soon she will be talking, too." She glanced over her shoulder at the footman. "Haines and Repper have offered to help move larger pieces of furniture."

Both men bowed toward Lord Warrick. They were trying to hide their dismay and shock at the state of the house, but failed.

"Thank you, my lady," Lord Warrick said. "There are a few pieces I want to shift to see what is behind them."

"Where do you want to start?"

"I thought we would begin in the attic, because you have seen the rooms on this floor that need the least work." He grimaced. "Least being only a comparable term, because I am coming to believe ripping the whole place down and beginning anew might be easier."

She glanced at the children. "I had not realized you would want to work up in the attic. I don't think it is suitable for Gil and Joy."

The butler cleared his throat. "Begging your pardon, my lady, but Mrs. Trannock asked me to tell you she would be glad to watch over the little ones while you are helping my lord."

"What a wonderful solution!" She caught Gil's hand as he ran past. "If you will show me the way to the kitchen, Wherry…"

Like a row of ducklings, they followed the butler past the dining room where, she was happy to see, the crumbling plaster had been cleaned off the table and broken chairs removed. The kitchen stairs were too steep for Gil's short legs. Lord Warrick squatted to allow the little boy to climb up to wrap his arms around the baron's neck. Gil shrieked with excitement as they bounced down the steps.

A short woman, Mrs. Trannock wiped her hands on a pristine apron as she looked up from kneading bread. Not a wisp of gray littered her black hair beneath a floppy cap, though she must be as elderly as Wherry. Her round face brightened with a smile when she greeted them.

"Ah, look at the adorable *babanas*," she said.

"Bananas?" asked Lord Warrick as he knelt to let Gil slide off.

"*Babanas*," Caroline replied, emphasizing the second *b*. "It's Cornish for babies." She looked at the cook. "I see you are busy, Mrs. Trannock. Will you be able to watch Gil and Joy while we work in the attic?"

"The bread is ready to rise, and I know one lad who will be glad to help me punch it." Mrs. Trannock winked at Gil, who giggled. "Don't worry, my lady. If we need any help, we will send for you straightaway. Between us, Wherry and I have more than a dozen nieces and nephews who have children of their own. We have bounced each of them on our knees." Her smile widened as she took Joy, who tugged at the cook's cap. "Aren't you a sweet one?"

"Kitties?" asked Gil.

The cook chuckled. "Let me put out some milk. They usually come as soon as the bowl touches the floor."

As Gil walked away with the cook, fingers settled on Caroline's sleeve. Lord Warrick's fingers. She knew instantly, as fiery ripples spread outward from his touch.

"They will be fine," he murmured, close to her ear.

She nodded, all power of speech gone beneath the dual assault of his splendid touch and his breath slipping along her skin. Only the cook returning with a cloth bag gave her time to regain control of her senses and herself.

"You will need these," Mrs. Trannock said as she held out the bag to Lord Warrick.

He took it. "What is in this?"

"Rags. Everything in the attic has years of dust on it. You can use these to wipe some of it away."

"I hope there are a lot of rags in here."

The cook grinned. "There is a good breeze today. Open the windows, and it may do the work for you."

"Or make us sneeze until we cannot stand up." He thanked her before he motioned for Caroline and the footmen to come with him up a set of steps from the kitchen.

The staircase led into a wing of the house that had suffered even more than the rooms she had seen before. A whole section of ceiling had collapsed, and water dripped through the opening.

When Lord Warrick assured her other sections of the upper floor were in better condition, she followed him to a central corridor. As she looked in both directions, she bit back her groan. The furniture in the hallway appeared as if someone had thrown the pieces against a wall. Some were missing legs, and she saw large chips out of the edges. The walls were bare of paint. Their surfaces had weathered to a sickly brown between the closed doors.

She wondered about the state of the rooms beyond those doors but did not open one. Lord Warrick would not mind if she did; however, she guessed the sight of the chambers would depress her.

"The rooms in this wing are actually in surprisingly good shape compared to the ones downstairs," he said as if she had asked. "The paint has stayed on the walls, and some of the furniture is salvageable. We can look around if you wish."

"No. Let's see what you have in the attic we can use. After that, when we have some idea of what pieces are available, we can figure out how to set up the rooms." She peered to her right. "And in that direction?"

"Many of the windows have been broken for years, leaving everything exposed to the weather."

"I would suggest you have a door put up to block the ruined hallways, so no one wanders through them."

"I had already planned to do that. Doors with sturdy locks." A gust of cold wind rushed toward them. "They will keep this floor warmer." He opened a nearby door. "The attic is this way. Watch where you step."

Caroline followed Lord Warrick up the stairs. The steps creaked beneath her feet, and more than one wobbled. She heard a muffled oath, then a loud crack. Looking back, she saw Haines extracting his foot from a broken tread with the help of Repper.

"Are you hurt, Haines?" she asked.

"No, my lady," the ginger-haired footman replied as he nodded his thanks to Repper. "Didn't expect it would give way."

"Stay close to one side or the other," Lord Warrick cautioned. "As you have discovered, the wood is weakest in the middle."

The two footmen nodded, one moving quickly to the left while the other edged right.

"To bring furniture down these stairs will be impossible," Caroline said.

"I thought it might be simpler to lower whatever we choose by a pulley hung outside one of the attic windows."

She smiled. "I should have guessed you already had devised a solution."

Lord Warrick paused when he reached the top of the staircase. A closed door blocked the way. He put his hand on the old-fashioned latch. "Ready?"

"As much as I shall ever be."

"Ah, there is your curiosity again. You know what they say about curiosity."

"That it killed the cat? 'Tis a good thing I am not a cat, then, isn't it?"

When she laughed, he said over his shoulder, "Let me warn you. It is a jumble."

"Most attics are."

He did not reply. Pushing the door open, he stepped aside so she could enter first.

She sneezed as dust coiled around her ankles. She looked around, not wanting to disturb more dust until she could determine where to start first.

"Oh, my!" she said as Lord Warrick and the two footmen entered after her.

Unlike Cothaire, the attic at Warrick Hall was one vast space divided only by stone pillars holding up the roof. She was accustomed to a warren of rooms with at least the appearance of order. Furniture and boxes and individual items had been put in Warrick Hall's attic haphazardly, as if someone had opened the door and shoved them inside before hurrying to shut the door to prevent them from tumbling down the stairs.

"Where do you want to start?" she asked.

"I don't think it matters, though I think we can ignore the paintings over there." Lord Warrick motioned to framed canvases leaning against a wall. "I examined them, and they are portraits of the dreariest group of people I have ever seen." Lifting the top box off a pile, he put it on the floor between them. He bent to open it, then held out his hand for one of the cloths they had brought with them. "Hold your breath while I get rid of some of this dust."

She put her hand on his arm to halt him, then jerked it back as the powerful tingle raced through her fingers and up her arm again. Oh, bother! She had warned herself not to touch him, and she had forgotten less than a minute after they entered the attic.

"Yes?" His voice was neutral. Had he felt the tingle, too? For the first time, she thought he might have.

The situation was getting out of hand. She could not let him think she was interested in more than friendship. Already, if Elisabeth was right, Mr. Hockbridge wanted to court her. Telling him she did not want him to do so was sure to cause bad feelings. To have to do the same with Lord Warrick would be even more difficult.

Squaring her shoulders, she decided to act as if

nothing out of the ordinary had happened. "I think we should start with the larger pieces while Haines and Repper get as many of the windows open as they can."

Lord Warrick did not look at her as he said, "As you wish, my lady. I saw some headboards in this direction." He went to his left.

"How many guests are you expecting?" she asked, picking her way around crates and draped items.

"Four. My stepmother, my brother and his wife, and his wife's sister."

"Is it likely they would bring anyone else with them?"

"They have not mentioned that, but it is possible."

"Then you would be wise to have a couple of extra bedrooms ready." She tapped her fingertip against her chin. "How many bedchambers do you have in the wing you plan to use?"

"Six or seven." He gave her a sheepish grin. "I have not taken the time to get an exact count."

"Either six or seven bedchambers will suffice, I am sure. Let's find what we need before it gets too dark to work up here." She pushed up her sleeves and smiled. "To work!"

Lady Caroline was as good as her word. Finding a length of thin fabric, she tore it into strips and gave them to Jacob and the footmen to wrap around their hands and tie around their heads like turbans. That would allow them to wipe away spider webs without getting the sticky filaments on their skin or in their hair.

Jacob admired her efficiency as she directed the footmen, and they hurried to obey her requests. She gave orders easily, but with a kindness that suggested the footmen were vital parts of the team.

Would he ever be able to do the same? He had no trouble barking out orders at the mines, but doing so at Warrick Hall made him uneasy. Someone, he could not remember whom, had told him a member of the *ton* must treat his servants as if they were invisible. It might have been Wherry, who seemed to feel it was not inappropriate to lecture a low-born baron on how to act in his own home. Those dressing-downs had been one of the reasons he had decided he needed lessons from Lady Caroline.

Every word she spoke reminded him how gauche he must appear to her. Suddenly he felt as if he had a dozen hands and half as many feet and did not know where to put any of them. His elbow bumped a box, tipping it to the floor where it cracked open. Straw scattered from it. Several cups shattered as they struck the floor. Before he could react, the footman rushed around the box and began to gather up the shards.

Should he thank the man or not? Before he could decide, he heard Lady Caroline gasp, "Look at this! It is a cradle!"

As she dropped the blanket covering it to the floor, he could see it was most definitely a cradle. If he had to guess, he would say it was not more than a few decades old. Thick oak planks had been used to construct its sides and hood. Delicately curved finials were set at each corner to allow someone to rock it. The dark stain was blistered on one side, and he wondered if it had gotten too close to a hearth or if the dampness had ruined the finish.

She ran her fingers along the smooth wood as she

looked at the beautiful interior carved with images from nursery rhymes. "It looks as if it has never been used. Did your uncle intend to marry and have a family?"

He shrugged. "You are asking the wrong man. My uncle never communicated with us."

"That is sad." She touched a carved flower on the inside and bent to admire the skill of the person who had designed and built the cradle. "And a surprise."

"Why do you say that?"

"We seldom saw your uncle, but he occasionally attended services at the Porthlowen church. I thought he appeared lonely, because he sat alone and seldom spoke. Some of the mining families came to our church even then, and they never greeted him."

"I have heard he was very eccentric."

"I think he was quite ill, especially toward the end of his life. Perhaps he did not feel well enough to engage in conversation or to receive guests in his home."

He curved his hand along her cheek and tipped her face toward him. Amidst her shock at his forward behavior, a softness filled her eyes and curved her lips in a fragile smile.

"You are amazing, Caroline Dowling," he said. "You always see the best in everyone."

"I try. We are urged not to judge others, for our own lives seldom can live up to being judged."

He watched as her lips formed each word; then he tried to shake off his fascination. She enticed him with every motion, but he needed to resist her allure. He knew that, but he wondered if he could have if one of the footmen had not called out a question to her and she looked away. Drawing in a sharp breath, he pondered how long he had been holding it as he gazed at her.

"I wonder what other surprises we will discover here," he managed to say when she turned to him again.

They began to inspect nearby items. He realized much of what had been stored in the attic was useless, and he was puzzled why anyone had brought it up the steep stairs instead of tossing it out.

"Look at this!" Lady Caroline drew a sheet away from what he had assumed was another portrait of a scowling ancestor.

It was, instead, a grand mirror. Almost as tall as she was, it was edged in a wood frame that must have been carved by the same artisan who had made the cradle. Flowers that ran through the scenes inside the cradle decorated the frame, along with animals, both real and imaginary. Each one was exquisitely chiseled from the wood, so that muscles and sinews were visible.

"This would be beautiful on the chimneypiece in the parlor," she said as she glanced over her shoulder.

"Getting rid of that ugly gilt mirror is a good idea. It looks as if the frame has been run over by a wagon."

Jacob returned to the search, glad they had found at least one item they could use. He had renewed hope that there would be others.

Caroline took another sip of the cocoa that had been waiting in the parlor when they emerged from the attic. She had no doubts that, in the kitchen, Gil's face was covered with chocolate. She hoped Mrs. Trannock had made enough for Haines and Repper, as well. The two footmen from Cothaire had worked hard, shifting crate after crate, as well as big pieces of dusty furniture.

At first she had been stumped on how to separate the pieces she wanted brought downstairs. Wherry had solved that when he brought tea to the attic for them. When he had seen her problem, he returned with a skein of faded blue yarn. She tied a length around the furniture she had selected. She had chosen enough for several rooms on the ground floor and for the bedrooms in one wing upstairs.

Other furniture should be brought from the attic before it was ruined, but it could wait until after Lord Warrick's family's visit was over. She thought of the cradle and wondered what other stories about the previous, very reclusive Lord Warrick would be discovered in the attic.

Lord Warrick entered the room and sat facing her. When she offered him a cup of the dark, rich cocoa, he smiled. "Mrs. Trannock makes the best hot chocolate in the world, and her chocolate cakes are almost as good."

"They sound wonderful."

"They are. I want to thank you for your help today, Lady Caroline. We were able to accomplish more than I expected. As I told you, I was daunted by the task."

"As you should have been when you took it on alone."

He took a sip, then said, "Wherry, though his heart is in the right place, cannot do heavy work like that."

"I agree. Have you considered hiring more servants? Wherry and Mrs. Trannock cannot manage this whole house themselves, especially when you have guests."

"I have been meaning to, but I have not had the time." He paused and cocked an ear.

She heard the faint sound of the beam engine. "Perhaps when matters at the mine don't demand all your attention, you will have more time for other things."

"I agree." He set his cup on the tray between them. "How does one go about such things as finding servants? Putting out the word that one is looking to hire or advertisements in newspapers? I am not sure how to begin."

"Both are excellent ideas, but it is simpler to ask for recommendations from your neighbors. There are always servants who wish to advance themselves and see opportunities at a house that is hiring."

"I will do that. My dear Lady Caroline, do you have any recommendations?"

She laughed at his somber tone. "I do, and, if you wish, I would be glad to interview them for you."

He shook his head. "I cannot ask that of you. You are already being generous with your time and expertise. I don't want to take advantage of your kindness."

"You are not. As I told you, I have found myself with too much time on my hands, now that Maris is taking over the duties of the lady of Cothaire. You would be doing me a favor to allow me to help."

He laughed. "Tell me. Will I ever be able to offer help graciously and make it sound as if *I* am doing *you* a favor by allowing you to assume my obligations?"

"If you don't keep missing your lessons."

"*Touché.*" He became serious again. "I would appreciate your help. I'm not even sure which servants I should hire."

"You need a footman or two as well as an assistant for your cook and two maids. Will your stepmother and the other women be bringing their own maids when they come to Warrick Hall?"

"I don't know."

"Then you might wish to hire three maids, so one can perform the duties of a lady's maid for your guests. That is the very minimum. You need to have a grounds-keeper by the time spring comes."

"I have hired a few men to repair the inside of the house, but I need more. I have gotten help from a few of the miners, but they already put in long hours at the mines. Do you know of any who are looking for work?"

"The Porthlowen fishermen cannot go out to sea once the winter winds stir up the waves. They are strong and unafraid of hard work. If you would like, I can tell Raymond about your interest in hiring men to help move the furniture and fix the rooms you plan to use. He will spread the word while he visits his parishioners."

"A good idea! What would I do without your help, Lady Caroline?"

"As I said, I am glad to help." Sipping the delicious chocolate, she hoped she was not being foolish as she asked, "Under the circumstances, do you think we could dispense with our titles and call each other by our Christian names?"

"Gladly." He smiled. "Gladly, Carrie."

She put her fingers to her lips in vain, because her gasp escaped.

Lord Warrick—Jacob—frowned, his brows lowering. "What did I do wrong now?"

"You called me Carrie."

"I thought—"

"Arthur is the only one who uses that name for me."

"Forgive me. I didn't know that."

"No need to apologize. It simply startled me." She

was the one who needed to relearn her manners. Making a scene about something incidental was silly. "If you wish, go ahead and call me Carrie, too."

"I am honored, but I will use it on one condition."

"What is that?" She relaxed when she heard his jesting tone return.

"Don't ever call me by the nickname my brother gave me."

"What is that?"

"Half-bake Jake."

She laughed so hard tears welled up in her eyes. With difficulty, she was able to promise around her laughter that she would never speak the silly name.

They spent the rest of the time while they finished their hot cocoa discussing his plans for the house. Only when darkness began to creep out of the corners of the room did she realize how swiftly the hours at Warrick Hall had passed.

As soon as Joy and Gil, who chattered about what he had done and seen in the kitchen, were brought, she checked that their wraps were in place. She thanked Jacob for his hospitality and asked Wherry to convey her appreciation to Mrs. Trannock for keeping the children busy and out of trouble.

The footmen were waiting outside by the carriage when the butler opened the door. A gust of wintry wind hastened into the entry foyer, and she held Joy's face closer to her own coat. Taking Gil by the hand, she turned to bid Jacob a quick farewell.

"Thank you for your help, Carrie," he said as he put his hands on her shoulders.

Did he feel her quiver at his wondrous touch? She bent to check Gil's coat as if it were simply a casual motion instead of an attempt to keep herself from step-ping even closer to him.

God, she prayed as she stood again, *don't let me forget what a disappointment I will be to any man who is foolish enough to be interested in me. Make me strong in my resolve and guide my steps along Your path.*

"As I have said time and again," she said aloud, "it is wonderful to have tasks to fill my time. I will also ask the Cothaire servants to spread the word that you are looking to fill positions here. I have no doubts we will have many suitable candidates within days."

"At least until they see the sorry state Warrick Hall is in."

"Have faith, Jacob. By the time your family arrives, the house will be ready."

"Are you sure of that?"

"Absolutely," she said, even though she was not. However, she knew he needed to have faith…as she did that all would resolve itself as it should. A half sob caught in her throat, because she knew everything resolving itself as it should would mean some other woman relishing his sweet caresses.

Chapter Eight

When Jacob arrived early at Cothaire for another lesson more than a week later, he was eager to tell Carrie that the furniture she had selected was out of the attic. It had been a greater task than he had guessed to get the largest pieces out through the windows and on to the rope attached to the pulley, but with the help of the men he had hired from Porthlowen, the job had gone well.

He asked the butler to have him announced to Carrie. He was surprised when the family's butler said that the earl wished to speak with him first. Surprised and unsettled. What could the Earl of Launceston want to say to him? He had met the man only a few times, because the earl suffered from gout, which kept him confined for days at a time to his rooms.

The only way to discover what the Earl of Launceston wanted was to follow the butler to a door. Jacob hid his astonishment. Usually, he knew from his few lessons with Carrie, a footman would be responsible for that task. Clearly the butler considered the duty important enough to do it himself.

When the door opened, Jacob realized he had been

in the room before. He had spoken with the earl's heir briefly there, and at that time, he had taken note of little about the room other than the huge portraits of horses and hounds on the walls. Other smaller pictures were scattered between them. It was a room meant for men, and the faint smell of tobacco suggested it was one where they could raise a cloud without bothering the ladies.

He noticed all that in the moment before he looked at the earl, who sat by the tall windows. The earl's dark hair, which he had bequeathed to his children, was woven with gray. His face was finely wrinkled, especially around his eyes, which were a peculiar shade of silver. That suggested he was a man who smiled often and easily, but his expression was serious.

"Lord Warrick," the butler intoned as if Jacob had initiated the meeting and his arrival were a surprise.

Jacob decided to ask Carrie about the butler's actions later.

"Thank you, Baricoat," the earl said, his voice deep and resounding.

The butler nodded and bowed his head before leaving the room, closing the door behind him.

"Sit, Warrick." The older man chuckled. "Despite what my children may have told you, I am no ogre."

"No one suggested you were," Jacob said quickly before realizing that the earl was jesting. He dropped into a chair close to the earl's.

"I can ring for tea, if you are hungry," the earl said, "but I am told that Caroline intends to include serving tea among her lessons with you today."

A heated flush climbed out of Jacob's collar. With Carrie, he could forget how silly it was for a grown man to need a tutor. He heard no disparagement in the earl's voice, but talking about the lessons made him uncomfortable.

"No need to look embarrassed, young man." The earl leaned back in his chair and pyramided his fingers in front of his face. "Any man who stops trying to better himself is a fool. I realize your uncle did nothing to prepare you for the role you have been given. You should be commended for your efforts."

"Actually, your daughter is the one who deserves praise. She is very patient with my fumbling attempts to absorb what she is trying to teach me."

Once more the earl laughed, and Jacob relaxed, pushing his spectacles into place yet again.

"My children can be quite single-minded when they have a goal. If I know my eldest, she will soon have you ready for court."

"I would rather avoid that honor."

"I understand completely, but are you planning to attend Parliament? Your uncle stopped going long ago, even though he received many requests to make an appearance. I know you did not know Maban Warrick, but he was a man who made his own rules and cared little about anyone else's."

Jacob nodded. "That is what I have heard of him."

"What I have heard about you, young man, suggests you are making excellent progress updating your mines."

"Thank you."

"It was sad to see your uncle pay less and less attention to the mines and the miners as his health and mind faltered. He did not leave Warrick Hall for the last decade of his life, and he received no one but his mine captain for the final five years."

"I did not know that." He wondered why nobody had mentioned this to him.

"From what my daughter has told me, I thought that might be the case. Your uncle was a broken-hearted man. He never recovered from the loss of his betrothed."

"I did not know he was ever betrothed." He thought of the cradle Carrie had discovered in the attic. Had his uncle had it made when he believed he would wed? "How did his betrothed die?"

"You would know that answer better than I because his betrothed married your father."

His eyes widened. He had no idea his mother had chosen one brother over the other. So much about his reclusive uncle suddenly made sense. Why would Maban Warrick want to provide support for the family of the woman who had married his brother instead of him?

"I did not realize," the earl said, "this would be a surprise for you."

"My father never spoke of his brother, and my mother died when my brother and I were fairly young." He wondered if his stepmother knew about the family's past.

"If I had known that, I would have been more tactful in mentioning the rift between Maban and your father, Austol."

"I appreciate knowing the truth."

"Good. From what I have heard of you, I thought that might be the case. Now tell me about your plans for Warrick Hall. Caroline mentioned that you are trying to prevent its further decline."

Jacob outlined what he intended to do. The earl interrupted him with suggestions for repairs Jacob should consider. When the earl changed the subject to the past in western Cornwall, Jacob thought of his own father entertaining them with stories in their cramped cottage. Neither he nor his brother had felt the pinch of poverty when Father had them laughing at his tales of someone he had met or something he had seen.

Not once had Jacob sensed the terrible loss his father must have felt every day of his life after he won the heart of his brother's betrothed. *How did you overcome it, Father, and live your life?* He lowered his head and changed the anguished question to a prayer to his heavenly Father. *Help me overcome the loss that haunts me, so I can live the life You want for me. I cannot believe You wish me to be mired in grief and guilt. Show me the way.*

He opened his eyes and focused on what the earl was saying about long-ago visits to Warrick Hall. In his mind he could hear Carrie urging him to have faith. He must while he waited for an answer to his prayer. He hoped it would come soon.

Carrie admired the arrangement on the bedside table. A trio of books were stacked next to a glass lamp. Draperies of the same green hung beside the two windows that reached from the floor almost to the ceiling. The books were histories of Cornwall she had found in a musty book-room. If Jacob's family was anything like him, they would enjoy reading such titles. She was pleased the tomes had aired out enough so she could place them in the bedroom.

Even a week ago, in spite of her words to bolster Jacob's hopes, she could not have imagined how Warrick Hall would be ready by the time his family arrived. The servants she had hired on Jacob's behalf had been a huge help with shifting furniture and cleaning. She had found other workers willing to paint the handful of rooms that had to be finished in time for Jacob's guests.

The gold parlor, a small dining room, a withdrawing room for the ladies and enough bedchambers were ready for Jacob and his family. Along with the corridors connecting them, the rooms had been emptied, scrubbed and redecorated. New mattresses had had to be obtained, because, despite the three cats' best efforts, mice were found nesting in every one.

The past fortnight had passed in a blur of getting Warrick Hall ready for guests, continuing Jacob's lessons, and spending time with her family enjoying the first weeks of Advent. She was relieved that Maris was handling the preparations for the annual New Year's Eve open house at Cothaire. Her sister-in-law had fewer and fewer questions for her each day, and Arthur was stepping with far more ease into the role as Cothaire's host as he prepared to take on that task for the open house as he had many of Father's other obligations.

"Ah, here you are." Jacob came into the bedchamber. He nodded to the maid who was folding freshly laundered blankets and placing them in the chest under the window, then smiled at Carrie. "You have worked wonders."

"I hope you don't mind that I took some paintings from the attic and brought them into the bedrooms.

With the new bedcoverings and draperies, the bare walls looked stark."

"You didn't bring any of the grim ancestors, did you? I fear they will give guests nightmares."

Laughing, she said, "No, I selected ones I thought would be soothing rather than frightening."

"The smartest thing I did was to give you carte blanche. Without your help, I would probably still be standing in the attic trying to decide where to begin."

"I doubt that." She adjusted the lamp, then appraised the tableau again. "What do you think?"

"It looks fine to me."

"I thought the books would appeal to your family because they are not familiar with Cornwall. The county has had an interesting history."

"Beverly is not much interested in history."

"I shall look for something else to put on the bedside table for this room."

He waved aside her words. "That won't be necessary. I doubt she will do much reading anyhow. She prefers conversation to words on a page."

"Of course, it is necessary." She wagged a playful finger at him. "Jacob, as the host, your only thoughts should be on the comfort and needs of your guests. Every minute of their visit."

"Is that what you do when I call?"

She laughed. "You are at Cothaire enough now to be considered a family friend. I noticed you addressing my siblings by their given names after you joined us for dinner last week."

"These 'Lord This' and 'Lady That' started getting tiresome."

"Wait until you go to London. You shall have 'Lord

This' and 'Lady That' and 'Sir So-and-So' and 'His Grace' as well as 'Her Grace' everywhere you turn." She paused, then asked, "Are you going to London for the Season?"

"I doubt it. As I am not looking for a wife now and I have pressing duties here, I see no reason to go. Are you thinking of going up to London yourself?"

"Me?" She shook her head vehemently. "No, thank you. I am beyond that nonsense. I prefer spring in Cornwall." Appraising the room again, she said, "This is set. The maids will keep dust out. If you allow the cats to continue to wander in here, they should make sure none of the mice return."

"Beverly would not appreciate that." He smiled. "My stepmother is a tolerant woman. Of most things, but mice are not among them."

"I am looking forward to meeting her."

"You will when they arrive."

"No, not then." When he started to protest, she hurried on. "Jacob, this is your first time being the host for your family since you became Lord Warrick. You don't need me nearby to make you nervous. You have learned so much, and it is time for you to put those lessons to work. In addition, you have not seen your family in many months. You will want time to be together."

"Miss Bolton will be here, and she is not part of my family."

"She is part of your brother's family. Also, Jacob, your family will be fatigued after their long journey. They will not wish to be put on display for your neighbors."

"You are right." He gave a terse laugh. "As you always are on these matters. Do you have any advice on making them feel at home?"

"Act as you always have with your family, and that will put them at ease. As for Miss Bolton, you must let her direct the course of your conversations. That is what a gentleman does when he is spending time with a young lady."

"Why didn't you tell me this before? I have not always let you lead the direction our conversations go in."

She slapped his arm with a chuckle. "Jacob, you and I are friends. We talk about what we talk about. It is not as if you are courting me."

Walking out of the bedroom so he had no chance to reply, she pointed out the changes she planned for the corridor. She was relieved when he approved each one, including the pale yellow she wanted to paint the walls above the wood paneling that probably had been installed when Queen Elizabeth ruled Britain.

"How is Gil?" Jacob asked, abruptly changing the subject.

"Did you see him and Joy downstairs?"

"No. I didn't realize they were here."

She peeked into a room as they passed and was glad to see it had been painted the light blue she had picked. Turning to Jacob as they continued along the hallway, she said, "Gil asked to come because he hoped to see you and thank you for the tool board you made for him. He has been having a wonderful time with it." She had been almost as delighted as Gil when Jacob had brought him a gift on his most recent visit to Co-thaire. On the board, Jacob had affixed bolts and nails connected with twine. "He loves loosening the nuts, and I found him using a shoe to pound on the nails."

"He is supposed to pluck the twine to make sounds."

"He prefers loud noises like the smack of a heel against the nails."

"That sounds like a boy."

"Several times," she said as they continued along the corridor past the other bedchambers, "he has asked if we could visit your engine house. He has heard everyone talking about it, and he wants to see it."

"Is he interested in science?"

She paused and faced him. "Maybe he is, but he wants to spend time with you. Perhaps we could arrange a time for him to visit."

"I would be honored to give the children a tour." His expression darkened. "Carrie, I must admit that I have done little to help in your search for the children's parents. I have asked some of the miners, but they have not been able to tell me anything new."

"I appreciate you talking to them. Someone knows the truth, and if we keep asking, someone may err and reveal it."

"I will do my best."

She almost reached out to put her fingers on his arm as she would have to anyone else she wanted to thank, but kept her hand by her side. "I know you will. Jacob, may I ask another favor of you?"

He rested one shoulder against the wall. "After everything you have done to help me, I would be a cad to say no. What can I do to help you?"

Had he moved away from her slightly because he had sensed she was about to touch him? Or had he guessed that she had restrained herself? Either way, she needed to change the subject to one less personal than her children.

"Would it be possible for you to bring the children from the mining village to the Porthlowen church so they can be part of our Christmas pageant? We are sending a wagon from Cothaire as well, but it won't be big enough to hold all the children who want to come."

His easy expression faded. "Won't they want to join in the celebrations at the church closer to the mines?"

"There is nothing being planned for children this year there. Mr. Minden still is feeling poorly, and spending extra time in a cold, damp church could make him sicker. Raymond offered to have the children come to the Porthlowen church, so Mr. Minden can concentrate on regaining his health before the worst of the winter cold arrives."

"I think that is wise. Do you think I should give Mr. Minden a look-in to see if he needs anything?"

She shook her head. "He would feel obligated to play host because you control his living. If you want to send him your good wishes, ask Mr. Hockbridge to deliver them. He mentioned to the Winwood sisters that would be the best way to let Mr. Minden know we are praying for him. The sisters spread the word."

"Mr. Hockbridge and the Winwood sisters have created a very efficient communications system." His words sounded clipped. Was he bothered about rumors about her and the doctor? The talk would not stop, and she had felt everyone's eyes on them when she greeted Mr. Hockbridge after church yesterday.

Jacob should know better. She had made it clear in every way that she had no interest in remarrying. Even if he failed to remember that, he should have seen for himself that she had no time for wooing while helping him and overseeing the children.

Her own voice was taut when she replied, "But you have not answered my original question. Can you provide a cart to bring children from the village to the Porthlowen church to practice for our Christmas pageant?"

"Of course, I will have someone drive the children to Porthlowen."

"Oh, I thought you might want to bring them yourself. We could use some help with making a stable to put in front of the altar."

Color slapped his face, and he looked out the window beyond the stairwell. Was he trying to avoid her eyes? "I will help where I can, but I don't want to make promises I cannot keep. If I am needed at the mines, I will be unable to help you. It would be better if I have Howell drive the children and help you at church. He is a good lad."

"Thank you. I appreciate you finding someone else when you will be busy with your guests here." She said the words automatically, but not the ones she wanted in order to ask further questions. What about driving the children from the mining village to Porthlowen had set him on edge? And why was he trying to hide the truth?

Jacob sensed Carrie's disappointment, and he yearned to tell her that the idea of him handling any vehicle filled with passengers made his stomach roil with guilt and shame. What if something went amiss as it had when he had driven out with Virginia on that ice-slicked road? Recently, a cart from Cothaire had lost a wheel on the road between the mines and the cove. Fortunately, no one was hurt.

"However," he said, as if his thoughts remained sanguine, "I do hope you don't mind if I pay a visit to watch at least one of the practices."

"That would be delightful. Gil and Joy will be there, and, as you know, Gil is always eager to see you."

Only Gil? he wanted to ask, but refrained. Carrie had been wonderful helping him with Warrick Hall and teaching him what he needed to know to fit in with the Beau Monde. He needed to respect her desire to spend time with the children and her family.

"They are in the parlor," she continued when he said nothing. "Do you have time to see them?"

"Go ahead. I have to check one thing, and I will meet you there."

When she nodded and went down the stairs, he curled his fingers into a fist on the banister. Frustration burned inside him like a torch. He ached to tell her the real reason why he could not bring the children to the Porthlowen church, but he could not endure the thought of her regarding him with the disgust that twisted his gut.

He was still waiting for an answer to his supplication. He had lost his way since the night Virginia died. He could see that now, but he had no idea how to find his way to the life God expected him to live. Would he stumble through the rest of his days without being able to come to terms with the past?

The sound of the children's happy voices drifted to Jacob, and he stepped away from the banister and his dark thoughts. Going to the room where he had discovered Carrie working, he sent the maid to the kitchen with a message for one of the footmen. She curtsied and rushed off to do as he bid.

By the time Jacob reached the parlor, Lawry, one of the recently hired footmen at Warrick Hall, was waiting with a crate from the attic. He motioned for the footman to follow him into the parlor.

Carrie sat with Joy on her lap and Gil at her feet. The picture of a happy family in front of the hearth. When had that last been seen at Warrick Hall?

Lawry set the box on the floor and handed Jacob the pry bar balanced on top of it.

Nodding his thanks before Lawry took his leave, Jacob smiled at Carrie and the children. "Who wants to see what is in here?"

Gil let out a squeal and jumped to his feet.

"What is it?" she asked, putting her arm out to block Gil from running to the box.

"It is marked toys. I found it in an area near the eaves which we have only begun to explore. As most boxes in that area have been labeled accurately, I assume this one is, as well." He slipped one end of the pry bar beneath the lid.

Pressing, he gritted his teeth when the top refused to move. He shoved again, and the top rose with the squeal of nails reluctantly pulling out of the wood.

"Wait," Carrie said as Gil tried to slip past her.

Grinning, Jacob said, "You are as curious as the children are about what is in the box, Carrie."

Relief ironed out the threads of stress in her forehead. He wanted to apologize for upsetting her, but doing so would require him to explain the reasons he acted as he did.

"Aren't you?" she fired back.

"Yes!" The word became a shout of triumph as the last nail gave way, and the top came loose. It spun into the air before falling onto the crate. "Stay away. I will get whatever is inside out."

Gil started to protest but halted when Carrie pointed to the rough edges and reminded him about a splinter he had gotten earlier in the fall.

Jacob leaned the lid against the wall. He knelt by the box and pulled out the straw on top. It was not, he was glad to see, filled with mold. If there truly were toys in the crate, they might not be ruined.

He felt fabric and brushed the straw away to reveal two handmade dolls lying side by side. What child had last played with them? His uncle and his father? Or had they been packed away even longer than that?

"What have you found?" Carrie asked.

"Two dolls."

Gil's button nose wrinkled. "Dolls are for girls!"

"Are you sure you don't want to look at these?" He drew the dolls out.

One was female and the other male. Their faces were painted on leather aged to a deep tan. From the man's hat, he guessed they had been made more than a generation ago. Both wore cloaks, the woman's once must have been a bright red, but had faded to a shoddy pink. The man's had weathered time better and was as deep a green as Miss Ivy wore. Their clothes were simple, as befitted peddlers. Their wares hung from their clothing, as well as a string stretched between their leather hands. Tiny pots and loaves of bread looked as real as any sold at a kitchen door.

Gil cooed with excitement when Jacob handed him the male doll. He began clicking the pots together, but dropped the doll to the floor when Jacob lifted out a handful of tin soldiers. The flat figures once had been brightly colored, but most of the paint was gone. Of the dozen Jacob set up on the floor, only one had a face.

That did not matter to the little boy. He began lining the figures up in a row. When Jacob handed him a tin horse, he giggled with anticipation. He picked up a soldier and held it on the horse. The platform at the base of the soldier's legs kept him from straddling the horse, but Gil's imagination clearly had taken care of that problem.

"Is there anything in there for Joy to play with?" Carrie asked.

"How about this?" He pulled out a brightly painted wooden top.

When Carrie set Joy at the edge of the rug, he spun the top. The baby bounced on her bottom with glee. She put her hands out to it, then pulled back when the top slowed and fell on to its side. Her face screwed up, but he was unsure if she was disappointed it had stopped or frightened. Hoping it was the former, he twirled the top again. She giggled with renewed excitement.

He pushed aside the remaining straw. "There is a Noah's ark along with some picture books and, of course, blocks with the alphabet on them." He set the toys on the rug, then picked up the crate and carried it out of the room.

Suddenly, he yelped. Two of the fingers on his right hand looked like a hedgehog with splinters poking out of them. He tried to pull the longest one out, but the fingers on his left hand were too clumsy.

Slender fingers reached past his at the same moment that a tendril of dark hair glided along his cheek. "Let me," Carrie murmured as she tilted his hand to get a better view. "Oh, my! You grabbed those splinters by the handful, I see."

"I never do things by halves."

"I have noticed." She stepped away and asked him to sit by the window where the light was best. Sending Wherry to get a needle from one of the maids, she thanked him when he returned moments later.

Jacob's hand was throbbing from the splinters, but that pulse centered in his throat when Carrie sat beside him on the window bench, took his hand, and settled it on her lap. Grateful that she could not see his expression as she leaned over his fingers to remove the slivers, he breathed shallowly. Each breath was scented with a delicate fragrance from her hair.

"Ouch!" he gulped.

"I am sorry," she said. "There are only a few more. Do you need a pause?"

"Go ahead."

She bent over his hand again. In less than a minute, she said, "There. That was the last one."

"Thank you."

"You are welcome." She raised her head.

His uninjured hand curved along her face as he gazed into her soft blue eyes. A man could melt into such eyes and lose himself forever. She was lovely, and her heart was giving, always leading her to think of everyone else around her before she thought of herself.

He tried to ignore a tugging on his sleeve, but it grew stronger. When a thread snapped, he tore his gaze away from hers to see Gil pulling on his shirt.

"Ouchie?" asked the little boy. "Kiss and make it better?"

How tempting it would be to answer that question with a resounding yes! A kiss from Carrie would make him forget about the pain in his fingers. He drew away, knowing a kiss would complicate everything else between them. It would suggest a promise he could not make to her or any other woman. Not when he had not come to terms with the part he had played in Virginia's death.

He forced a smile and held out his finger to the little boy, making sure it was one that had not been sliced by a sliver. When Gil gave it a loud kiss, Jacob thanked him. He turned to say the same to Carrie, but she had already set herself on her feet and moved away.

He should be grateful that at least one of them had the good sense to recognize the danger of him giving into his craving to hold her.

But he was not.

Chapter Nine

Jacob paced in the parlor. He could see the road leading through the wall surrounding the estate house and across the moor toward Porthlowen. A closed carriage had appeared along it almost fifteen minutes ago.

How long did it take for four people to emerge from a carriage and to be brought to where he waited? Without his lessons with Carrie, he would have gone out to greet his family right in front of Warrick Hall. She had told him that would require him to have the household servants flanking him in order for his family to be welcomed properly. As he did not want to interrupt the work continuing throughout the house, he had decided to wait and have his guests escorted to him.

Had something gone amiss? Unlikely, because Wherry was as well versed as Carrie in the proper way to welcome guests. The footmen she had engaged were well trained, so they would not loiter or forget to bring his guests to the parlor.

He went to the window and peered out past the draperies like a naughty imp peeking through the newel posts at his elders when he was supposed to be in bed.

The carriage was drawn up by the main entrance. Mud splattered it, and scrapes along the sides revealed that the family's long journey from Cumberland had included narrow roads edged by unkempt hedgerows.

Letting the draperies fall into place, Jacob knew Carrie had been right. She should not be present when Jacob welcomed his family to Warrick Hall. His stepmother and her nieces would be exhausted from their journey, and they would want to look their best when they met the daughter of an earl.

Even so, he wished she was standing beside him as he waited for his family to be shown into the refurbished parlor. She would have directed the conversation so that he made no social solecisms, and she would assure that his family had a warm welcome.

But that was not the only reason he would like to have her by his side. When she was not nearby, his life seemed dull and colorless. She walked into the room, and every hue of the rainbow burst forth. It might be her laughter or her pretty smile or the love she gave the children or even the effort she had put into helping him and Warrick Hall be what his family expected. An aura of gentle warmth surrounded her.

Muffled voices came from the direction of the entry hall. Jacob gave the room one final glance. The large mirror Carrie had discovered behind the cradle hung over the fireplace. The shelves along one wall were filled with books that had been aired, so the musty odor had vanished. The stench of strong pipe smoke was gone as well from the furniture that had spent every possible moment on the stone terrace behind the parlor. The three strong footmen had helped him rescue the settee and upholstered chairs from a sudden downpour on several occasions.

The furniture had been placed on the rug to hide scorched marks and other stains that could not be removed. Lamps glowed warmly on tables scattered throughout the room, making the space cozier. Everything was exactly as Carrie had asked for it to be arranged. He could not imagine how anyone would find fault with it, even his stepmother.

He halted that thought. Beverly might be exacting, but she meant well. She had been more pleased than he was at the announcement that he was the heir to a baron who had recently died. At her insistence, he had left Cambridge in the middle of the term to go up to London to be invested with his title and the family estate before coming to Cornwall. She might not have given birth to him and to Emery, but she loved them deeply.

His promise to his father to look after his family and provide for them rang through his mind. He had failed to protect Virginia. He would not fail his family.

The door opened, and Jacob drew in a deep breath. He released it as Wherry stepped in.

With a bow that must have made his old bones creak, the butler said, as formally as if he were announcing guests at Almack's, "Mrs. Warrick, Mr. and Mrs. Warrick, Miss Bolton."

His effusive stepmother rushed past Wherry, who regarded her with the same dismay as a dowager finding a burglar in her bedchamber. Beverly paid him no mind as she embraced Jacob.

"My dear boy, we have missed you!" She wore a dark traveling outfit, which gave her light brown hair a ruddy glow. More silver among the strands glittered in the lamplight than the last time he had seen her. She was a woman who was politely called handsome because her nose was too long for her face, and her eyes tended to squint. She was too vain to wear spectacles as he did.

"It has been less than six months since the last time you saw me," he replied.

"It seems a lifetime."

He smiled, accustomed to her extravagant exaggerations. "It is good to see you."

Beverly kissed his cheek, then eyed him. "You look thin, Jacob. Are you getting enough to eat?"

Emery laughed. "Do you really need to ask that? I doubt he has eaten or slept much since he got here and found out how much work the mines needed. Every letter he has written to us has been filled with explanations of the multitude of tasks he faces." Clapping Jacob on the shoulder, he chuckled again. His younger brother was growing wider around the middle, and a balding spot peeked through his black hair. "And it has sounded as if you are enjoying every minute of your time in Cornwall, big brother."

"I have." He was astonished to realize it was the truth. Even before Carrie had come to play such a large part in his life, he had been fascinated with the stark moors and the vast sea. Problems at the mines and working to make the mining families' homes more comfortable were tasks he enjoyed because his mind was challenged to find solutions. And the time he was able to spend with Carrie and the children was an extra blessing he had not expected.

"You will give us a tour of the mines, won't you?"

Emery asked. "After what you have written to us, I am curious to see these great gashes in the earth myself."

"Gash? I would not describe a tin mine that way. They look more like a small hole leading to a bottom-less pit."

"You cannot be thinking of going into the mines." Helen Warrick was a younger version of her aunt, though she smiled far less often than Beverly did. She took every situation seriously. As Emery did not, they were a good pair.

"We have come to Cornwall," his brother said, "and I intend to see the source of its greatest income throughout history." He winked at Jacob. "Besides, if my older brother, who always has hidden his nose in a book, is willing to go underground, how can I not do the same?"

Helen opened her mouth, and Jacob guessed she was about to remonstrate with his brother, giving him a list of reasons why he was wrong.

Before she had a chance to say a single one, Beverly drew the other young woman forward and said, "Allow me to introduce Miss Faye Bolton." She did not nudge him with her elbow, but the look she gave him suggested that she had. "Faye, this is my stepson Jacob, Lord Warrick."

Jacob would have known that she was Helen's sister without any introduction. Like his sister-in-law, she had a thin face and large, luminous brown eyes. Unlike her, Miss Bolton did not have a hawkish nose. Slender and tall, she moved with the grace of a willow, but did not say more than a quiet greeting in a voice that was pleasant on the ear. She remained by his stepmother's side, her eyes lowered demurely.

I wonder if she has had as much fun as I have learning proper manners. Jacob silenced the thought that would have rewarded him with a frown if Carrie heard him say it aloud.

Your only thoughts should be on the comfort and needs of your guests. Carrie's voice, filled with both gentle amusement and frustration at his many questions, popped into his head.

Yes, my lady. Again he was struck by the yearning to laugh, and again he submerged it.

"Welcome to Warrick Hall, Miss Bolton." He took the hand she held out to him and bowed over it as Carrie had taught him. When he straightened, he saw surprise and delight in Beverly's eyes.

"Thank you, my lord." Her voice was soft and wispy, pitched to intrigue a man.

Quickly releasing her hand, he turned to greet his sister-in-law. Helen had been watching, wide-eyed, as he bowed over her sister's hand. With a wink at his brother, he copied the motions he had made with her sister.

Unlike her sister, Helen giggled before saying, "You certainly act like a baron, Jacob."

"And I want you to act like a baron's guests. The staff at Warrick Hall is here to do your bidding. Would you like something to eat? If you prefer to rest, I can have a light repast sent to your chambers."

"Having our meals delivered to our rooms would be lovely." His stepmother beamed as if she had instilled lordly manners in him herself. "Our journey has been long and tiring. Perhaps we should reconvene tomorrow at breakfast when we have had a rest."

"You ladies go ahead," Emery said. "If you do not

mind, I will stay here a while longer. That way we brothers can talk."

Curious why his brother, who looked as fatigued as the women, was forgoing the opportunity to rest, Jacob picked up the brass bell that sat on a nearby table. He rang it once, then a second time. From beyond the door, he heard hasty footfalls before a knock was placed on it.

Killigew, the most recently hired footman, came in and bowed his head properly. "Yes, my lord?"

"Will you have the ladies escorted to the rooms that have been made ready for them?" he asked. "I am sure they would be interested in seeing the vases in the short gallery on their way."

The young man nodded hard, and Jacob guessed his message had been conveyed. Killigew must take the Warrick ladies and Miss Bolton only by the prearranged path to their chambers. They must be allowed no hint that the rest of the house did not match the grandeur of the few rooms prepared for their visit.

After Jacob urged them to ring if they needed anything and to make themselves at home, the ladies took their leave. Helen aimed an inquisitive glance at Emery but followed the others.

A second footman arrived with a tray topped by a hearty tea. He set it on a low table beside the chairs arranged near the hearth, then left without saying a word.

Emery watched with wide eyes. When the door closed behind the footman, he said, "I knew your life would be different after Uncle Maban left you his title and the estate, but I never imagined you having servants. A butler and footmen as well as the stablemen."

He glanced at the tray. "And a cook and maids, also, I'm assuming."

"Warrick Hall is a big house, and it requires many people to keep it running." He hid his astonishment at how he had come to accept the changes in his life. Even a few weeks ago, he had questioned if he could give orders to his staff and not feel uncomfortable. With Carrie's help, he had learned better how to live a life he never had imagined.

"I doubt I could emulate a fine milord as well as you do, Jake." He grimaced. "Or are you addressed now only as Jacob?"

"If you prefer to call me Jake, do."

"What does that fine family in the great house we passed call you?"

"Jacob or Warrick, depending on which one I am speaking to."

"Does one of the earl's daughters call you by your Christian name?" He winked. "Or does the earl have only sons?"

"He has daughters, one married and one a widow, as well as two sons." He chose his words with care. "You will meet the Trelawney family when we go to church in the morning."

Emery chuckled before selecting a sandwich and taking a generous bite. After swallowing, he said, "It sounds as if you are fitting right in here."

"I'm learning." He motioned for his brother to take a seat.

"No, thanks. I have been sitting in that accursed carriage for longer than I care to think about. I know Father and his brother wanted to make sure they did not encounter each other, but Father did not need to travel to the far reaches of northern England before he settled down."

Jacob wondered how much his brother knew of why the two brothers had become estranged. He would tell Emery the truth before his brother and the rest of the family returned north with Miss Bolton.

Miss Bolton… He sighed. That was a problem he needed to deal with quickly, but he must not hurt the young lady's feelings.

"What do you think of Faye?" asked his brother as he wandered around the room, looking at each item Carrie had selected for the space.

"You expect me to have formed an opinion when we have spoken scarcely a score of words to each other?"

"No love at first sight?" Emery snapped his fingers. "You didn't look at her and fall like that?"

"Of course not."

"You haven't changed completely, Jake. You always have been the careful one. No pretty lady is going to sweep you off your feet and urge you to throw caution to the wind."

Jacob selected a sandwich. "Even you, the one who is well-known for taking risks, courted your wife for over a year before you asked her to wed."

"True." He finished his sandwich in a few large bites, then said, "Maybe we should sit."

His brother did not look in his direction as he took a chair by the hearth. Jacob sat facing him and noticed how Emery's hands opened and closed into fists, a sure sign his brother was nervous.

"What is wrong?" Jacob asked, seeing no reason to dissemble.

"I need to speak to you of an important matter." His

brother lowered his eyes and rubbed his hands nervously on his thighs.

"What is it?"

"I am, as I have heard it said, sitting on a penniless bench."

Jacob stared at his brother in disbelief. His brother had no money? How was that possible? Even though their uncle had made no effort to get to know his closest living relatives, he had provided for Emery as well as his heir. A bequest of more than £20,000 had been provided for Emery, an amount that had emptied a good portion of Warrick Hall's coffers, leaving Jacob needing to watch every penny. That had been not much more than a year ago. How could one man spend that amount of money in such a short time?

He asked the question aloud. When his brother did not give his usual quick answer, Jacob said, "I don't understand, Emery. You need to explain to me. Were you robbed?"

"Yes, but willingly."

"I don't understand."

Emery set himself on his feet and walked to look out the window at the early twilight settling on the moors. "I know you don't. As you said, you don't take risks."

"I have." He did not add more, because he never had confided to his brother about the risk he had taken the night Virginia died. He recalled the carriage rocking wildly, which suggested they had been traveling at a rapid rate. He should have kept Virginia, who was unaccustomed to driving, to a slower pace. Or had he tried? He wished he could remember for certain.

"I am sure it was a calculated risk." Emery paced the room as Jacob had before the family's arrival. "You always consider every possible outcome before you make a decision."

"Not always."

His brother did not seem to hear him because he went on, "I am the one who jumps in without looking, though this time I thought I had examined the variables before I invested. Still, I have ended up with nothing."

"Emery!" he said sharply to get his brother to focus on him. "What did you invest in?"

"Horses."

Jacob sighed. He should have guessed the truth. Emery had always admired finely boned horses, especially if they were fast. "Did you lose your inheritance by gambling on horse races?"

"No!" Emery faced him and scowled. "I am no fool, in spite of how it might appear. I despise gambling because one might as well throw away one's money. I bought horses to breed into an excellent line of racers."

He kept his groan silent with the greatest of efforts. As much as his brother appreciated horses, he had never spent much time with them except when he was riding or driving. It had been Jacob's chore to tend them and feed them because straw made Emery sneeze. When Jacob had moved to Warrick Hall, he had urged his brother to hire someone to oversee the care of the family's two horses. Instead, Emery had used the whole of his inheritance to buy more horses.

Saying nothing, Jacob listened as his brother recounted his woes with buying horses that had proven to be too skittish to train and others that had failed to deliver foals with the potential to win races. The costs of stabling the horses and paying for their care had quickly eaten up his dwindling funds. Emery had attempted to sell some horses in order to concentrate on the best ones, but even that had failed to help. One by one, he had sold the animals, getting far less for them than he had paid. When the final bills were tallied up, he had had enough money to keep the family through the previous winter. Now, even that was gone, and he had only his small income from tutoring students in their village.

"Helen and Beverly don't know our dire situation," Emery said with a sigh as he sank into the chair. "They think this is solely a visit to enjoy the holidays with you."

"Beverly must suspect something is amiss."

He shook his head. "She has been too intent on other things."

Jacob did not need to ask what, because he knew his stepmother had been busy making arrangements to have Miss Bolton come with them on this trip. He sighed. Telling his stepmother that he had no plans to wed now would be doubly hard when she learned how Emery had squandered his inheritance.

"She never noticed," Emery went on, "that some of the nicer pieces in the cottage have been sold."

"But those were gifts from Helen's family. Surely she has noticed."

"If she has, she has said nothing of it."

"Whatever gave you the idea to invest in race horses?"

He shrugged as if they spoke of nothing more important than what hour the sun would rise in the morning. "The risk seemed negligible, and the rewards would have enabled us to live as grandly as you do, brother. Now I don't know what we will do. The only thing of value we have left is the cottage itself."

Jacob considered, for a moment, giving his brother a tour of the unrepaired sections of the house, but doing that would be petty. The part of Warrick Hall that Carrie had helped him get ready for the family was many times the size of the cottage where he and Emery had grown up. Even though he had to be cautious with money, there was enough to enable him to live comfortably as well as update the mines and the terrace houses in the mining village.

Rising, he put his hand on his brother's shoulder. "You are welcome to stay here for as long as you wish, of course."

"Thank you." He glanced around. "You certainly have enough room for everyone."

"Eventually, when the whole of the house is repaired, there will be enough room so we each can have our own wing of the house."

Emery smiled feebly. "I mean it, Jake. I appreciate you opening your doors to us."

"You are family. This is the family's estate. The solution seems obvious."

Getting to his feet, Emery clasped Jacob's hand. "Thank you. This is not the first time you have saved me."

"You would do the same for me."

Emery released his hand and looked away, his shoulders hunching again.

"Is something else amiss?" Jacob asked.

Shaking himself, Emery smiled weakly. "Isn't that enough? Will you promise me one thing?"

"If I can."

"Don't say a word to Beverly or Helen about us staying here." His voice grew steadier as he said, "I need to be the one to explain why it is necessary. It is my fault."

"If you want me there to reassure them, say so."

"No, but thank you. Helen is likely to react badly, and you don't need to be a target of her anger. I know you, Jake. You will feel like you need to do something to ease the situation, so I don't feel guilty. I know you have enough guilt, whether you should have or not. I am not going to add more now."

Jacob nodded, unable to speak. His brother had come to his rescue the night of Virginia's death. Emery, unlike the rest of the family, knew exactly what had occurred.

When his brother asked him to excuse him, Jacob nodded again. He dropped heavily to a chair and stared into the fire. Emery's words reminded him of what he must never, ever forget. There had to have been something he could have done to keep Virginia from dying.

If only he could remember so he did not make the same mistake again.

The interior of the church was bright with sunshine but chilly. Winter seemed determined to lay claim to Cornwall, even though the official start of the season was more than a week away. Carrie moved her toes closer to the metal box, which held stones heated in a fireplace at Cothaire. Drawing Gil nearer, she moved her black wool cloak around both him and Joy. She hoped cuddling together would keep them warm enough through the whole service.

When she heard the whispers around her, Carrie kept her eyes on the pulpit where her brother soon would stand. She had no doubts that Jacob and his family were entering the church. Only strangers could elicit the low buzzing sound as the parishioners murmured their curiosity.

Gil was not circumspect. He shoved aside her cloak and clambered to his feet. Before she could halt him, he called to Jacob, who sat at the rear of the church.

On one side of Jacob were a man who must be his brother, because they resembled each other, though the younger man had a pudgier face, and a woman. Was that his brother's wife? Even as Carrie looked, the woman turned up her collar and hunched into it. A wave of sympathy rolled over her. The back pews were even colder than the front ones because each time the door opened, the wind blew in. To Jacob's right, two other women were seated. The older woman must have been his stepmother and the younger, his sister-in-law's sister.

Her heart tightened when she saw how lovely the younger woman was. There was an inherent grace in every movement she made, even the slightest motion of her hand. She appeared to be the perfect choice to be the wife of a baron who would depend on her to oversee his household and make sure his guests felt at home.

Would he change his mind about marrying, now that he had met Miss Bolton? Whatever made him determined to delay taking a wife might matter far less now.

And Jacob looked dashing, with a dark cloak over his greatcoat. His hair had been mussed by the wind, giving it a rakish appearance. Easily she could envision him, dressed as a feudal lord, standing on a curtain wall around his estate, daring the invaders to come closer. She turned her eyes forward as her mind formed the image of herself in medieval garb standing beside him, her hand over his on the wall.

Trying to swallow past her suddenly constricted throat, she realized, when she heard chuckles from the nearby pews, Gil was waving enthusiastically to Jacob.

Behind her, Mrs. Thorburn sniffed in disapproval. "Children who cannot behave properly should not come to church," she said loud enough for Carrie to hear.

Carrie whispered to Gil to sit again, unsure she could have spoken more loudly even if she wished.

"Jacob sit here," he said as he nestled against her.

"Not today."

He pushed away. "Gil sit with Jacob."

"Not today. Shh," she whispered when Raymond walked into the sanctuary, the signal the service was about to begin.

The little boy subsided, but the moment the benediction was done, he jumped from the pew and rushed behind Raymond up the aisle toward the door. Smiles followed him as he stopped in front of Jacob and held up his hands. He giggled when Jacob shook one, then he ran to Carrie.

Tousling the little boy's hair, Carrie stood. She took care not to jostle Joy, who had fallen asleep. She joined the others filing out of church. They had gone about halfway to the door when Gil halted not far from the Winwood sisters.

"Boat," Gil said with excitement.

She shook her head. "It is too cold for going to the cove today, Gil."

"Boat." He tugged on her coat and raised his voice. "Boat."

She bent and put her fingers to his lips. "Let's talk about the boats later."

He pouted for a moment, then took off again, weaving among the parishioners until he reached where Jacob stood by the door. He pointed at Carrie and loudly said, "Boat."

Jacob scooped him up and whispered something in his ear. Gil giggled before throwing his arms around Jacob's neck.

"Lord Warrick dotes on the boy," Miss Hyacinth said with a broad smile as Carrie paused to let the elderly twins step from their pew.

"Anyone with eyes can see that," Miss Ivy added.

"And the baby, as well. He always has a special smile for her."

"As he does for you, Lady Caroline."

"A very special smile."

Knowing she had to put a halt to the course of the conversation before others began paying attention, Carrie said, "If you will excuse me, I need to get the children home while the rain is holding off."

"Go," Miss Hyacinth urged. "Damp is not good for children."

"Or anyone else." Miss Ivy laughed.

"Better rain than snow, though."

Miss Ivy grew serious. "Snow is coming. You can see it in how heavy the clouds are."

"Yes, we should leave ourselves."

"Excuse us, Lady Caroline."

"Have a pleasant Sunday."

Carrie thanked them, but she doubted they heard because they continued their conversation as they went along the aisle. If they saw the indulgent smiles in their wake, they gave no sign.

After stopping to thank her brother for an excellent service he had led, she looked around for Gil. He was sitting on Jacob's shoulders, chatting to Jacob's family as if he had known them since the day he was born.

She stopped long enough to pull her cloak over Joy who was sound asleep; then she crossed the churchyard to where the Warrick family stood near the lychgate. Introductions were made quickly, and Jacob gave her a clandestine wink when he handled them as etiquette required.

"Welcome to Porthlowen Cove," she said with a smile. "I assure you not every day is as gray and dreary as today is. When the sun is shining, this is one of the prettiest places you will ever see."

The senior Mrs. Warrick eyed her closely. "You are the earl's oldest. Is that right?"

"Yes."

"But your husband has been dead… That is, the children are young…" Color rushed up her face.

Jacob interjected, "These are two of the children I mentioned to you at breakfast. Some of the ones found in the small boat floating in the cove."

"Oh, now it makes sense." Mrs. Warrick's color returned to normal. "How good of you to take in these waifs, Lady Caroline!"

"I am the one blessed by having them in my life."

Jacob's family excused themselves, and Carrie guessed Mrs. Warrick was embarrassed. When she said the same to Jacob, who lingered behind as he set Gil on the ground, she urged him to reassure his stepmother that she was not distressed by her comments.

"Maybe you should give my whole family lessons in deportment," he said as the wind caught his cape and flapped it behind him like dark wings.

She laughed. "Don't judge anyone else by the standards I have been teaching you. I appreciate plain-speaking people. Your stepmother was curious about the children, so she asked."

"And she is curious about you. As you know, my family has not had much interaction with the peerage."

"Jacob, stop apologizing for them. Nobody said anything I found uncomfortable. A widow of almost six years having two such young children would create questions wherever I went beyond Porthlowen. Here, everyone knows the story." Her smile broadened. "Did they find the redone rooms comfortable?"

He visibly relaxed as he nodded. "Quite. Now I only need to convince them *not* to go into the other parts of the house."

"The best way is to keep them busy."

"Will you help me find ways to entertain them?"

"Certainly. I have helped you thus far. Why would I stop now?"

When he smiled and her heart did a dance, she knew she may have made a big mistake. She must be certain this was the last time she assisted him. She was enjoying it far more than she should.

Chapter Ten

Silence held the moor in its thrall when Carrie drew in her horse. She had come out on the cold day in an effort to clear her head. At Cothaire, preparations for the holidays kept the staff busy. The most delicious smells came from the kitchen. Many of the dishes were being put into cold storage to await the feast on Christmas Day or to be given to their neighbors for their own celebrations. The house was being cleaned from top to bottom, the wood polished, the brasses shined, and the windows in unused rooms opened to air any last heat from the summer out.

She felt as if she were in everybody else's way. She had never guessed she would experience such a feeling in the house where she had lived her whole life, even during her marriage. Maybe it was because everyone else seemed to be moving forward, and she spun her wheels in the same rut. She did not understand why she felt as she did, so she had no idea how to change.

Taking a long ride to sweep the cobwebs from her brain had always served her well, but today, not even riding her favorite horse, Marmalade, across the bare expanse of the moor helped.

Carrie scowled as she cocked her head so the wind did not rush beneath her bonnet. She heard nothing but the crackle of dead growth beneath Marmalade's hooves and the distant crash of the sea against the shore in the wake of last night's storm.

The beam engine had stopped.

Knowing she was breaking the vow she had made to herself after church not to get further involved in Jacob's life, she gave Marmalade the order to go in the direction of the engine house. She found a track and urged the horse even faster.

They climbed a small hill in the heart of the moor. At the top, she drew the horse in. Shading her eyes, she looked across the open landscape to where the beam engine building rose high above everything else around it. She smiled when she saw a distant motion coming from the building. Straining her ears, she could discern a steady thump.

Not from the direction of the mine but from behind her. She looked over her shoulder to see another rider coming at a neck-or-nothing speed, his cloak rippling wildly behind him. Recognizing the rider, she was astonished the always careful Jacob Warrick was riding at such a pace. She was about to wave to him when he took an abrupt turn toward her. His black horse made the change easily.

Carrie waited for him to draw even with her. She was about to greet him when she saw his scowl.

"What are you doing out here by yourself?" Jacob asked sharply.

"Good morning to you, too," she replied.

His frown eased only a smidgen before he asked again, "What are you doing out here alone?"

"I was riding, and I realized the beam engine had stopped. I thought I would come and see if there was anything I could do to help." She hurried on when his eyebrows shot skyward beneath his windblown hair. "I know you don't need me tinkering with the engine, but I thought I could get you and Pym something to eat. I halted when I heard the engine start up again."

"Pray *this* time it will keep working."

"Have you discovered what is wrong with it?"

"Yes. It is a worthless piece of junk."

She laughed, then quickly apologized when his frown deepened even more. "I am sorry. I know the situation isn't funny, but I did not expect you to say that."

"Why not?" he asked in the same irked tone. "Just when Pym and I have the beam engine working well, it stalls again. My family is beginning to think I am avoiding them. I have spent more time at the mine than with them at Warrick Hall."

"I am sure they understand more than you believe."

He edged closer, and Marmalade suddenly seemed as small as a pony beside his magnificent horse. Looking at her, he said, "You never answered my question. You should not be out here alone."

"You fret too much, Jacob. I have told you I have been riding across this moor since I was a child."

"But you are no longer a child. Any man, including those with evil intentions, would notice that fact immediately."

Heat slapped her cheeks, but she did not lower her eyes as she fired back, "You need to stop being over-protective of those around you."

"I don't see why when you do dangerous things like riding alone."

"There are no highwaymen lurking about when the sun is high and there are no trees to hide them." To halt his next comment, she said, "I do appreciate your concern."

"Even if you think I am overreacting?"

"Yes."

It was his turn to laugh. "Now *that* is an answer I did not expect." He motioned for her to follow as he set his horse to a walk along the track. "I will ride with you to Porthlowen. The parson sent a message yesterday asking if there were any additional blankets in the attic. The need is great with winter cold arriving early. I want to let him know there are several more crates full."

"Why did your uncle have all those blankets?"

"You met the man. I never did. If you cannot answer my question, there is far less chance that I can."

"We probably will never know the truth, but it is wonderful the blankets are being put to good use now." She smiled up at him. "I brought Marmalade out here to let her stretch out at a speed faster than this." Her horse nodded as if in agreement. "Shall we?"

"Shall we what?"

"Give them their heads and see what they can do."

His eyes grew wide again. "Are you challenging me to a race? Shadow is a very powerful horse."

"So is Marmalade."

"I think you are misguided in your assessment, my lady. Your horse is a fine animal, but she cannot compare with Shadow."

"No?" She slapped her hand against Marmalade's flank and shouted.

Her horse leaped forward in a cloud of dust. Behind her, she heard Jacob command his horse to run. All sound vanished beneath the pounding hooves on the hard earth.

Leaning forward, she let Marmalade pick the best path through the gorse. Carrie did not want to guide her into a chuckhole. A victorious shout rang in her ears as Jacob sped past on his horse. Beneath her, Marmalade added speed, clearly not ready to cede the race to the larger horse.

Her bonnet slid off her hair and bounced on her back, held on by the ribbons tied around her neck. Hairpins popped, unable to fight the wind tearing through her hair. She did not release the reins. Shaking her hair aside, she sped onward.

She could not recall the last time she had felt free. The cold wind scored her face, but she kept going, even though she knew her horse had no chance of catching Jacob's.

Marmalade must have realized that, too, because she began to slow. Carrie drew her to a stop and dismounted. She threw the long train of her riding outfit over her arm before she stroked Marmalade's neck and murmured what a wonderful horse she was. The horse's ears pricked up each time Carrie spoke her name.

Jacob must have been watching, because he turned Shadow toward her. When he drew even with her again, he dismounted. "Shall I be a gentleman and call it a tie?"

"No! I beat you."

He gave a mock scowl. "We left you far behind."

"Oh, did you think it was a race to a finish line?" She shook her head with a superior smile. "It was a

contest to see which horse could start more quickly."
She patted Marmalade's neck. "We were the clear winners."

"Clearly."

They burst into laughter together.

"That was fun!" she declared.

"It was." Slanting toward her, he ran his thumb along
her cheek and grinned. "You look like Joy when she
is working hard at trying to walk, rosy and happy and
yet determined."

"I have not ridden like this in longer than I can remember." She was well aware they were in clear view
of anyone else on the moor, but as his skin brushed
hers, she did not care who saw them close together.

"Because you are the very responsible Lady Caroline Trelawney Dowling."

She wrinkled her nose. "Oh, that sounds like the
most boring person I can imagine."

"I have to disagree. I find the very responsible Lady
Caroline Trelawney Dowling extremely intriguing."

His gaze invited her closer, but she began walking
Marmalade toward Porthlowen. Again he set Shadow
to the same pace beside her. He paused once, and she
did, too, when she guessed he was listening for the
beam engine. She did not hear it at first, then the deep
rhythm reached her ears.

"Good," he murmured as they continued on. "Pym
is keeping it going this time. I had promised Beverly
I would take them to Penzance this morning. Maybe
I will be able to fulfill that promise this afternoon,
though why she wants to go eight miles each way simply to look at the sea when she could visit Porthlowen
is beyond me."

"She probably wants to see as much of Cornwall as she can on her visit. I know I would want to explore as much as possible if I went to another part of England."

His voice became grim. "She will have plenty of time to see whatever she wants to see."

"Are they staying past the holidays?" She tried to halt her stomach from cramping at the thought that one good reason for them to remain at Warrick Hall longer was because Jacob had given into his stepmother's plan to have him marry Miss Bolton.

"Long past the holidays."

She scanned his face. "Does that please you?"

"That they will be here, yes, but not the reason why." His gaze caught hers, and she saw uncertainty in his eyes. "May I confide in you? I told Emery I would say nothing to the family or Miss Bolton, so you must be as reticent with them."

"I have spoken to Mrs. Warrick and your brother's wife only that one time at church, though I know Maris plans to invite them to Cothaire." She slowed her horse even further. "But I can keep a secret, Jacob." *I have been keeping my inability to conceive a secret for almost ten years.*

When he related what his brother had told him, she listened without comment. She sensed Jacob needed to share with someone beyond his family, someone who would listen and confirm he was doing the right thing.

She was touched she was the one he had chosen, that he respected her insight and opinion. If their situations were reversed, she easily could imagine herself seeking him out to get his point of view on an important matter.

"I wish," he said after outlining his brother's situation, "Emery had come to seek my advice before he was imprudent."

"He may not have wished to give you an additional burden, especially if he knows about the troubles you have had with the mine."

He looked at her directly for the first time since he had begun speaking of his brother. "He knows. I have poured out every bothersome detail in my letters to him. Maybe I should not have."

"Don't be absurd. He is your brother, and he would want to know how you fared. Aren't you upset with him because he did not confide his problems to you before now?"

"Carrie, you keep astonishing me with your insight. How do you do that?"

She gave him a supportive smile. "It is simple. I think how I would feel if I had to deal with the quandary. Like now, I know I would be distressed if one of my siblings faced such circumstances and I hadn't known about it. Maybe I could not have done anything to change what happened, but I could have been there to stand by their sides and to hold them up in prayer." She shook her head. "But I don't understand one matter. You said the horses he bought were as fine as your Shadow. If so, I don't know how he lost his money so quickly."

"Nor do I, but dealing in horses is a complex and tricky business. There are, as I have heard, very unscrupulous men who will take advantage of a man as unfamiliar with horse breeding as Emery is. None of that matters now. However he managed to let the money slip through his fingers, it is gone. I am grateful he could not use the entailed property as a stake to start over and try again to succeed."

"What will he do at Warrick Hall? He sounds like a man who wants to be useful."

"I have asked him to learn how to work with Pym and me to oversee the engine house. I want to replace the ancient machinery at smaller mines with new steam ones, and I will need more eyes and hands to keep them running."

"Amazing!"

"What is amazing?"

"That you plan to replace the old engines with new ones after you have had such trouble with the steam engine you already installed."

He gave her a crooked smile. "Maybe my brother and I are not different after all. He risked everything on a line of racing horses while I invest in modern equipment to make the mines more productive and safer."

"No one is trying to assign blame, Jacob."

"I see now, even though I have assured him and my family—and you—I sympathize with his situation, I have been blaming him for being careless. I need to rethink this." He gave her a smile and reached out to take her hand and squeeze it. "Carrie, thank you for opening my eyes."

"I am glad for any help I could give you at this difficult time." The words were trite, but the emotion behind them was not. Nor was her delight as they continued to hold hands while they followed the road to Porthlowen.

Gil and Joy were playing with Irene on the day nursery floor. Carrie was not surprised to find them alone in the nursery, because Maris had taken Bertie with her on a call to the parsonage. Raymond had been pleased to hear Jacob's tidings about the extra blankets and arranged to send someone to Warrick Hall to collect them.

Jacob had asked to see the children, and she knew he missed spending time with them as much as they missed him. That was confirmed when Gil dropped his toys and clambered to his feet. He ran past the sleeping kitten and threw his arms around Jacob's legs. He began firing questions at Jacob about where he had been and when he was going to take Gil to see the mine and how his cats at Warrick Hall fared.

Jacob swung the little boy high in the air. Gil crowed with excitement and begged him to do it again. Tossing him up, Jacob caught him and settled him gently on the floor.

"Do again!" Gil cried in excitement.

Irene interjected softly, "He ate not too long ago."

"Later," Jacob said with a conspiratorial wink.

When Gil started to pout, Carrie put an arm around his shoulders. "Have you been having fun with Irene today?"

The question diverted him, and he began talking about every toy he had played with since Carrie left him and the baby in the nursery so she could ride on the moor.

"Ac-oob!" Joy chirped as she held up her arms and bounced on her bottom in her excitement.

All of them, even Gil, turned to look at the baby.

"Did she say what I thought she said?" Jacob asked.

"Ac-oob!" Joy's tone was more insistent as she waved her tiny hands.

Carrie chuckled. "If you thought she said your name along with a request for you to pick her up, then I would say you are right. You should be honored, Jacob. Your name is her first word."

Wonder lit his face as he bent to scoop the baby up in his arms. Joy patted his coat before grabbing a lapel. She began to chew on it, leaving a line of drool along the dark green wool.

When Carrie reached to take his lapel gently out of the baby's mouth, he said, "She cannot hurt it."

"You are spoiling these children with fresh toys and fresh teething surfaces."

"I spoil them no more than you do, I dare say."

"Children need to be loved and to know that no matter what they do, they will remain loved." She looked from Gil to Jacob, who held Joy tenderly. "Most especially these children who have lost so much."

His mouth hardened before he said, "You are assuming they were loved before you found them." He put Joy on the floor where she picked up a block and stuck one side of it in her mouth to chew on. Waiting for Gil to scurry to sit next to the baby, he took Carrie's arm and drew her out of the nursery and beyond the children's earshot. She understood why when he asked, "How could anyone have loved them and put them in a boat that could have sunk at any second?"

"They were loved, Jacob. I know that for a fact."

"How?"

"There was a note pinned to Joy's shirt. It must have been written by one of the parents."

"You cannot assume that. I have discovered only a few of the adults in the mining village know how to do more than read and write their own name, and I doubt it is different elsewhere along the coast."

"But you built a school for the children. They are learning to read and write. Maybe one of them wrote the note."

He gave her a dubious frown. "Do you think any child could keep the secret of where these youngsters belong? Many people have asked. Certainly a child would have revealed the truth by now."

"True, but if one of the parents didn't write it, who did?"

"Do you still have the note? May I see it?"

Telling him to wait there, she went to her private rooms. She retrieved the note from her desk and took it to where Jacob now sat in the middle of the floor, much to Irene's amusement as well as the children's. He was trying to get Joy to say his name again, and the baby was staring at him as if he had lost his mind.

"I warned you she is stubborn," Carrie said as she entered the nursery.

Jacob got to his feet, his smile fading. She held out the many times folded page to him. The holes where the pin had gone through it to attach it to Joy's clothing showed more signs of wear than the rest of the page.

"Careful," she cautioned. "This is the original one. We made copies, but I thought you might be able to discern something we overlooked by seeing the actual note."

He unfolded the page and read the few words on it: *Find loving homes for our children.*
Don't let them work and die in the mines.

"It is very specific," he said as he handed the note

to her. "Very specific about everything but who wrote it and why."

"The why seems obvious to me. The parents wanted the children to have a better life than they were living, and, in their desperation, they believed such an outrageous method was the way to get it for them."

"They have achieved that goal, because your family has given the children loving homes." He sighed. "If the parents are among my miners, I wish they had come to me before doing something drastic."

"We can't know where they are from until we discover who they are."

"I promised you that I would help with your search, and I meant it, Carrie."

"I know." She looked at the note and the words she had memorized and scrutinized time and time again in the hope of discovering something she had overlooked before. She was unshaken in her belief it was written by the parent of one or more of the children, but she was beginning to wonder if they ever would find the children's families.

Or, if after almost six months, they should even be trying any longer.

Jacob yawned widely as he walked into Warrick Hall. Handing Killigew his hat, he pulled off his gloves and gave them to the waiting footman before shrugging off his coat. Hours in the saddle, riding from one mine to the next and talking to anyone he chanced to see, had gained him nothing. Either nobody knew the truth about the children, or they were not telling. He was unsure which.

As the footman took his coat, Jacob turned to climb

the stairs. It was an hour until tea, and he had paperwork that needed doing as well as correspondence to answer. Several peers he had never met had already invited him to functions in London after the beginning of the new year. Parliament was open, and he had a duty to be there, but did not want to leave Warrick Hall until the beam engine worked consistently.

"Jacob!" called his stepmother.

He paused as she swept into the entry foyer. When she held out her cheek, he gave her a kiss. "How are you today, Beverly? I hope you are enjoying your time here."

"I would enjoy it more if we saw more of you." She gave him the stern expression she had when he, as a child, had done something that disappointed her. "We did not travel here simply to be waited upon by your servants."

"Tomorrow I should be able to spend the whole day with you." He explained about the work awaiting him in his rooms, but did not tell her that he had spent more than an hour at Cothaire with Carrie and the children before he had set out to try to discover the truth behind the cryptic note.

"Having these obligations is why your father never wanted to be burdened with the family's title. He always hoped his brother would marry and have a son, so neither he nor you were saddled with the duties that come with this estate." She smiled sadly. "But you have always been the dutiful son, and I expected you to be very serious in assuming the responsibilities here."

"Thank you." He was unsure what else to say. Had Emery spoken to Beverly and his wife yet about them moving permanently to Warrick Hall? He wished he had never promised his brother to say nothing of the matter until Emery had a chance to talk to them. That vow made every conversation more difficult than it should be.

"But you have another obligation," his stepmother said. "No, obligation should not be used to describe what you should see as a pleasurable interlude. Faye is waiting for you in the parlor."

"Will you offer her my apologies? I must—"

"No. She has been patient for too long while she waits for you to spend an hour or two with her, so you can get to know each other better. You must spend some time with her." She tapped one foot against the floor, a familiar sign she was distressed and disappointed with him. "You have not, since we arrived, and it has been almost a week. She will think you have no wish to know her better."

He was not interested in courting the young woman, but Carrie had taught him a host must set aside his own needs and ensure his guests' needs were met. That did not include an offer of marriage, he knew, but it behooved him to spend some time with Miss Bolton.

"Very well," he said, earning a bright smile from his stepmother. "You are right, Beverly. I have neglected my duties to my guest."

"I ordered a nice tea for the two of you." She patted his arm, then gave him a gentle push toward the gold parlor.

Miss Bolton was sitting in a pose of perfect patience and elegance when Jacob entered the room. Her gown was the delicate pink of the first light at dawn, and it accented her cheeks, which were a similar shade. She had chosen, he noted, the very same chair where Carrie had sat on her first visit to Warrick Hall. Now the room was a pleasure for the eyes instead of a part of a house filled with discarded furniture and trash.

Thinking of Carrie was the wrong thing to do, though he had no idea how *not* to think of her.

"Good afternoon, Miss Bolton," he said, taking the hand she held out to him and bowing over it *exactly* as Carrie had taught him. He sat across from Miss Bolton, *exactly* as Carrie had taught him. He waited for Miss Bolton to speak, *exactly* as Carrie had taught him.

If Miss Bolton was disappointed he did not sit beside her as a *beau* would, he saw no sign of it in her serene expression. He realized he seldom had seen any emotion on her face. But, he reminded himself, he had not spent any time with her.

"Thank you for taking the time to share tea with me, my lord," Miss Bolton said in her wispy voice.

He missed the straightforward warmth of Carrie's voice. Confound it! He owed Miss Bolton the courtesy of giving her his full attention.

"It is my pleasure," he said. "Are you enjoying your visit to Cornwall?"

"Yes." She folded her hands on her lap. "I would guess it is far prettier in the spring than it is now."

"It is. Once the moor flowers in shades of bright yellow and green, it is like walking on the largest carpet you could imagine. You must come to Warrick Hall in the spring to see it."

"Thank you. I would like that."

Hoping she had not read more into his words than he intended, he asked if she would like to pour the tea. Carrie had instructed him about that, as well. He kept his laugh to himself. It was futile trying not to think about Carrie, because she had become so much a part of his life as Lord Warrick.

He took the cup Miss Bolton held out to him and thanked her. Silence fell between them. He searched for something to say, but what? The weather? He had tried once before, and his questions had fallen flat because Miss Bolton seemed to have little interest in what was happening outside the window. What about the young miss's plans for the holidays? He knew them already, because the family planned to spend Christmas and Boxing Day at Warrick Hall and New Year's Eve at Cothaire. Letting Miss Bolton direct the course of the conversation did not work when she said nothing.

What do I do now, Carrie?

He got his answer when Miss Bolton began a long story about friends and what they were doing for the holidays. As he never had heard of any of the people she mentioned, his participation was limited to nods and the occasional, "Oh, I see." She seemed to require no more from him, and he listened with only half an ear as he began to make a mental list of the tasks he needed to do after he finished this obligatory tea.

His attention was drawn to Miss Bolton when she said, "I trust your visit to Cothaire was pleasant." She held up a plate topped by Mrs. Trannock's thick sandwiches. Her face was bland, but her eyes sparked with ill humor.

"Yes, it was." He would not lie, even though her expression made it clear she was vexed.

"You visit there often."

He took a sandwich, then asked, "Have you heard about the children who were rescued from the Porthlowen Cove?"

"Yes, it is an extraordinary tale."

"I have become quite close to the youngest boy, who is named Gil. He has a quick and curious mind, and I enjoy his unique view of the world. Today, the baby, who may be his sister, spoke her first word. It was my name. I must say I was delighted." He was babbling as he once had with Carrie. Since then, talking to her had become as easy as talking to himself.

"You clearly enjoy being with children."

"Yes. Do you like children?" It was too personal a question, but he would say almost anything to keep the conversation moving forward.

"I am looking forward to spoiling my sister's babies," she said with more enthusiasm than he had ever heard from her.

"When the first one comes, it will be a happy day for both of our families."

"Yes, it—" Her voice broke off, and he heard what she must have already.

Footsteps were racing along the corridor toward the parlor. He stood, curious what necessitated such speed in the house.

When Carrie rushed into the room, Miss Bolton's brow furrowed in the hint of a frown, but her face remained as placid as before. She came to her feet as Carrie stopped and scanned the room.

Jacob's greeting was interrupted when Carrie asked, "Is Gil here?"

"Here?" he asked. "What would Gil be doing here?"

"He is missing. I had hoped he came here." She glanced around the room again as if she expected the little boy to be hiding behind a chair.

Crossing the room, Jacob grasped Carrie by the shoulders. "When did you see him last?"

"At least two hours ago. We thought he was napping, but he is gone." She gripped the lapels of his coat. "Jacob, if he isn't here, I have no idea where he might be."

Chapter Eleven

Carrie whirled to run out the door. She had been sure Gil had come to Warrick Hall because the little boy had been talking about "my friend," as he called Jacob, since morning. If the child was not here...

A strong hand caught her elbow and halted her in midstep. She did not have to look to know the hand belonged to Jacob, because the now familiar buzz undulated along every nerve from where he touched her.

"Carrie, stop a minute," he said.

"I can't! I need to find Gil before he wanders into danger."

Gently he turned her to face him. Beyond him, she saw Miss Bolton regarding them with a furious scowl that distorted her pretty face into a caricature of itself. Was it possible Miss Bolton was upset because Jacob was not paying attention to her *now*? A little boy was missing. Nothing mattered but finding him.

Her attention riveted on Jacob when he said, "We need to do this logically."

"There is nothing logical in the mind of a child of his age."

"Gil is not given to flights of fancy. What makes you certain he is not at Cothaire? Your home has plenty of places for a child to hide."

"His coat is gone. He would not have taken it if he intended to hide in the house."

"I agree. Gil is very practical. But it is our logic, not his, that must be called into use here. You must have some idea of where he was going. You came to Warrick Hall."

"Yes! Because I can tell how he misses you because he had not seen you in several days before this morning, and then you left quickly."

"To search for answers to the mystery of the children's parents. You know that."

"I do, but Gil doesn't. He sees that you came and you left after a short time. He had grown accustomed to your longer visits."

She could not fail to notice how the other woman's frown deepened. If the young woman was vexed because Jacob had spent time at Cothaire before Miss Bolton arrived at Warrick Hall, that was between them. Her own heart contracted painfully as she thought of Miss Bolton and Jacob as a single unit.

Not now, she told her heart. Now she must think solely of Gil.

"He may have gone to the mine instead of coming here." When her face became as cold as the wind, he hurried to say, "I will send Howell there while we look through the house."

"Hurry! There are many dangers for a child between Cothaire and the mine."

Jacob turned to Miss Bolton, whose face became

pleasantly blank again. "Forgive me, but I must help find Gil."

"Of course you must." Her voice gave no suggestion she had ever frowned. "The dear child must be terrified if he is lost."

"Thank you for understanding," Carrie said, her gratitude genuine.

"You are welcome." The crisp words made it clear she would not be cooperative if Carrie interrupted her time with Jacob again.

Refusing to respond to such silliness, Carrie wanted to tell Miss Bolton she had no reason to be jealous. Jacob did not intend to wed anyone now, and, if he changed his mind, he would not be marrying Carrie.

Not ever.

Jacob put his hand on Carrie's arm and steered her to the door. He shouted for a footman. When Killigew appeared, he listened as Jacob gave him a message to take to Howell in the stable. He ran off to deliver it.

A familiar flush of guilt rose within Jacob. Little Gil might be in danger because of him. He could not believe it was happening all over again. He had to make sure this potential tragedy had a happy ending.

Still holding Carrie by the arm, Jacob rushed both of them toward the entry hall. Another footman was waiting with his heaviest coat. As he reached for it, he heard a soft gasp behind them.

He looked over his shoulder to see Beverly staring at him and Carrie in astonishment.

"Good afternoon, Mrs. Warrick," Carrie said.

"Lady Caroline! I—" She clamped her lips closed, but her frown spoke volumes.

"Beverly," Jacob said, taking his coat from the footman who also held his hat and gloves, "Gil, the little boy I was playing with at church last week, is missing. Car—Lady Caroline thought he might be here."

"At Warrick Hall? Why would he come *here*?"

Carrie did not wait for him to jump to her defense again. "Gil loves Jacob. All the children do. When I discovered Gil was missing, my first thought was he would come here." She took a deep breath. "Jacob believes he might have gone to the mine instead."

"The mine!" His stepmother's irritation vanished like lightning from a storm sky. "You must find him, Jacob!"

"We will. Beverly, will you alert the rest of the servants and ask them to search the house and grounds?"

With a nod, she rushed away.

"Don't worry, Carrie," he said, slamming his arms through the sleeves of his greatcoat. "We will find him."

"Alive and unhurt." Tears glistened in her eyes.

"That is what I am praying for."

"Me, too." She dipped her head, but he saw the tears tumbling from her eyes.

His thumb beneath her chin raised it so he could see her face. He wiped away a tear with his fingertip. "Where is my brave Lady Caroline?"

"She has been shown to be a fraud. I am scared, Jacob."

"I know. I am, too."

Tears rushed into her eyes anew at his admission few men would willingly make. He was not going to hide the truth from her and make her feel worse. If that was even possible.

"We need to find him before dark," she said.

"Is he afraid of the dark?"

She shook her head. "No. I honestly don't think he is afraid of anything because he is too young to realize the danger he could face. If we don't find him before dark…"

"We will." He absently shoved at his spectacles. "Between Beverly and me, we will set every soul to the task."

As he opened the door, Killigew burst in. "Howell asks for you to come to the stable, my lord."

"Why hasn't he left for the mine already?"

"He said you will understand when you come out to the stable."

"Kittens," Carrie said.

"What?" Jacob had no idea what she was talking about.

"The kittens. Gil knows you have more than one cat here. He has been talking about getting another kitten for the nursery. He believes his is lonely because it doesn't have a baby as your mother cat does."

Jacob grasped her hand and pulled her outside. Snow spit tiny, sharp flakes against his face. For the first time he wondered if Gil had taken a scarf and mittens when he left Cothaire. Carrie had mentioned he had his coat, but could the little boy button it closed on his own?

"I hope Howell knows enough to keep Gil from slipping away again," she said as the wind tried to snatch her words away.

"I am sure he does." He squeezed her fingers gently. "The lad has a good head on his shoulders." He did not release her hand as they rushed together to the stable and was glad she did not pull her fingers out of his.

Right now, he knew she needed the touch of someone who loved Gil as much as she did. And he needed the same. That connection strengthened him, a constant reminder they were a team with a common goal.

Howell met them at the stable door. The lad seemed to grow taller and thinner each time Jacob saw him. His bony wrists protruded from his sleeves when he motioned for them to follow him into the stable.

"Is Gil here?" Carrie asked.

With a nod, Howell smiled. "I saw him here just before Killigew came with your message, my lord. This way…"

Jacob put his hand on Carrie's back as they walked past the stalls and toward the haymow. She looked up at him once. Her expression was both hopeful and unsteady.

When they reached the three steps to the haymow, he heard a childish giggle. Carrie must have heard it, too, because she ran up the stairs. She called out Gil's name and rushed to where he sat in a corner, playing with a half dozen kittens.

"Cuddle kitties." The little boy smiled as if he came to the haymow every day. "See me cuddle kitties?"

"Yes, I see." Jacob thanked Howell quickly, then went to squat beside the child. "Do *you* see Carrie's face? Do you see how scared she has been since you left Cothaire without telling anyone?"

"I told someone."

"Who?"

Gil squared his narrow shoulders with pride. "I told Bertie and Joy. Told them I come to cuddle kitties."

Picking up a gray kitten that was launching an attack on his coat, he handed it to Carrie. "Gil, you must tell Carrie before you leave Cothaire."

"Tell Carrie?" His eyes grew round, and Jacob guessed the little boy was finally comprehending how he had frightened them. He got up and gave Carrie a hug. "Carrie, cuddle kitties. See Gil cuddle kitties."

"I see." Her voice was gentle and patient. "But next time, Gil, tell me *before* you go."

"Tell Carrie. Cuddle kitties," he repeated solemnly.

"Yes." She gave him a warm smile. "Don't forget."

"Gil not forget. Tell Carrie. Cuddle kitties?"

Nodding, she said, "Cuddle kitties now."

"Make sure you don't scare Carrie again," Jacob added, "and I will take you to visit the beam engine at the mine day after tomorrow. Would you like that?"

"Yes!" The little boy grinned before throwing his arms around Jacob once more.

"As long as Carrie says you can come."

"Of course." Her smile was for both of them, but it warmed his heart where cold had existed too long. "That sounds like fun."

She set the gray kitten on the stone floor, and it raced back to the rest of the litter with Gil in pursuit.

"Do you think he understands?" Jacob asked quietly.

"About coming here to visit the kittens? Yes, but he is too young to realize he should tell me before he leaves the house for other reasons. One lesson at a time."

"Like with me?"

Her laugh was soft and weary. "I hope I don't have to explain every detail of every possible scenario to you."

He looked at the little boy, who was laughing again

as he played with the kittens. "The easiest way to keep him from coming here on his own might be to let him take one of these kittens."

She smiled and said, "If I take one, I need to take two. Bertie will want a kitten of his own if Gil brings home another. Thankfully, Joy is too young to expect one." As he turned to go to speak to Gil, she added, "But he should not take them today. I don't want him to think he will get a reward when he has done something as naughty as leaving the house without telling me where he was going."

"Come back whenever you wish with the boys. We have such a crop of kittens, and there will be more in the spring."

"I'm sure Bertie will want to select his own." Her smile wavered as she added, "Jacob, I am sorry I intruded on you and Miss Bolton."

"Your arrival gave us the excuse to put an end to the stilted conversation neither of us was enjoying. I can tell she is only pretending to be interested in what I have to say, and to own the truth, she was talking about people I have never met."

"A gentleman—"

"Allows a lady to lead the course of the conversation. See? I have listened to your lessons, Professor Dowling."

"It seems you have no more need of my tuition, for you have learned your lessons well."

"I am sure I have many more lessons to learn."

"We each learn something new each day."

As he watched her collect Gil, who reluctantly left the kittens, he pondered her words. Did she have any idea that what he had learned today was how much

she and the children had become vital to his life? He
had no idea how to change that without hurting them.
Maybe it was as simple as telling Carrie the truth about
his greatest ignominy; then she would understand why
he could not offer her his heart. He could not face the
possibility of losing her as surely as he had Virginia.

Light danced off the church windows as wind
slipped through any gap around the glass. Clouds hung
low over the cove but swept through the sky as if fleeing. In the village, every cottage was lit against the
storms threatening Porthlowen.

Inside the church, there was laughter and anticipation and chaos. The first rehearsal of the children's
choir was underway, and Carrie was glad Elisabeth had
offered to assist. At first, Carrie had hesitated, knowing how many other aspects of Advent and Christmas
a parson's wife had to oversee. Elisabeth had been suffering from a stomach ague prevalent in the village, but
she seemed fine as she auditioned the older children
for speaking roles in the Nativity play.

Carrie stood in front of the altar rail where she had
gathered the other children to practice the carols they
would sing on Christmas morning. She had made sure
everyone knew the same words and tune to "The Coventry Carol" and "This Endris Night."

"Everyone together one more time." She raised her
hands to get the children's attention.

Most of them quieted immediately, but some of the
boys had to jostle each other before obeying. A frown
in their direction quelled them. As they sang, their
enthusiastic voices filled the church. They would be a
wondrous addition to the Christmas morning service.

She was about to start them on another carol when Elisabeth asked to speak to her. Telling the children to sing "The Coventry Carol" another time, she turned to her sister-in-law.

"Do you know that woman?" asked Elisabeth as she glanced toward the rear of the church. "She asked to speak with you."

Carrie's eyes widened when she saw Beverly Warrick standing by the porch door. "That is Mrs. Warrick."

"Lord Warrick's stepmother?"

"Yes. Let me find out what she needs. In the meantime, will you have the children sing the final verse again? I don't think the younger ones have learned the words yet."

Elisabeth nodded and gave her a bolstering smile before turning to the children. Her sister-in-law's cheerful voice accompanied her up the aisle.

Carrie greeted Mrs. Warrick.

"I was told I would find you here," said Mrs. Warrick with a smile. She looked at the children, who had begun the next song under Elisabeth's direction. "How adorable! A children's choir is a wonderful idea."

"We have one each year. The children enjoy it as well as the chance to be in our Nativity play."

"Do you have mummers in Porthlowen on Christmas Day?"

"They perform on New Year's Eve. I know most places have mummer plays on Christmas Eve or Christmas Day, but Porthlowen has always had mummers with the New Year's celebration."

"Interesting…" She glanced around the church again. "Jacob tells me the church is always as full as it was when we attended on Sunday. Are you considering adding on?"

"That decision will be Father's and Raymond's, but the congregation is growing. Many new members have joined us temporarily from the parish on your family's land. Once the parson there is well enough to hold services again, they will likely return to their own parish." She halted herself, knowing a discussion of expanding the church was not the reason Mrs. Warrick had asked to talk with her. "Is there something I can help you with?"

"Yes. I want to talk to you about Jacob. He is in love with you, you know."

She flinched and stared at the older woman. "We are friends, nothing more."

"Does he know that?"

"Why wouldn't he?"

Mrs. Warrick glanced toward the altar. "Perhaps we should discuss this elsewhere."

"Yes."

She slipped her arm around Carrie's and walked out of the church. The wind off the land was colder than when it came from the sea, and Carrie shivered.

She forgot about the chill when Mrs. Warrick said, "I like you, Lady Caroline. You are a mature woman who comprehends the ways of the world. That is why I am going to speak candidly."

"I appreciate that, and I will be as candid when I say Jacob and I are friends. We both know what is the best for us, and marriage is not in our plans. Certainly not to each other." Even as she spoke, she could not keep from imagining Jacob drawing her into his arms.

No! Allowing such fantasies into her mind would

only lead to heartache. She had nothing to offer a man who loved children as Jacob did and would want some of his own.

"I know you believe you are only friends," Mrs. Warrick replied, "but he has changed."

"Of course. He has responsibilities and a life he never thought would be his. Leaving the university and coming here to where he has the livelihood of so many people dependent on his decisions would change anyone."

"I agree, but for most of his life, he has preferred spending time with books rather than with people. Now he uses any excuse to go to Cothaire to see you and your children. Do not misconstrue my words when I say you and the children are not what he needs. He needs a wife, and my beautiful niece would be perfect for him."

"Miss Bolton is lovely." What else could she say? That Mrs. Warrick should warn Miss Bolton how she would drive Jacob away if she pouted whenever he talked to another woman.

"I agree, as does Jacob, but he insists he has no interest in marrying now. I could accept it if I believed it to be true. When I see how he glows with happiness in your company, I wonder if he is being honest."

"Jacob does not lie."

"How quickly you come to his defense, Lady Caroline! Are you sure your feelings toward my stepson are mere friendship?"

"Yes." *They cannot be anything else!* She could not be Jacob's wife. After the work he had done to repair the mines and Warrick Hall, he must do the proper thing and choose a woman who could give him children. "Let me assure you, Mrs. Warrick, I have no plans to marry again. My life is full with my family and the children and my friendships."

"I understand loving children you did not carry in your womb. I love Jake and Emery as if I had brought them into the world myself, but I know, as much as Jake enjoys spending time with your little boy, he must have a son of his own." She sighed. "I know you are accustomed to the needs of succession with a title, but I find it uncomfortable to talk about Jacob needing an heir after he came close to dying once."

"He almost died? When?"

"It was quite a few years ago. A tragic carriage accident. He was severely injured. Fortunately he recovered."

She wanted to ask why, if Jacob had survived, Mrs. Warrick called the accident tragic. There could be but one reason. Someone else had died. Was that the cause of the pain she had seen half hidden in Jacob's eyes when he thought nobody was watching? She considered the times when he had reacted strangely if she spoke of him driving a carriage or another vehicle. He had resisted, vehemently, if he might have passengers with him.

Mrs. Warrick went on, "God was watching over him, and I believe it is because Jake—I must remember to call him Jacob now that he is a baron—is meant to give our family the way of life and social status it would have had if my husband and his brother had not been driven apart by arguments."

"Is that what happened?" she asked before she could halt herself. Such a personal question was rude.

"I am surprised you didn't know." Mrs. Warrick

seemed to take no offense at Carrie's question. "Maban Warrick was your family's closest neighbor his whole life."

"He may have told my father what happened, but I seldom saw him other than at church."

"You spend so much time at Warrick Hall now I assumed you had when my husband's brother was alive." She folded her arms in front of her. "I see I was wrong. However, I am not wrong about how Jacob feels about you."

Before Carrie could think of a suitable answer, she heard Jacob ask, "What are you two doing outside in the cold?" He strode toward them with a smile. "I know you are both intelligent and know enough to come in out of the cold."

Had he heard his stepmother's comment? Carrie replayed it in her mind. If he had overheard her last few words, he might not realize Beverly insisted he was in love with Carrie.

"We did not want to distract the children from their practicing," Carrie said quickly. "Would you like to come inside and listen to them?"

"No, I need to get to the mine." He raked his hand through his hair. "The beam engine is stopping again for no reason I can see. I have to postpone Gil's and your visit."

Aware of Mrs. Warrick watching them, Carrie said, "I will let him know."

"I'm sorry to disappoint him."

"I know." She forced a smile. "Maybe he will forget tomorrow is the day you planned to take him to see the beam engine."

"Thank you for understanding." He bid them a good

afternoon before he hurried to his horse tied to the lych-gate.

Carrie watched him ride away and wished there was some way she could ease his frustration with the beam engine. As hard as he worked to make life better and safer for the miners as well as his own family, she wanted him to succeed.

A sniff pulled her gaze from him to his stepmother, who arched her brows as she said, "Only friendship, you say. Look in the mirror, my lady. If that is mere friendship on your face when you look at Jacob, then I am the king of England." She strode away.

Putting her hands to her abruptly hot face, Carrie backed toward the church's porch. She could not be falling in love with Jacob. She must not.

Not ever.

Chapter Twelve

Why hadn't he told her the truth?

Jacob listened to the even beat of the beam engine, but he saw only Carrie's face. He was as sorry to disappoint her as he was Gil. The little boy might mistake the day, but she knew he was unable to do as he had promised.

"Pym, go home and have your supper," he said. "I will watch over the beam engine until you return."

His assistant shifted uneasily as he glanced at Yelland, who must have come in while Jacob was lost in reverie. When Pym opened his mouth, Jacob cut him off by repeating his order. The short man nodded as he edged past Yelland, who gave him a condescending smile.

When the mine captain was about to follow, Jacob said, "Wait. I want to speak with you."

"Are you going to do my duties, too, my lord?" His drawl turned into a sneer on the last two words. When Jacob did not react, he frowned. "I have work to do."

"Apparently you have been a very busy man."

Yelland glowered at him from narrowed eyes. "Why

don't you say what you mean? Your uncle always did. I liked that about him."

"Really? I would have thought you liked the fact he seldom came to the mines and left you to your own devices."

"I won't lie. I did like it. The old baron, he trusted us. He didn't breathe down our collars every day. He took a miner at his word. If a miner said he would have a fathom worked out by a set date, the old baron left him to do his job and checked only when the job was done."

Jacob tried to keep from clenching his teeth. How could Yelland have overlooked the truth right in front of him? Because of Maban Warrick's indifference and failure to keep the mines safe, men had died. Miners and their families had come close to starvation. The most desperate had turned to crime and paid a horrible price.

"There is no sense arguing about my uncle's ways and mine," he said as calmly as he could. "He is dead, and I am Lord Warrick now. I do not appreciate you trying to thwart my work."

"Thwart you? How?"

"Questioning my orders or refusing to follow them."

"I have followed your orders."

"No message was ever delivered to Lady Caroline as I asked the night when the beam engine stopped for the longest time." He could not keep from adding, "So far."

Yelland glowered at him even more. "I gave your message to one of the lads. He told me that he delivered it. Until now, I thought he had." He slammed one fist into his other palm. "I will teach the lazy cur to lie to me."

Jacob tried to discern if the mine captain was being honest or playing his part like an expert actor. Too bad he did not have Carrie's clear insight into people. Again he tried to push her out his thoughts. Again he failed.

"Leave the lad be," he ordered.

"But—"

"I said, leave him be. It is over and done with. What I am more interested in is what *you* know about the recent failures of the beam engine."

"You are talking to the wrong man. Pym is your assistant, not me."

"However, you have been in the engine house frequently when I am here. It makes me wonder if you are here as frequently when I am not here. Because of your visits, nobody would notice if you came in. It would give you the opportunity to wreak havoc on the machinery."

"Me? Wreck the machinery?" His face turned red with fury. "Why would I do that?"

"I don't know. Why don't you tell me?"

"I cannot tell you, because I have not damaged the beam engine. No one hates when it isn't working more than I do. I have miners complaining to me how they cannot go into the mine when the water is rising. They fear they will not get their work done on time, and they will not get paid. Do they come to you? No! They come to me." Yelland's hands fisted at his sides, but he did not raise them. "You should be more like your uncle. He stayed away, and we could do our jobs. The system worked well. Everything has fallen apart since you decided to intrude."

Jacob laughed tersely. "Everything had fallen apart

before I got here. The housing, the mine shafts, the beam engines."

"I am not talking about that. I am talking about a system that worked fine until you came along."

"Really?" Jacob leaned against the railing, letting the shadow of the beam engine crisscross him and the floor in front of Yelland. "You say the men come to you to complain. They also come to me."

"They are not supposed to."

"Maybe not, but they have. Some of their complaints are silly. Others, though, have been insightful and worthwhile. Those ideas I have begun to implement."

"What ideas?"

"Like making sure every team has one man keeping an eye on the walls around them at all times."

"If they are watching, they are not working."

"Every man is allowed a break during his shift. If he scans the walls to make sure no change signals a potential collapse, that does not keep him from resting. There are enough men there, so someone can be on watch."

Yelland reluctantly said, "Not a bad idea. Sounds like something Semmens would have suggested."

Impressed at Yelland's knowledge of the men who worked beneath him, Jacob said, "Semmens was the one who came to me with it. He also suggested the walls be inspected at the beginning of each team's work so they don't start digging at a weak spot. I told him to talk to you about that so the practice can be begun as soon as possible."

"He asked to speak to me tonight when he comes up."

"Semmens isn't the only one who lost someone from

his family in the big cave-in the month before I arrived in Cornwall. His son is of an age to begin work in the mine soon, and he doesn't want to lose him, too. You should listen to the men, Yelland. Some of their ideas are brilliant."

"And you should heed me, my lord. I have done nothing to halt the beam engine." He glanced up at the huge beam. "Wouldn't know how even if I wanted to, but I don't want to. If the men fail to meet the date they gave you in their bid, I don't get paid, either."

Jacob nodded. He had forgotten that one important fact. But if Yelland was not the one causing damage to the beam engine, who was?

Carrie's bed bounced. Hard. One. Twice. Again and again.

Another gunpowder explosion?

She had not heard anything, but she had been deeply asleep. Her dream had been wonderful. It had been… The images faded away even as she tried to grasp for them. All she could recall was Jacob smiling at her in the dream.

The bed bounced again.

Opening her eyes, she stared at Gil. He was standing next to her and watching her.

"Snow!" he shouted.

For a second, she wanted to tell him unless it was snowing from the canopy of her bed, she was not interested; then she saw the glow of happiness on his round face.

She put her finger to her lips. "Don't wake Joy. Let's keep the snow our secret!"

"Snow," he repeated but in a whisper.

Holding out her hands, she smiled when he tugged on them. She pretended to have to fight her own weight to sit up. He laughed, then clamped his hand over his mouth.

The children usually slept in the nursery, but last night, Carrie had allowed them to stay with her. Joy had been running a slight fever and was cranky as her first tooth tried to poke through again, so Carrie had wanted her nearby in case she woke. Gil had insisted on being with "his" baby. A small cot and Joy's cradle had been set up in her room.

Carrie went to the window. She shouldered away the heavy draperies and looked out. In the gray light before dawn, snow came straight down. Not a hint of wind stirred the fuzzy flakes. So far, only the tops of the bushes and grass were covered with the white icing. As fast as it was falling, she guessed several inches would accumulate by midday.

"Go out!" urged Gil.

She wanted to groan at the idea of trading her warm room for the cold hour before the sun rose. "Why don't we wait until there is more snow? If we go out now, as soon as we touch it, it will melt away and be gone."

He considered her words, then nodded. "Go out later."

"That is a good idea. For now, though, shall we get more sleep?"

"In your bed?"

Again she smiled as she closed the draperies. "If you don't wiggle." She tickled his sides but stopped when he squealed with laughter. If they woke Joy, any chance of sleeping would be gone.

She lifted him on to the high bed and watched him

walk to the middle where she had been. On every step, the mattress shifted. He had not been bouncing to get her attention before. He had been trying to reach her.

Lying beside him, she drew the covers over them. He nestled against her. His small body seemed the perfect size for her arms. As Joy's did. She leaned her cheek against the top of his head and listened to him chatter about the things he wanted to do in the snow. She loved moments like this with the children.

It was her last quiet one. Joy became fussy, and Carrie could find nothing to soothe her. Irene had the idea of wrapping a piece of ice in a cloth and letting Joy chew on it. That seemed to ease the baby's discomfort.

Gil was eager to get outside and play in the snow. Every two minutes, he asked if they could go out now. Again the nursery maid came to Carrie's rescue, volunteering to keep Joy in the nursery while Carrie took Gil outside. When Carrie offered to take Bertie, too, Irene told her that he was with Arthur and Maris, who had left late yesterday to pay a call on Arthur's long-time friend, Gwendolyn Miller, and her husband for a few days.

Thanking Irene again, Carrie dressed Gil and herself in their heaviest clothes before she led him outside. Someone had shoveled the snow away from the door. She had no idea whose duty it was because, until the past few winters, she could not recall it snowing often. When it did, the scarce inch quickly melted.

She guessed there was already six inches of damp, heavy snow on the ground, and more fell on the brisk wind, which had raised drifts against the side of the house. It might be a record accumulation for Porthlowen.

Gil was having trouble plowing through the deeper drifts. Carrie picked him up and carried him around to the side garden where the snow was untouched. He chortled with delight as he ran about in a circle.

"That looks like fun." A deep laugh was not muted by the falling snow.

Whirling, Carrie gasped. "Jacob! I didn't expect to see you today."

"I am from the north. A little bit of snow does not keep me confined to the house. I was at the mine, and I decided to take the long road home." He watched Gil racing through the snow. "I wanted to make sure he was not too disappointed. I can see he is not. You have been giving me many excellent lessons. I thought I might call and give one to Master Gil."

"Me?" asked the little boy as he leaped through the snow toward them. "Cuddle kitties?"

"No, but I think you will like this, as well." He bent and scooped up a handful of snow. "Try this." He packed a snowball in his hands, then began to push it along the ground.

Carrie helped Gil copy Jacob's motions. The little boy dropped the first snowball and fell on top of the second when he tried to turn it through the snow. She kept him from giving into frustration and tears by quickly making a third snowball and assisting him until the snowball had become almost as tall as he was.

"Perfect," Jacob announced. "Now step back."

Gil did and fell in the snow. He was laughing when Carrie picked him and set him on his feet again.

By that time, Jacob had hefted the large snowball she and Gil had made. He set it on top of the bigger one he had rolled. Calling Gil over to him, he helped the boy make another ball. He put this one on top of the other two. From his greatcoat pocket, he pulled out some small, dark stones. He put them on the uppermost ball to make a face.

Gil stared in disbelief at the snowman, which was taller than he was.

When the little boy did not speak, Carrie knelt beside him. "Look what you made. It is a man made out of snow. What should we call him?"

"Gil?"

She laughed. "No, that is your name."

"Toby?"

"How about Mr. Winter?" suggested Jacob.

"Mr. Winter! Mr. Winter!" Gil danced around the snowman.

"I guess he likes that choice." Carrie got to her feet.

"That is one kind of snow people. Let me show you another." He picked up the little boy and then bent to set Gil in a pristine section of snow. Lifting him again, he turned Gil to see the imprint. "Look! It's a snow Gil."

"Snow Gil! Mr. Winter!" He tapped Jacob on the chest. "Snow Jacob now!"

Setting the child down, Jacob grinned as he fell back, his arms spread wide. Snow billowed up in the air around him.

Gil clapped his hands in excitement.

When Jacob got carefully to his feet, Gil moved closer and stared at the shape he had made in the snow.

"Snow Jacob!" he said with glee. He ran to Carrie and tugged on her hand. "Make a snow Carrie!"

Jacob glanced at her with uncertainty. "Ladies don't—"

"Let anyone stop them," she said as she went to where the two silhouettes were side by side in the snow. With a laugh, she stretched out her arms as Jacob had and let herself topple into the snow.

It was deeper than she had guessed, and flakes flew in every direction around her. She breathed in the fresh, cold scent, feeling as young as Gil. She had played with Arthur under their nurse's supervision, and they had teased to remain outside until their teeth were chattering with the cold so hard they could barely form a word.

When snow trickled on to her face, she knew she could not stay in her memories of the past. She sat up and saw the delight on Gil's face. She wanted to pull him into her arms and hug him, but it would ruin her Snow Carrie.

She tried to stand, then realized she had not considered how much more complicated it was for her than Jacob and Gil. Neither of them had to contend with a coat that brushed the top of their toes or several other layers of clothes. She sat in the snow to figure out how to rise without damaging her silhouette.

"Let me help." Jacob reached a hand out to her from where he stood beyond the heels of her imprint. When she grasped it, he pulled her easily to her feet and toward him.

She swayed, and he steadied her. When she had her feet underneath her again, he released her arm. She was about to thank him when his thumb traced the curve of her cheekbone as his gaze held hers. Their breaths fogged and merged between them, binding them together in some inexplicable way as time seemed to stop in one perfect moment.

His eyes sparkled like the snow as his finger caressed her face, tipping it toward his. So many reasons why she should not be standing like this with him flew through her mind, but the single reason why she should was the only one that stayed. Being here beside him made her happy. She leaned toward him.

"Snow Gil! Snow Carrie! Snow Jacob!" Gil's chant sent time careening forward again as he pulled on her coat. "Look! Look! They hold hands. Make Snow Gil hold hands, too."

Carrie stepped away from Jacob, belatedly remembering to thank him for assisting her to her feet. Her breath caught when she looked at the imprints and realized Gil was right. Her left hand had hit the snow right next to Jacob's right hand, so it looked as if the two figures had clasped each other's fingers. Gil's smaller imprint stood beneath their hands, and the image was of a family standing close to one another.

Jacob picked up Gil again to keep the little boy from prancing through the snow shapes. "Watch where you step. We need to be extra careful."

Was he talking only about not damaging the snow people? If not, she did not need his warning. She knew the danger she risked if she gave into her yearning for him to court her.

He must have, as well, because when she said it was time to go inside before they froze into real snow people, Jacob agreed.

"I have not spent as much time with my family as

I would like," he said before he handed Gil to her and took his leave. He glanced back with a smile so warm she was surprised every snowflake did not instantly melt.

She walked, as if in a waking dream, into the house, savoring the sensations that had flowed through her when they had stood face-to-face in the perfection of the sparkling world of the fresh snow. The entry hall was full. Susanna and Elisabeth had come to visit, along with the children.

Gil rushed to the other children and began telling them about the different snow people they had created in the back garden. They pelted him with questions. Their voices rose with their enthusiasm until they were too loud for anyone else to talk without shouting.

Carrie took control of the situation by sending for Irene. With the help of a footman and the butler, the nursery maid herded the children upstairs to where they could prattle to their hearts' delight and play with the toys.

"I will get Gil into some dry clothes," Irene added over her shoulder. "You may want to come up for the children's midday meal, Lady Caroline. Miss Joy's tooth is close to breaking through. One good bite should break it free."

"I shall be there!" Carrie's smile widened as she saw the excitement on the other women's faces. Their shared love for the children made every event special.

Taking off her coat and bonnet, she handed them to the waiting footman, who was almost invisible beneath the garments he held. She walked with her sister and sister-in-law to the small parlor where a fire warmed the room, but barely heard what they were saying as she replayed over and over in her mind every word she and Jacob had spoken in the snow.

But her attention was yanked to Elisabeth when her sister-in-law spoke the words Carrie had yearned to say for so many years, "Yes, it is true. I am going to have a baby!"

Chapter Thirteen

"**W**hat wonderful news, Elisabeth!" When Carrie hugged her sister-in-law, she wore a genuine smile. As much as she had longed for a child of her own, she knew Elisabeth and Raymond were equally eager to add a baby to their family as a sibling for little Toby. It was a blessing for all the Trelawneys.

"I thought I had the sickness plaguing the village," Elisabeth said, her face aglow with happiness, "but it was not that."

"Morning sickness," said Susanna with a smile.

"All-day sickness is more like it."

Going into the parlor, Carrie rang for a footman to bring cocoa. The hot drink would make for an excellent celebration. She urged Elisabeth to go in and put up her feet.

"Not you, too!" her sister-in-law said with an emoted groan. "Raymond is hovering over me as if he fears I will shatter. I tell him to save his doting for the baby, but he will not listen."

"Or he cannot." Carrie smiled. "He loves you so much."

"He does." An odd expression crossed Elisabeth's

face as she pressed her hand to her middle. "Maybe I should sit. Not moving lessens the queasiness." She reeled into the room and sat heavily by the hearth. Leaning her head back, she closed her eyes.

As Carrie was about to follow, Susanna drew her aside. "How are you?"

"Me? I am a bit chilled, but the cocoa will take care of that."

"Stop it, Caroline!" When a maid turned to look at them with concern, she lowered her voice. "You do not have to pretend with me. Do you think I didn't notice how often you looked as if you had been crying? You are my big sister. I watched everything you did because I wanted to be exactly like you. I saw your unhappiness, and I asked Mother about it. She told me I must never speak to you of it because she was sure that time would eventually give you reason to dry your tears."

"She said that?" Carrie had never guessed Mother had ever mentioned her oldest daughter's inability to conceive.

"Yes. I didn't know what she was talking about then, but I have figured it out in the ensuing years. I know you are happy for Elisabeth, but..."

"There is no but. I am very happy for Raymond and Elisabeth. Beginning, middle and end of the story." She smiled at her sister. "You are sweet to think of me, but I plan to be one of the first to hold the baby."

"I am relieved to hear that." Susanna paused, then asked, "Is not being able to have a child the reason you have never remarried?"

"It is not prudent to marry when one has not found the right person."

She waved her hand to dismiss Carrie's trite words. "You are being evasive. Answer me."

"I thought I did."

"Perhaps you gave me *an* answer, but you haven't given me *the* answer. The real answer. I saw Lord Warrick with you and Gil. You looked happier than I have seen you since John died."

"He has mentioned several times he does not wish to marry now when he has to devote his time to the mines."

"Yet he has time to play in the snow with you and Gil. Would you marry him if he asked?"

She shook her head, unable to say the words, which would shut the door on her heart's desire.

"Tell me one thing," Susanna said. "How do you know you cannot conceive?"

"I was told by the woman who was the midwife in Porthlowen at the time. She said after so many years of trying, it was unlikely I ever would, especially as I was past thirty years old then."

"She may be wrong."

"She may be right. I cannot marry when I am not sure."

"So you are making the decision for you and Lord Warrick without giving him the courtesy of telling him the truth?"

Carrie forced a smile. "You are talking about something that has not happened and is unlikely to happen. As I told you, Jacob has no interest in marrying now. If he were to change his mind, his marrying Miss Bolton would please his family."

"But what would please him? I see him with you

and the children, and there is no doubt he is happy with you."

Not wanting to repeat the conversation she had had with Beverly Warrick, Carrie excused herself. Why did no one else understand that no matter how happy Jacob might be with her now, his happiness would sour when he learned the truth? They could not wed, and when he decided to marry someone else, their friendship would have to change.

She intended to relish every moment, knowing each one could be the last.

Jacob listened for the sound of the beam engine over the waves on the shore. He had spent yesterday afternoon and half the night working with Pym to get it running again.

Beverly had not hidden her vexation when he had excused himself from a family gathering with Miss Bolton in the parlor yesterday. His stepmother's complaint he spent less time at Warrick Hall than he did elsewhere probably was valid, but her accusation he was at Cothaire too often was not. He had not called there as frequently as he would have liked.

He knew he could not leave matters as they were. He had caught irritation festering in Miss Bolton's eyes when she thought he was not looking. Other than their one curtailed tea, they had not been alone together once.

Maybe Pym was right when his assistant said Jacob did not need to come to the engine house whenever the steam engine stopped. Certainly, almost every time, Pym was the one who discovered the source of the problem and could fix it without help.

Even if his assistant was correct, Jacob knew he could not remain away when the beam engine halted. The first thing he did each time was to make sure everyone had escaped the mine. The thought of someone dying while he did nothing left him nauseated.

However, spending time with his family was important, too. He wanted them to feel at home. Again he wondered if his brother had revealed the truth to the others. The next time he had a chance to speak with Emery, he must ask.

"Listen," Jacob urged, looking at his family who stood by the closed carriage not far from the Porthlowen church. They had a splendid view of the cliffs' double curve which sheltered the cove. They were bundled up against the cold. A resonant boom came from the base of the outer cliff. "That is the sound the water makes when it builds up in a tunnel within the cliff. The tide washes in, leaving more water than can drain away before the next wave. When the tunnel cannot hold any more, it explodes out."

He waited for them to respond. No one spoke, and he had to admit they looked miserable.

With a sigh, he wondered how they could insist he spend time with them and then act as if they wished they were anywhere but with him. They had agreed when he offered to give them a tour of the area and now exhibited no interest in anything he showed them. So far, he had taken them to see the engine house and the foundations from an ancient settlement on the moor before coming to the cove.

Helen and her sister had complained about the dirty floor in the engine house, and he could not help thinking of Carrie sitting there when she had brought the meal they had shared with Pym. Beverly had no interest in walking across a field to see the foundations, because her boots were too low for the deep snow. He had hoped the tunnel in the cliff would intrigue them, but they clearly were too chilled to care about anything but returning to Warrick Hall. Helen and Miss Bolton had done nothing but grouse about the wind and the cold.

He was about to suggest they curtail the rest of the tour when the happy sound of bells came from the road leading to the village. Two sleighs came over the crest. One rushed past, and Arthur and his wife waved before they were quickly out of sight.

The other sleigh slowed. His grin returned when he heard Gil shout to him over the bells. The little boy was sitting next to Carrie, who held the jingling reins. She stopped the brightly painted sleigh close to the carriage. It had a single seat and a flat area, making it look more like a wagon than a buggy.

Miss Bolton put a hand on his arm, startling him so much he recoiled. She tightened her hold on his sleeve, but her face wore the same cool smile it always did when Carrie was present. When he glanced at Beverly, his stepmother was looking from him and Miss Bolton to Carrie, clearly waiting to see what would ensue. His brother and Helen climbed into the carriage in an obvious attempt to get warm, but his sister-in-law peeked past the lowered curtain on the door.

"Good afternoon!" Carrie called. "I have wonderful news to share, Jacob. Joy's first tooth came through this morning. She is proud of it and showing it off to anyone who will stand still long enough to look into her mouth."

"She should be proud," he said with a laugh. "She suffered for that tooth."

Beverly laughed from behind the scarf she had pulled up over the lower half of her face. "Now maybe you can sleep better."

"Not likely." Carrie rolled her eyes. "Another one is already bothering her."

"If it is next to her first tooth, it should come in more easily," his stepmother assured her.

"I hope you are right. She has many more to go." She paused as Gil stood up and whispered in her ear. She nodded, then asked, "Would you and your family like to join us, Jacob?"

"Where are you bound?" he asked as Miss Bolton stiffened beside him.

"Gil and I volunteered to collect holiday greens for the house while Arthur and Maris help Elisabeth with scenery and costumes for the Nativity play. You are welcome to come along with us and see where we find our greenery. You can gather some for Warrick Hall."

He was astonished when Miss Bolton said, "That sounds lovely."

Beverly stared at the young woman by his side, and her eyes narrowed. Was his stepmother as dumb-founded as he was by Miss Bolton's words? Only moments ago, she had been complaining about the cold and saying how eager she was to get indoors before the wind chapped her lips and cheeks.

Telling himself not to ponder on the mysteries wrapped up in Miss Bolton, he checked with Beverly and his brother and Helen before he told Carrie they would follow her. He assisted his stepmother into the carriage, then offered to do the same for Miss

Bolton. She did not release his hand as she turned in the cramped space to face him.

"Do ride with us, *Jacob*," she cooed, but her eyes suggested it was more of an order than a request.

"I have my horse."

"You can tie it to the carriage."

He withdrew his hand from her grip, wondering momentarily what he would do if she refused to relinquish her hold. She did let go, and her eyes snapped with vexation.

"I will ride Shadow," he said as he stepped away.

"Are you sure?" Beverly asked. "You are welcome to join us in here. We can make room."

"I am sure."

He strode to his horse after telling the coachman to follow him and the sleigh. When he signaled to Carrie, she edged the sleigh into packed snow along the road. He followed and smiled when Gil waved eagerly to him again. Cheerful jingling filled the air along with the creak of the carriage lumbering after them.

Shadow shook his mane impatiently, and Jacob let his horse catch up with the sleigh. Shadow never liked not being in the lead.

"Thank you for the invitation," he said to Carrie as he drew even with her.

"I thought coming with us would offer your family a chance to see more of the area," she said.

"Perhaps, but they have not appreciated the tour I have given them thus far." He outlined what he taken them to see.

When she laughed, he was perplexed. "What is funny?"

"I see I forgot one important lesson for you. When

you are someone's host, you need to entertain them with what *they* would enjoy. Not what you enjoy."

He chuckled, amused by her comment, but even more delighted by her crimson face. The bright red accentuated her high cheekbones and her eyes the color of a blue sky through an icicle. There was nothing cold about them, however, for they burned with the heat at the very heart of a fire.

"I will keep that in mind, Professor Dowling," he said, then asked Gil what he had been doing.

The child talked with barely a pause to catch his breath. His little voice mixed with the sleigh bells to make a joyous holiday melody. More than once, Jacob had to hold back a laugh at Gil's impressions of the world around him, and he saw Carrie's lips quirk.

Jacob's eyes widened when Carrie turned the sleigh away from the road. Ahead of them was a tree-filled oasis amidst the raw desolation of the moor. The valley was little more than a cleft between two massive cliffs flanking a stream flowing into the sea. In its sheltered confines, greenery and trees grew with abandon as if to make up for the stark moorlands.

"I had no idea there was such a place this close to the cove," he said as he stared around him.

"The soil here is richer and thicker than on the moor," Carrie said as she stopped partway to the trees. "Here, trees can put down roots and survive the winds off the sea. Whenever I read a tale of fairies as a child, I always imagined they lived here."

He swung from the saddle. "Did you ever find one?"

"No, but not for a lack of trying."

When he held up his hand for the reins, she gave them to him. He tied them to a tree and turned to help her out. As she put her hand in his, the carriage arrived and halted where the wagon tracks ended. He did not have to look in its direction to know Miss Bolton would be watching closely while he assisted Carrie from the sleigh.

Confound it, he could not live his life to the expectations of a woman who seemed dedicated to a single idea: that he would ask her to marry. He treasured his friendship with Carrie.

Is it truly only friendship you feel for her? asked a small voice within his mind. He ignored it now as he had each time it nagged him.

"There is a saw as well as a hatchet in the back," Carrie said as she lifted Gil from the seat. "Do you want to use one?"

"I will take the saw." He reached into the rear of the sleigh and pulled out both tools. Handing her the hatchet, he asked, "Gil, do you want to help me?"

"Yes!" Gil bounced, sending snow flying in every direction.

After Carrie outlined what she needed to decorate Cothaire, he took the little boy's hand. He paused when he heard his stepmother call his name.

He looked over his shoulder. Beverly looped one arm around her daughter-in-law's as they and his brother walked to where Carrie had begun chopping sprigs of holly off a nearby bush as she sang a bright tune he recognized as a children's song. When Gil joined the singing, Jacob wanted to as well, but he did not need a glance from his stepmother to know what she expected of him.

Putting the saw in the sleigh, he told Gil to wait. The little boy, confused, nodded, and Jacob glanced at him again and again to make sure he did not wander off while Jacob plowed through the snow to the carriage.

The door was open, and Miss Bolton sat as still as a statue. He waited for her to look at him, but she continued staring forward until he asked, "Miss Bolton, may I hand you down?"

She shook her head. "No, thank you. It is too cold to be larking about." She turned toward him and gave him a smile. "Would you drive me to Warrick Hall, my lord?"

"You want to leave? Without everyone else?" He hid his amazement she would insist the others come and, as soon as they arrived in the dale, ask to leave. Comprehension came when Miss Bolton affixed a glare in Carrie's direction. She wanted to keep him away from Carrie.

"Why, Lady Caroline can bring them when she is finished here. She seems interested in being such a good neighbor. This will allow her the opportunity."

"There is not room for everyone in the sleigh."

"Then send the carriage back for them." She reached for his hand.

He clasped them behind him. "An excellent idea."

She smiled broadly, but it faded when he went on.

"I will let the others know you wish to leave. If they want to go with you, then they can. Have a pleasant journey." Stepping back, he called to the coachee to bring extra blankets from the boot for Miss Bolton. He told the driver to return after he had delivered Miss Bolton and anyone else who intended to leave immediately for Warrick Hall.

He walked to where Carrie was directing Emery on which clumps of mistletoe to cut out of a high notch in a tree. His brother held a piece over her head and winked. Jacob acted as if he had not seen either motion as he asked his family if they wished to return to Warrick Hall because the carriage would take any of them who did not desire to remain outside.

When they said they wanted to stay, he gave the signal to the driver to leave with his single passenger.

"Isn't Miss Bolton joining us?" Carrie asked as she gave Gil a small piece of holly to carry to the sleigh while the Warricks moved to collect some ivy wrapped around a tree.

"No." He lowered his voice, so his words did not reach his family. "She wanted me to take her to Warrick Hall and leave the others for you to bring when you were done."

"Oh."

"Is that all you have to say? Oh?"

"Jacob, have you told her you have no intention of marrying now? You must, you know. For her sake as well as your own."

"You are right." He needed to be honest with Miss Bolton that he was not going to ask her to be his wife. He would as soon as he returned to Warrick Hall.

Carrie put her hand on his arm and gave him a gentle smile that set off fireworks in his center. "I will keep both of you in my prayers, because I know how difficult it will be for Miss Bolton, as well as you."

"Thank you," he said, then asked, "How much do you need to gather? Enough for Cothaire and the church?"

"Just Cothaire." She swung the hatchet at a dense section of the shiny, green leaves. "Raymond would allow greenery to be placed in the sanctuary, but it would distress some of the older parishioners who cling to the tradition that holly, like mistletoe, doesn't belong inside a church. Some parishioners would like to have it, but, even then, it should go into the church only on Christmas Eve."

"But you plan to bring holly and other greens into Cothaire before Christmas Eve."

"If we waited to begin decorating, we would spend the whole night hanging holly and ivy and mistletoe instead of lighting the Yule log and enjoying our other traditions. In addition, some of the servants wish to celebrate Christmas Eve with their families. We always have extra holly, so they take it home with them to decorate for Christmas and the new year."

Jacob got the saw from the sleigh and went to work, helping Carrie and his family pile greenery on the snow. He carried branches to the sleigh and placed them in the back.

"Holly!" came an excited cry as a sprig slapped against his leg.

Looking down, he smiled. "An excellent piece, Gil. Do you want to put it in the sleigh?"

The little boy nodded, so Jacob lifted him high enough to let Gil drop the small piece of holly on top of the longer pieces.

"More!" Gil rushed to where Carrie worked.

The sleigh was almost full when the carriage returned. It did not take long for the men to stack greenery on top and tie it in place. As soon as they were finished, his family climbed inside, eager to return to Warrick Hall.

"You should go with them, Jacob," Carrie said.

"And leave you with only Gil to safeguard you?"

Her eyes twinkled like sunshine on the snow at

the idea the toddler could protect her. "They are your guests. More important, they are your family."

"I am beginning to think the rules of being a host are designed to make someone do what they don't want to do."

She laughed. "Now you finally have learned what you need to know."

He chuckled with her before going to where Shadow waited patiently. As he swung up into the saddle, he almost jumped down again. If he did, Carrie would be disappointed in him. He did not want her ever to feel that way about him, so he waved farewell and followed the coach out of the valley, though his heart was begging him to stay with her.

Carrie watched until the carriage and Jacob were out of sight. She gave Gil a smile. In the most cheerful voice she could manage, she said, "We need more holly. Let's cut it."

"What about Jacob? Where is he going?"

"Home."

"Why?"

"The others are too cold." She forestalled his next question by saying, "We cannot stay much longer ourselves. Let's collect as much holly as we can before we have to leave."

She went through the motions and even managed to tease Gil, but her heart ached. That Jacob had done as she taught him was excellent. He was putting his family's needs first. She should be proud of him, and she was, but she could not help wishing he had not been quite so attentive a student.

Lord, let me rejoice in what Jacob has accomplished

instead of being tangled in my yearnings for his company. I need to be as selfless as he is, and I don't want to do anything to jeopardize our friendship. Help me remember that.

Carrie's shoulders felt lighter after she had shared her quandary with God. She started singing again and smiled when Gil sang along with her.

Within an hour, the wind was strengthening, which was a good reason to leave. Gil climbed in while she loosened the reins from around a tree. The jangle of the bells accompanied her as she sat next to the little boy.

She started to turn the horse in the narrow space between the trees. Suddenly it shied and jerked to the left. She did not see what had frightened it as the sleigh snapped like a riding crop. She ducked as it swung beneath some low tree branches and grabbed for Gil with one hand as she struggled to hold on to the reins with the other.

Gil cried out in terror as the sleigh slammed sideways into the trees. A loud crack echoed through the woods, and the concussion vibrated through her. The reins whipped out of her hand. The horse vanished toward the road, dragging the traces in its wake.

"Are you hurt?" she asked Gil.

He shook his head and clung to her. She winced as she moved her left hand to check his limbs. Both her elbow and her wrist were going to be bruised, but they had suffered no other injuries. Sending up a prayer of gratitude, she pushed aside the branches and climbed out on Gil's side. Her side was pressed up against the tree, misshapen and cracked.

Carrie took a deep breath but could not make her knees stop shaking as she looked at the damage. Even if the horse had not run off, the vehicle was useless. One runner was bent and the other broken off and lying in the snow. Cut greenery was scattered in an abstract pattern around them.

Gil picked up a piece of holly and held it out to her. "Holly."

"Yes." She took it before she hugged him again.

"Ouchie," he said, pointing to the sleigh.

She nodded. "It definitely has an ouchie. We will have to send someone to get it and our greenery. Let's go. It is a long walk to Cothaire." She could stop at any cottage in the village, but even that would be a walk of at least a mile. Looking up, she saw the sun was not far from the western horizon, and clouds were gathering.

Gil wanted to walk on his own, but Carrie lifted him on to her back as she had seen Jacob do. He clung while she pushed her way through the snow. Each step was difficult, and, by the time she reached the road where the carriage had stopped, she was panting as if she had run at top speed from Porthlowen to London.

Making sure Gil was secure, she headed toward the village. She set him on his feet when he insisted because she did not want to waste strength arguing. When he tired, she would carry him once more.

Suddenly he ran forward.

She cried out and gave chase as hoofbeats came toward them. If the rider did not see Gil, he could be run down.

The horse slowed, and she heard the little boy shout, "Jacob!"

Stumbling to a stop, Carrie watched as Jacob halted his horse. She stayed where she was when he jumped down and hugged the little boy. He asked Gil a question she could not hear past her heart that pounded even faster, when, after lifting the little boy and setting him on his shoulders, Jacob strode toward her.

He had put a cape over his greatcoat, and it flowed behind him like a dark stream. His hazel eyes focused on her face. She fought every instinct that urged her forward to embrace him as Gil had. How she longed for those strong, tender arms around her, holding her close to him!

Instead of doing as she wished, she said, "You came back."

"Are you all right?" Jacob asked, and she was glad he did not respond to her foolish comment. "Gil says you hit a tree."

"We were bumped about, but we are fine. The horse broke free."

"I know. I saw it racing home. That is why I rushed here at Shadow's top speed."

"But why are you here?"

"You didn't think I would leave you here alone, did you?"

"I have told you I am safe on these hills." When he arched his brows, she sighed. "It is true the sleigh slid into the trees, but we could have reached Cothaire before dark."

He set Gil on top of his horse. "I am sure you could have, but you would have been half-frozen."

"I do appreciate how concerned you are for us."

"Who taught me a gentleman should think first of a lady's needs?"

She smiled. "Not me."

"Quite to the contrary. You told me I should always follow a lady's lead in conversation and make sure she is greeted properly." He gave her a lazy grin. "You did not teach me I should rescue a lady from a sleigh mishap, but I could infer that from your other lessons."

"I am glad."

"I am, too. Let me get you up on Shadow and take you two to Cothaire."

Exhausted, she nodded as she stepped closer. She drew in his warm, masculine scent as she put her hands on his shoulders. When she put her boot on his clasped hands, he lifted her as easily as if she weighed no more than Gil.

He undid his cape and told her to wrap it around herself and the child. When she protested, he insisted he would be kept warm on the lee side of the big horse. She was grateful for the thick wool when the wind grew stronger as they reached the village. She picked out the lighted windows in the great house and watched as they came closer.

Gil cheered when they went through the gate. He began to babble about how he intended to share their adventures with Bertie and Joy.

They stopped not far from the front door. As soon as Jacob lifted Gil from the saddle, the little boy ran to the house. The door was opened, and he vanished inside.

Carrie leaned forward to put her hands on Jacob's shoulders so he could assist her from the tall horse. Snow crunched beneath her boots when her feet settled on the ground, and she stood between him and the horse. She was about to thank him for coming to their rescue when he cupped her chin, tilting her mouth toward him. With a gentleness that set her heart to beating like a storm wave upon the shore, he brushed his lips against hers. He drew back for a moment. To let her decide? Didn't he know she already had decided she wanted him to kiss her? Not once and not as lightly as he would the children. She wanted him to *kiss* her.

Her hands slid up to his shoulders and along his nape. He smiled in the moment before she stood on tiptoe and pressed her lips to his. His kiss remained gentle, but it deepened as he drew her into his embrace. She had no idea if seconds or an eternity passed before he raised his head. All she knew was even her dreams had never been as glorious as this moment.

He kissed the tip of her nose, and she laughed. That sound turned into a gulp when she saw in his eyes how much he wanted to kiss her again.

Had she lost her mind completely? She should not be kissing a man she could not marry. When she stepped away from him, his eyes narrowed.

"Carrie?" he asked. "If I did something wrong, tell me, because I cannot imagine kissing you being a mistake."

She shook her head, unable to speak. This time, there would be no lesson for her to explain to him what he had done wrong. He had not made a mistake.

She had. The biggest one she could, for she was falling in love with him, even though she knew there was no future for them other than as friends. Letting him think anything else was possible had been wrong, even though she had not intentionally led him on.

Running into the house, she went up the stairs as fast as she could. She heard Jacob behind her in the entry hall, but did not slow until she had reached her bedroom. She went in and closed the door. Sinking on to the closest chair, she hid her face in her hands.

She had not guessed how truly alone she had felt

since John's death. She had known it seemed as if half of her was gone, but she had never examined those feelings to discover their depths. Maybe she had been afraid to. Maybe she had seen the futility of it when there was no one to fill the void left behind.

Then the children had come to Cothaire, and she could have the family she had dreamed of. It was an improvised family, but better than the life she had been living. However, until Jacob had asked for her help, she had not accepted the truth of how much she missed having a man look at her as if she were the only woman in the world.

Lord, I have lost my way. And my heart, but You know I must never follow it into Jacob's arms. Help me. I cannot do this by myself any longer.

Chapter Fourteen

Usually Carrie treasured having a few minutes to herself, but she did not the day after Jacob kissed her. She wanted to be busy so she had no time to think. She tried to keep herself occupied, which should have been easy in the week before Christmas. Every task she thought of was already being done by someone else. Which was why, in spite of her efforts, she found herself alone in the solar in the middle of the afternoon, staring at the snow falling against the windows. Neither of the children had protested taking a nap, and the rest of her family was busy with tasks of their own.

Was this what the rest of her life would be like? A desperate race to fill every hour so she had no time to rediscover how lonely being alone could be?

Last winter, before the children's arrival and her brothers and sister marrying, she had enjoyed long conversations with them and her father by a cozy hearth. When his gout bothered him, she had kept him company so he could concentrate on what she had to say instead of the pain. She had not spent an afternoon with her father for almost three months because her life had been caught up with taking care of the children and with helping Jacob.

She went to the smoking room where Father spent his afternoons, but he was not there. Hoping the gout had not returned, she went to the suite of rooms attached to his bedchamber. Baricoat stood on guard at the door and shook his head as she approached.

"His lordship is with the doctor, and he asked they not be disturbed during the examination." The butler unbent enough to add, "The earl is feeling fine, my lady, but Mr. Hockbridge asked for privacy."

She nodded, then walked away. Maybe she should get a book. She usually had time to read only before her nightly prayers. Reading aloud to the children was not the same as enjoying a book herself.

Choosing a volume of poetry from the book-room, Carrie sat by a window where the light was best. She turned a few pages, but her gaze was caught by a motion beyond the garden. A rider! Her heart thumped wildly as she watched him. Was it Jacob?

Instantly, she forced her gaze to the book. She rubbed the bridge of her nose as pain throbbed across her forehead. Whether it was Jacob or not should have no bearing. She was being an air-dreamer to allow herself to fall in love with him. Doing that risked losing him completely because it was sure to tarnish their friendship.

"I hope I am not intruding," said a male voice from the doorway. When the man stepped forward, she realized it was the doctor.

"Mr. Hockbridge, do come in," she said, closing the book without having read a single word. "What may I do for you today?"

"I would like to speak with you a moment, if I may."

"Certainly." She did not ask the questions clamoring against her lips. Mr. Hockbridge had been with Father. Had he found something about her father's health he wished to discuss with her? "Shall I ring for tea?"

"That would be nice." He smiled. "I had very little to eat for breakfast, and I was forced to skip the midday meal. With the sickness in the village and surrounding area, I have been even busier than usual."

While waiting for the tea, they conversed about the ague and the weather. The hearty tea was delivered, and the subject changed to the upcoming Christmas service at the church, especially the children's choir. Mr. Hockbridge spoke of how many children he had tended to who were eager to feel good enough to participate on Christmas morning.

"It should be enthusiastic," Carrie said with a chuckle, "though I cannot guarantee they will sing the same words at the same time. Elisabeth told me that she postponed practices until more of the children are well enough to come."

"Only a few are confined to bed now, so you should feel free to hold practice whenever you and Mrs. Trelawney wish."

"I will let Elisabeth know. Thank you."

He nodded as he wolfed down a pair of roast beef sandwiches. Carrie tried to keep the conversation going so neither of them felt uncomfortable in the silence.

"Lady Caroline," the doctor said, interrupting her tale of Joy's first tooth, "I have something very important to speak to you about, something I discussed with your father before I came to see you."

"Is Father all right?"

Mr. Hockbridge smiled, but he was abruptly so tense the expression looked macabre. "The earl is fine. In fact, I would say he is doing better than he has for the past two years."

"I am happy to hear that."

"I hope you will be as happy to hear what I came to talk about with you." He straightened his shoulders. "My lady, the topic I spoke about with the earl was you."

"Me? Why would you need to discuss me? I am not ill."

"No, you most certainly are not. However, you are alone, and it is not a state the good Lord wishes for us. I have admired you from afar since my return to Porthlowen, and I have always counted your kindness—dare I say friendship?—among God's blessings to me. I would not want to ruin our friendship, but I can remain silent no longer. I am hoping my esteem is returned, and you will agree to let me court you."

"Court me?" Unsteady laughter scraped her throat, but she silenced it when she saw the truth on Mr. Hockbridge's face. He was serious in his far from romantic request.

"Your father has given me his blessing, if the situation is pleasing to you."

She stared at him, unable to speak. Maybe once, maybe before she had spent time with Jacob and felt her heart soar when he was near, she might have been willing to reconsider her stance on remarriage. Especially with someone like Mr. Hockbridge, who would like children but did not require an heir as a peer did. It would have been a logical, convenient arrangement where she would live close to her family, and neither of them would be alone and lonely.

But now she knew it was not enough not to be lonely. The words she had spoken in the solar burst from her memory. *I suspect there is a different sort of being alone if one marries someone they do not love.* She had been using that as an excuse to conceal her real reason for not planning to marry again, but the excuse was also the truth. She did not want a practical arrangement. She wanted what she had discovered with John. A deep and abiding love was a precious gift from God.

She wanted to be *in* love…as she was with Jacob. Accepting anything less would mean unhappiness for her and for Mr. Hockbridge.

"I am honored by your request, Mr. Hockbridge," she said as gently as she spoke to the children, "for I do hold you in the highest esteem. However, I must say no, because I do not intend to remarry."

"Ever?"

"Ever." Seeing him look so dismayed, she hurried to add, "I decided after John's death it would be for the best for me to remain at Cothaire."

"Leo."

"Excuse me?"

"My name is Leo. Can we consider ourselves good enough friends that you might use it?"

She realized she had forgotten what his given name was. Everyone addressed him and spoke of him as Mr. Hockbridge. When they were children, surely she must have known his name, though he was sent from Porthlowen to attend school at an early age.

Certainly allowing herself to call him by his first name would not be troublesome; then she knew she was fooling herself in an effort to spare his feelings. Her use of his name would suggest to others a connection between them that did not exist. It might make the situation easier for her, but looking at his face, she saw her saying yes to his request meant too much to him. He held on to the hope her agreement would be the first step toward her reconsidering his proposal.

"I am sorry, Mr. Hockbridge," she said, coming to her feet. As he leaped up, she added, "I am so very sorry."

"I will respect your wishes, my lady. Thank you for giving me a chance to express my feelings." He bowed his head toward her and took his leave without another word.

She sank back in her chair, knowing she had done the right thing, but feeling more alone than ever.

Staring at the page in front of him, Jacob could not comprehend a single word he tried to read. His mind jumped from one thought to the next too quickly to settle on a report of the new shaft being dug in a small mine to the west of the mining village. He had sat there for half the afternoon and made no progress.

A knock came on his office door, and he put the page aside gratefully as he called, "Come in."

Emery walked in and, glancing around at the stacks of paper and account books, whistled. "You need a secretary and an estate manager, brother."

"Interested in the position?"

"Possibly."

Jacob was shocked. He had intended his question to be a jest, but obviously Emery had not taken it that way.

Gesturing for his brother to clear a space on the settee, he waited until Emery was sitting before he spoke.

"Is handling the estate accounts something you truly want to do?" He felt obligated to add, "They were in a disastrous shape when I arrived, and they are not much better now. I cannot believe you would want to tackle the job."

"Go ahead. Ask me what you really are thinking."

"That was what I was thinking."

Emery shook his head. "We are brothers. You can be honest and say you are worried I will bankrupt this estate as I have the rest of the family."

"The thought never crossed my mind. I know I chided you for being a risk taker, but I have come to see in recent weeks we are not so different. You took a chance on your dream. No man should be faulted for that, even if it does not turn out as he hoped."

"It failed utterly, you mean." He bristled.

"Don't keep putting words in my mouth, Emery. We have always been forthright with each other. Something Father insisted on, and I understand why, now that I know why he and Uncle Maban were driven apart. If you want to take on the position of estate manager, I can think of nobody I would rather have working with me." He offered his brother his hand.

Emery lost his antagonistic pose and smiled as he shook Jacob's hand. "Nor can I imagine anyone else I would rather work for."

"Work *with*. This is the family's estate, and we are the last of a long line of Warricks who are responsible for it."

"I cannot wait to tell Helen. She has been making hints about how much she would like to stay here instead of returning to our cramped cottage." Emery stood, then sat again. "I came here to tell you that Faye has left."

Jacob was unsure what to say, so he fell back on the hackneyed. "I am sorry she was unhappy here."

"She was miserable. Unlike the rest of us, she despised everything about Cornwall. The food, the people, the weather, even Warrick Hall. She would have endured it all—her words, not mine—if she became Lady Warrick. When she saw that was not going to happen, she packed this morning and left. Apparently, she plans to go to London after the new year to try to find a rich or a titled—or both—husband."

"I am not both. When you go through the accounts, you will see money is tight."

Emery chuckled. "If you had been rich as well as titled, I don't think she would have given up as easily."

"What a thing to say about your sister-in-law!"

"I didn't say it. Helen did."

Laughing with his brother, Jacob felt a great burden roll from his shoulders. It should have been flattering to have a lovely young woman eager for his attentions, but it had been nothing but annoying to deal with her moods.

"Beverly must be upset," he said, shoving his spectacles up his nose as he did so often.

"Surprisingly, no." Emery shook his head and grinned more widely. "Maybe she has decided she would rather be known as the mother-in-law to an earl's daughter than to have Faye join the peerage by marrying you."

"Or she realized I meant what I said when I told her I was not planning to marry any time soon."

"Does Lady Caroline know that?"

"Yes."

Emery's brows shot upward. "So how does she feel about you courting her when you don't intend to marry her?"

"I am not courting her." He did not regret their kiss, because the thought of it sent happiness resonating through him. However, he could not forget how distraught she had looked when she had turned on her heel and fled from his arms.

"You could have fooled me."

"Enough, Emery!"

His brother raised his hands in surrender as sarcasm seeped into his voice. "Yes, my lord."

"I didn't mean it that way."

"I know." Emery smiled as he stood and put one hand on Jacob's shoulder. "But you need to figure out what you do mean before you break another woman's heart."

After his brother left, closing the door to leave the room in silence, Jacob folded his hands and bowed his head over them. He did not want to break Carrie's heart. He had believed himself to be in love with Virginia, and that had ended in tragedy. He did not understand why he had agreed to let her drive, but he had. Something had happened, and the carriage crashed, leaving her dead. Could he have halted the events? There must have been a choice he could have made that would have prevented the accident.

But, no matter how deeply he searched his mind, he could not recall the series of events which had unfolded that night.

Dear God, help me overcome the loss that haunts

me so I can live the life You want for me. I cannot be-
lieve You wish me to remain mired in grief and guilt.
Show me the way.

How many times had he prayed those words in desperate yearning to be released from his pain? More
times than he could count.

While he waited for an answer, he must do what he
had avoided for too long.

When a footman came to announce Lord Warrick
wished to speak with Lady Caroline, Carrie was playing with Gil and Joy in the small parlor. She was unsettled by Mr. Hockbridge's request to court her so
soon after Jacob had kissed her...after *she* had kissed
him eagerly. Since yesterday, her life had spiraled out
of control. The only constant was the uncomplicated
love the two children offered her.

Why was being able to express her feelings so simple with these darling children and so perplexing otherwise?

"My friend Jacob!" Gil jumped to his feet and ran
to the door as Jacob walked into the room.

He must have, she noted, given his coat to a footman before coming to the small parlor. As a proper
gentleman should, and as a proper lady, she could not
comment on it.

Gil skipped beside Jacob as they came to where she
sat with Joy at her feet. Before she could say anything,
Gil pointed out the baby's new tooth. Joy opened her
mouth wide and giggled when Jacob complimented
her on such a beautiful tooth.

Only then did he look past the children to her. His
eyes were hooded, so she could not guess what he was

thinking. Was he upset she had fled from their kiss? Was he glad she had come to her senses and wanted to tell her that he had done the same? Thoughts, each one more ridiculous than the last, flew through her mind.

"May I?" he asked, motioning to the settee where she sat.

"If you wish…"

He perched on the very edge of the settee and leaned one elbow on the arm. She was not fooled by his careless pose, because his jaw was taut.

"Would it be possible to speak to you alone?" He looked at the children. "All alone?"

She nodded and rang the bell on the table beside her. In only a few minutes, Irene came to take Gil and Joy to the nursery. Neither child wanted to leave, but Jacob reassured them he would come to see them before he left Cothaire.

"If possible," she heard him add under his breath as the children and the nursery maid left.

Her brows lowered in a frown as she noted how tense he was. Something was horribly wrong. Had he heard of Mr. Hockbridge coming to Cothaire to ask to court her? Nonsense. If someone had listened in on the private conversation, gossip could not move that fast even through Porthlowen. Mr. Hockbridge was the cause of her being unsettled, but what was distressing Jacob?

Had he come to apologize for kissing her? She hoped not, because she did not want to believe he thought the wondrous kiss was an error. It should not have happened; yet, she treasured the memory of those moments in his arms.

He cleared his throat once, then twice. Looking at

his hands splayed on his knees as if they were the most interesting things he had ever seen, he said, "I am not sure where to begin, Carrie."

"Wherever you wish."

"That is the problem. I'm not sure how I wish to put this."

"Be forthright, as you always are."

He glanced at her swiftly, then away. "As you wish. You know, Carrie, how much I treasure our friendship. I would not want to do anything to damage what we have. Don't you agree?"

"Yes," she whispered. His words were almost identical to Mr. Hockbridge's. Did he intend to ask her, too, if he could court her? The answer had been simple with the doctor, but now her heart begged her to say yes while her common sense warned her nothing had changed. She must find the perfect words to tell him that she appreciated his request more than she could say, but she could not be the wife he needed.

The doctor had been hurt by her refusal for him to court her. She did not want to hurt Jacob, too.

"Even though I overstepped the bounds of propriety to kiss you," he went on, "I cannot say I will ever regret I did. Our kisses revealed so much to me about the state of my heart."

Her own beat harder, eager for him to say the words that had sent dread through her when the doctor had spoken them. The warnings from the prudent part of her mind were muffled by its powerful pulse.

Knowing what she risked, she said, "It opened my eyes to my feelings for you, too, Jacob."

"I am sorry to hear that."

"What?" She had not expected him to say that.

"Because I don't want you to wait for me to propose marriage to you when I cannot."

"Cannot?" The single word stuck in her throat. She had been certain that, beginning the conversation as Mr. Hockbridge had, he intended to make her the same offer. She had prepared herself to turn him down gently in an attempt to salvage their friendship. Shocked, she blurted out her first thought, "Did you ask Miss Bolton to marry you?"

"No, and you should know she decided to leave Warrick Hall to return home."

"She did? When?"

"Earlier today." He put a single finger to her lips to silence her next question. "Carrie, please, say no more."

Turning her face from his touch, though she longed to lean into it, she asked, "How can you ask that of me? So many times you have told me that you admire my curiosity. Now you are telling me to quell it."

"I don't want to hurt you."

"The truth cannot hurt me more than silence will."

He stood and walked to the far side of the room as if he could not bear to be close to her. "You are right. I have been trying to persuade myself I am protecting you by not speaking the truth, when I am clearly protecting myself from losing your esteem." He turned to look at her, his face long with misery. "I made a vow one horrible night I would never again ask a woman I cared about to be my wife, because I might make the same mistakes I did that night."

"The night you wrecked your carriage?"

"You know about it!" Shock heightened his voice. "How?"

"Mrs. Warrick mentioned you nearly died, and she said it was because your carriage crashed."

"So you understand, then, how my mistakes led to the tragic accident."

She came to her feet as she shook her head. "I don't understand, Jacob. Why do both you and your stepmother call it tragic?"

"Because my betrothed, Virginia Greene, died that night, and it was my fault. If I had made different decisions, she might be alive. I should have kept her safe. It was my place to protect her, and I did not."

Again, words failed her. His powerful pain was almost tangible, a living presence in the room that had opened a chasm between them she had no idea how to bridge.

Somehow, she managed to whisper, "But you said yourself it was an accident."

"I cannot remember, Carrie. So much that happened before it and afterwards is nothing but a blur. If my brother had not come when he did, I would be dead, too. However, I am certain of one thing. If I had been as cautious as I should have been when the roads were covered with ice, she would not have died that night. There must have been something I could have done to prevent the accident. Something to protect her."

His words hung in the air between them, widening the abyss until she felt she would have to shout for him to hear her across it. He must have sensed it, too, because he walked to her, then halted and recoiled as if he had run into an invisible wall.

"I am sorry," she said, wanting to reach out and take his hands. "No wonder you are obsessed with keeping the miners safe."

"I like to think I would have had compassion no matter—" He turned to look at the glass doors to the garden. "Listen!"

"I don't hear anything."

"Exactly! The beam engine has stopped again. I must—"

This time, he was interrupted by the hallway door crashing against the wall. Baricoat burst in, his eyes wide as they scanned the room.

"Lord Warrick!" the normally placid butler shouted as she had never heard him do before. "Thank the good Lord you are here. You are needed at the main mine. There has been a cave-in!"

Chapter Fifteen

Carrie did not hesitate. An accident in the mines could turn deadly within seconds. Already the message had needed time to travel to Cothaire. "Baricoat, have Mrs. Ford make plenty of coffee and sandwiches. Get any medical supplies you can gather quickly, as well as blankets. Send every available footman to the mine to assist."

"I will." The butler ran out the door as quickly as he had entered.

She started to follow, but Jacob halted her by grasping her arm.

"Wait here," he said.

"I am not sitting at home while others are rescuing the men."

He grasped her by the shoulders. "Carrie, please. I don't want you in danger."

"I won't be." She put her hands over his and gazed deep into his eyes where the thick walls of pain had concealed so much. "But those families need someone beside them to bolster their hope."

"There may not be any hope."

"There is always hope. I believe you can find a way to rescue the men in the mine."

His hand cupped her cheek as he breathed her name. "Such faith you have in me, even after what I just told you."

"What you just told me could not change how I feel about you. Nothing could." She gave him a push toward the door. "Go," she urged. "We will follow you."

Everyone in the mining village, save for the men who were in the shafts, was gathered around the mine entrance when Carrie drew Marmalade to a stop by the engine house. She looked from the fearful faces to the great wooden beam that hung motionless above her head.

She slid out of the saddle and tied her horse's reins to the rail on the steps. Hearing the rattle of the wagon from Cothaire, she motioned for the driver to bring the load of food and supplies to where she stood.

Some of the villagers turned to watch the wagon arrive. She waved to them to help unload it. She began lifting out the few baskets of food the kitchen had been able to prepare before the wagon left. More food and supplies would follow. As she worked, her eyes searched the crowd by the mine entrance.

Where was Jacob? She had thought he would be in the very center, working out a plan to rescue those underground. Rushing up the steps, she threw open the door of the engine house.

"Jacob?" she called. "Pym?"

Neither man answered. Where were they? She had assumed Pym would be working on the beam engine, even if Jacob was busy elsewhere.

What was going on?

"Lady Caroline?" asked a deep voice from behind her.

She whirled to Yelland, the mine captain. "Where are they? Lord Warrick and Pym?"

"I don't know where Pym is, but Lord Warrick has gone into the mine to bring up the men." Yelland's face was as white as the falling snow. "I warned him not to go, but he would not be halted."

Her knees threatened to buckle beneath her, but she locked them in place. Jacob was determined no one else he was responsible for would be killed. So determined he was ready to turn his back on love to punish himself for what he believed were his mistakes. She should have known he would not remain outside the mine when miners were in danger.

She wanted to give chase, but she would be a liability in the mine. She had no choice but to wait.

"What happened?" she asked.

"As far as we know from the men who were closest to the cave-in, one of the supports failed, and the ceiling collapsed. At least a half dozen men are on the other side of the fallen rock." He glanced up at the beam and gulped. "If they are alive, they will drown as soon as water fills the shaft."

"Get the beam engine running!"

"I am not sure how."

"Then find Pym! Surely he did not go into the mine, too."

Yelland shook his head. "He is too much of a coward to step a toe in the mine. That is why he works here."

"Find him!" She pushed past him and hurried to where women were waiting by the wagon. Without greeting them, she said, "Open the baskets and put the food out."

"Where would you like it, my lady?" asked one woman whose face was stained with salt from her tears.

"Do you have tables you can bring outside?"

When heads nodded, she said, "Bring them. We can set up the food on them. That way, when someone is hungry, they can eat while watching the rescue."

"If there is one," murmured one of the women.

Carrie restrained herself from scolding the woman when her words brought muffled sobs from others. Tears seared her eyes, too, but she was not ready to give up hope. Not yet, when her prayers had a chance to be answered.

Climbing into the wagon, she handed out the baskets she could not reach from the ground. The footmen carried other supplies closer to the mine entrance so they would be there when the first men were brought out. Around her, she heard soft fragments of prayers. When Raymond arrived, and she knew he would come as soon as he heard of the cave-in, he would comfort the frightened families.

"...more orphans," one woman said as she bowed her head by the wagon. "God, you know we don't need more orphans."

Another woman put an arm around the woman's shoulder and said, "There is no confirmation anyone is dead. The mines are in better shape than they were after the old baron gave up on them and us. Things have changed. We won't need help from a pair of old prattling cats again now that we have Lord Warrick—"

"Who may not come out alive," groaned the first

woman. "He has done so much, and now he may be gone."

Carrie brushed tears from her eyes. Sending up another prayer for Jacob's safety along with the trapped men's and the other rescuers', she climbed out of the wagon. Another slowed behind the one from Cothaire.

For an irrational moment, she thought the silhouette of the driver belonged to Jacob and he was safe; then she realized the man holding the reins was his brother, Emery.

"Can your men unload these supplies, Lady Caroline?" he yelled as he jumped down. "I need to see where Jake wants help. Where is he?"

"In the mine."

The curse his brother snarled would have shocked her under other circumstances, but she understood his dismay.

"Why would he do something so chuckle-headed?" he demanded.

"He wants to save the miners."

"There are plenty of experienced miners to do that."

She sighed as she began unloading heavy baskets of food and handing them to the women. "But Jacob feels it is his duty to protect everyone as he could not protect Miss Greene in the carriage accident."

Mr. Warrick spat, "Absurd! The accident was not Jacob's fault."

"I agree. He said there was ice on the road."

He shook his head. "No! That is not what I mean." He dropped his face into his hands. "I should have told him the truth before, but I was afraid he would shut me out of his life as Uncle Maban did our father. Now he could die thinking he cost Miss Greene her life when it was my fault."

"Your fault?" She pressed a basket into another woman's hand, then looked at Mr. Warrick. "*You* caused the accident? But you did not get there until after Miss Greene was dead. Jacob told me that himself."

"Because he doesn't remember what happened." He raised his head, tears running down his face. "I was testing out a new team of horses I had borrowed from a breeder, and I wanted to see how fast they could go. I had no idea anyone else was on the road. When I came around the corner, my carriage clipped the rear wheel of his. The collision threw both vehicles. I was on the inside of the hill, so my carriage struck bushes and stones. Jacob and Miss Greene were on the outer edge, and their carriage careened over the hill. I can still hear the horrible sounds it made as it broke apart."

"He will blame himself for not reacting fast enough."

"He could not have done anything differently. Miss Greene had the reins." He took a shuddering breath before going on. "My lady, I know he has forgotten so much because of the injury he sustained to his skull. He does not remember Miss Greene insisted he offer her marriage. When he said he did not love her as a husband should a wife, she rushed away and got into his carriage. He gave chase because he feared she would hurt herself. He jumped in, but she refused to relinquish the reins." He sighed. "Several people witnessed it."

"Why didn't you tell Jacob that?"

He quaked with sobs before he said, "He believes

they were betrothed and that he was happy about it. Why take that good memory from him?"

"He needs to know the truth."

"I know, but I don't know if I am strong enough to tell him."

She put her hand on his arm. "You are Jacob's brother, and you were strong enough to come to him and admit you needed his help." When he looked up, astonished, she added, "He told me about your circumstances, but swore me to secrecy. Mr. Warrick, only a strong man can admit he is a failure and seek to remake his life."

"You are kind, but…"

"Once Jacob and the other men are safe, let me take you to my brother. Raymond is an expert on seeking forgiveness and God's grace."

For a moment, he did nothing; then he nodded.

Carrie did not hear him if he spoke further, because she saw a familiar form walking toward them.

"Pym!" she cried as she ran to Jacob's assistant. When she reached him, she said, "You must get the beam engine started."

"I thought Lord Warrick would have by now when the men in the mine—"

"He has gone to rescue them! He must have assumed you would get the pumps going while he brought the survivors up."

"Lord Warrick went into the mine?" Pym's face lost every bit of color. "Why would he do that? He could die."

"I know." She bit her lip to keep her sobs from escaping.

"If he dies, the mine will close." Pym looked as if he were going to be ill. "We will lose our jobs."

Before she could say it was silly to worry about a job when men needed to escape the mine, Pym ran into the building. The door slammed in his wake. She hoped he could get the engine running again. If he did not, every man in that mine, including Jacob, was doomed.

"There."

The man behind Jacob held the lantern higher. In front of them, the shaft ended in a death fall of stone. Men were tearing away the rocks, but slowly. He knew they could not go faster because moving the wrong rock could bring down more.

He coughed in the fetid air and stepped forward. Something crunched under his feet. A discarded pasty crust. He started to move through the narrow tunnel, then froze as a glitter caught the lantern's light.

He moaned. Water seeped between him and the trapped miners. If Pym did not get the steam engine pumping again soon, the men would drown, along with their rescuers. The climb up would take longer than the rate water was rising. Pym had made amazing repairs before. *Please, God, guide him to make another and save these men's lives.*

He went to work beside the miners, moving stones until his hands bled. Beneath his feet, water rose first over the soles of his boots, then over his toes. He tried to pay it no attention as he shifted rocks.

When the water reached his knees, he ordered the shorter men up the shaft. They soon would not be able to move in the deep water.

He fought the weight of the flood as he yanked another stone. Smaller stones tumbled, one striking his right foot. Pain burst though him, but he ignored it as light burst past the wall. He cheered with the miners beside him at the sight of a lantern being held up on the other side.

Agony sliced up his right leg as he stood on tiptoe to grasp the pair of hands stretching through the opening. He wobbled and struck the pile of stones, sending more pain from his knee along his leg, but he caught the hands and held on.

Around him, the miners pulled down more of the wall, releasing water. It rose faster and faster.

Jacob pulled the man through as soon as the opening was large enough. The miners beside him seized other hands and let the water's current help them pull the men out. He gripped another pair of hands as men began scrambling away from the rising torrent. Behind him, shouts came to get out while it was still possible.

"I am the last one, my lord," gasped a man as Jacob dragged him over the stones and into the now waist-deep water.

"Are you sure?"

"Aye. There were six of us, and we drew lots to see who would go first if someone freed us. I was number six."

"Go!" He pushed the man ahead of him and half swam toward where the shaft rose.

The man ran. Jacob tried to as well, but his first step on his right foot sent him to his knees. He pushed his head above water and caught outcroppings on the side of the wall to pull himself forward. A second try told him that his right leg would not support him. He pushed his hands against the wall and tried hopping on his left foot up the tunnel.

Ahead of him, sounds faded. He could not keep up with the fleeing miners. Light remained strong, and he saw a lantern someone had left behind to mark the way. He picked it up. As he tried to straighten, he wobbled and struck the wall. Dirt sprayed on him. An ominous rumble came from the tunnel.

He collapsed to the floor, putting his arms over his head. Trying to make himself as small as possible, he choked on the dirt flying through the air as rock and wood collapsed around him. Light vanished, and his thoughts faded. His last one was of Carrie, and how, no matter how he had tried, he could not protect her from a broken heart at his death.

"Forgive me," he whispered before darkness dropped around him.

Every inch of him hurt.

Jacob struggled to open his eyes, but he was unsure if he should. He did not want to see Virginia's broken form on the ground. So close, but too far away for him to touch.

Not looking would not change anything. He forced his eyes open and stared with incredulity at light blue eyes searching his face. Light blue? His brother's eyes were brown. It was supposed to be Emery leaning over him, urging him to hold on to his senses.

But it wasn't.

"Carrie," he whispered, wanting to believe his blurred vision. "Carrie, is it you?"

Something cool settled on his forehead, but her fingers were warm as they brushed his skin, pushing back his hair. "Hush. Lie still. You have a badly bruised foot and knee. Praise God nothing was broken."

"I am alive?"

She put her hand over his heart and smiled. "If this thump-thump-thump is any sign, I would say you are among the living."

It took almost all his strength, but he raised his own hand to place it over hers. Tears welled up in her eyes. "I thought I was going to die without ever telling you how sorry I am."

"You have nothing to be sorry for."

"I do, but…" He closed his eyes when the room began to spin around him. When he opened them again, Carrie still stood beside him. "How did I get out?"

"Yelland went to find you when the other men emerged and you didn't."

"Yelland risked his life to save me?"

"He insisted he go instead of the other men who volunteered."

"Who volunteered? I want to make sure I thank them."

She smiled gently as she handed him his spectacles. "They all did."

"All?"

"Every man except Pym, who managed to get the beam engine started before you drowned." She moved away from the bed.

For the first time, as he put on his spectacles, he realized he did not recognize where he was. The walls were covered in dark red silk to match the curtains on an elegant tester bed. Tall windows gave him a view of the gray sky and the snow falling from it.

Carrie put another cool cloth on his head. "Your

brother is working to get the shafts pumped out, and he agreed you should come to Cothaire because Mrs. Ford's stillroom has many remedies not available at Warrick Hall." She smiled gently. "You should rest."

He caught her hand. "Stay, Carrie. Stay and talk to me."

"About what?"

"Anything."

"I am not leaving." She set a chair by the bed and sat. "Shall we talk about the night Virginia Greene died?"

"But we already spoke of what happened."

"No, we spoke of what you *thought* happened." She explained what Emery had told her.

He was stunned that Virginia had demanded he propose. He was even more taken aback when Carrie shared the rest of what his brother had told her. Why had his brother waited so long to reveal the truth?

As if he had asked aloud, Carrie said, "Your brother did not want to chance repeating your father's and your uncle's mistake of letting bitterness come between them. He wanted to prevent you two from being driven apart for the rest of your lives."

"So it truly was an accident," he said softly.

"Yes. It has troubled your brother as much as it has you. Only when he thought you would die without knowing the truth, he broke his silence." She removed the cloth from his forehead and replaced it with another, easing the pain. "I suggested Mr. Warrick speak with Raymond because he wonders if you will be able to forgive him for the accident or his silence."

"Of course I forgive him. He did not mean for it to

happen. Why would he think I would withhold forgiveness from him?"

She folded his hand between hers. "Because he saw how you withheld it from yourself."

He could not argue with her when she was right. Since the accident, he had been furious with himself. He thanked God for learning the truth, and he knew he had more lessons to learn, including how to offer and receive forgiveness.

You know the way already. The way out of darkness is going toward light, toward love.

The voice was not his own, but it came from within his heart. God was using his heart to remind him of what he should know. For the first time, he believed—truly and deeply believed—he might escape the prison of sorrow where he had been incarcerated since the tragic night.

Go toward love.

That was advice he would gladly follow, but he had no chance as the door opened and an excited shout rang through the room and through his aching skull.

"Quietly, Gil," Carrie said as the little boy and the nursery maid came in with Joy. "Jacob is hurt, and he needs quiet." She took Joy from the maid, then looked at him. "The children chanced to see you being carried into the house, and they were frightened."

"Not my Gil." He pushed himself up to sit. The room whirled again, and he was glad to lean on the plump pillow Carrie put behind him after setting Joy on the rug by the bed. Making his voice light, he added, "My Gil is not scared of anything."

"Gil brave," announced the little boy, his thin chest jutting out.

"Ac-oob!" The baby tugged on the covers as she pulled herself to her feet.

Carrie picked her up so Joy could see him.

"Ac-oob!" She waved her hands at him.

"One kiss, Joy." Carrie slanted the little girl toward him.

He made a buzzing kiss on her cheek, and Joy giggled and repeated his name. He doubted he ever would tire of hearing her say it. Taking the baby, he set her on one side of him, then held his breath to keep from groaning as Gil bounced to sit on his other side.

"My lady?" came Baricoat's voice from the doorway. "What do you wish me to do with him?"

Jacob was about to ask who "he" was, but Carrie said, "Show Mr. Pym up. Tell him he cannot stay more than five minutes."

The butler hurried away to do as she wished.

"Pym is here?" Jacob asked.

"Yes. He refused to leave. He says he has to talk to you."

When Pym entered the room, he looked as out of place as a rabbit in a chicken coop. He stepped forward, then halted and whipped his cap off his head before bowing toward Carrie.

"Thank you, my lady," the short man said.

She held up her hand with her five fingers extended.

Pym gulped. "I came to tell you I am sorry, my lord. I never meant for anyone to get hurt."

"What are you talking about? Get to the point, man." He did not try to curb his impatience.

"Yes, my lord. I... That is, the troubles with the beam engine... I mean..." He took a deep breath, then said in a rush, "They are my fault. I would loosen a bolt or open a valve so it would stop running."

"But why, Pym?" he asked, too surprised to say more.

The man worried the brim of his cap and stared at his feet. "The old baron got angry with me when I asked for new equipment because the engine was not pumping out the deeper shafts. He told me to get out."

"My uncle dismissed you?"

"Yes, but then those men were killed, and he needed someone to watch over the beam engine, so he gave me back my position." He raised his head and met Jacob's eyes. "Then you came, my lord. You know as much about keeping the equipment running as I do. Maybe more, once you got the new steam engine."

"So," Carrie whispered, "you thought Lord Warrick would dismiss you as his uncle had."

"Aye, but I figured if he thought he needed me to keep the engine running, I would keep my position."

"No wonder you always knew what was wrong and could fix it fast." He frowned, then winced at the pain. "Why did you take so long to repair the engine when we almost had a riot because the miners grew so impatient?"

"That wasn't me. She broke on her own. Like today." He sighed. "You don't need to dismiss me, my lord. I will leave all quiet and like. I won't come back."

Jacob said, "That will not be necessary. Everyone makes mistakes, Pym. Sometimes we are blessed, and nobody else is hurt. Other times, we pay the price of suffering regret for the rest of our days."

"You mean I can stay?"

"As long as there are no more troubles with the engines than they cause by themselves."

Pym smiled more broadly than Jacob had ever seen, and he realized the man had been terrified of being dismissed the whole time Jacob had known him. He kept thanking Jacob until Carrie lifted her hand with her forefinger raised. Bobbing his head, he backed out of the room.

Jacob breathed a sigh of relief when the man left. His head rang from Pym's babble. "He never said much, and now he is chatting like a pair of old cats. I swear he could out-talk even the Misses Winwood."

"Boat!" said Gil with a smile.

"No," he began, "it is too cold to—"

"Oh, by the stars!" Carrie looked at him, her eyes wide.

"What is it?"

"I think I know who put the children in the boat."

"Boat," echoed Gil as Joy tried to copy the word.

He sat straighter, even though pain lashed through his head. "You do? How?"

"Old cats! I heard two women talking about orphans and how old cats came to their rescue. I didn't have a chance to think about it because your brother arrived then, but hearing you say it again…" She sank to the chair. "Gil often says 'boat' when he sees the Winwood sisters. I think the women by the mine were talking about them taking care of some orphans."

"But it makes no sense, Carrie. I have seen the Winwood sisters with the children. Why would anyone who loves those children put them in a boat and push them out to sea?"

"That is what we need to find out." She glanced at

the snow falling past the window. "It is too late tonight, but in the morning."

"On Christmas Eve?"

"What a Christmas gift it will be for the children's parents! They will be happy to have the children back. We…" Her voice broke when she could no longer pretend, even to herself, that she could bear the idea of returning Gil and Joy to their families.

She saw her pain reflected in Jacob's eyes. When he held out his arms, she went into them, leaning across his chest as she wept.

Chapter Sixteen

On Christmas Eve morning, the village of Porthlowen looked as if it were blanketed in a field of diamonds. Snow sparkled beneath the bright sunshine. The blacksmith was shoveling by his door, though no customers were out. Children frolicked, tossing snow at each other and laughing.

Carrie waved when the youngsters called greetings to her, but she was numb. Beside her, Jacob wore a grim expression. He walked with a decided limp, but he had refused to stay behind when she went to speak with Miss Hyacinth and Miss Ivy. She wanted to take his hand and remind him, as she had reminded herself, that not seeking the truth would not change anything. Last night, while sleep refused to come, she had tried not to pray she had been mistaken about the women's words and about Gil's reaction to the elderly twins. She must accept God's will.

Even so, her heart asked, *Why would You bring these children into our lives only to have them taken away again? I love them, and they are my sole chance to be a mother. To lose that...* She never allowed her thoughts to give voice to the despair within her.

She and Jacob had agreed that they would say nothing to anyone else until they had a chance to speak with the Winwood twins. Upsetting her family needlessly was something she wanted to avoid, especially on the day before Christmas. They had left Gil and Joy with Arthur and Maris, who were decorating the house, and they slipped out of Cothaire without anyone knowing where they were bound.

A short walk through the village brought them to the Winwood cottage. It was close to the road, and the short walkway had been shoveled. She wondered if one of the twins had cleared the snow away or if a neighbor came to help.

The cottage door opened before they reached it. Miss Hyacinth, as always dressed in some shade of purple, stood in the doorway. "Come in from the cold."

Jacob hung back so Carrie could climb the front steps first. As she entered the cottage, he followed in silence. It was a cozy space with room only for a pair of upholstered chairs and a table with two wooden chairs and a bench. A fire burned merrily on the hearth, warming the herbs hung overhead. The whole cottage smelled of Christmas. She guessed the cloths on the table hid fruitcakes and pies.

"So chilly out there this morning," Miss Ivy said from where she sat by the hearth. The blanket over her lap was dark green, and she wore a quilted shawl of the same color.

"The snow is early this year." Miss Hyacinth walked slowly to where her sister sat. She motioned for Carrie and Jacob to join them by the fire.

"Too early by far," concurred her sister.

"You seem to be warm here," Carrie said.

"Warm enough," Miss Hyacinth answered.

"Our bedrooms are on the other side of the fireplace, so they stay comfortable."

"Mornings the floors are cold, though."

"I knit you those thick socks, sister. You should wear them."

Miss Hyacinth shook her head. "The wool makes me itch."

"It is in your imagination. The socks I knitted are soft enough for a newborn baby's skin. You don't want to wear them."

"If you want me to wear the socks, I can show you the rash."

Before Miss Ivy could defend her socks further, Carrie said, "We are sorry to call without an invitation."

"You are always welcome, my lady," Miss Hyacinth said with an annoyed look at her sister.

"And you, too, my lord." Miss Ivy shot back a frown as vexed as her sister. "It is always pleasant to have company."

"Most especially at this special time of year. Please, sit."

"Yes, sit." Miss Ivy chuckled. "I am straining my old neck peering up at you."

Carrie hesitated, then sat facing the twins. Jacob put his hand on the chair, and she hoped he was not dizzy after the walk from Cothaire.

"We are here about the children," she said.

"Those dear babes," cooed Miss Hyacinth.

Carrie did not give Miss Ivy a chance to speak.

"You should know Lord Warrick and I know the truth about your participation in bringing the children to Porthlowen."

It was a bold comment. If the twins denied her words or were confused by them, she would have to apologize and begin the search for the truth again.

But she realized her intuition was right when Miss Ivy began to weep, and her sister put a consoling arm around her shoulders. Carrie wished she could retract her words and say them again more gently, but the secret had lasted long enough. Somewhere, families must be grieving for their missing children. No matter how much it broke her heart, she had to think of the children. They belonged with their families.

"We intended only to help," Miss Hyacinth said.

"Help. The children…and…the families." Miss Ivy's voice broke on each word.

The story tumbled out of the twins in their usual manner of speaking. Miss Hyacinth would share some information, and then Miss Ivy would confirm it as she added a bit more.

Carrie listened without halting them as the elderly sisters spoke of the many children in the villages around Porthlowen who had lost their parents in the mines or at sea. She imagined Gil's grief if Jacob had perished in the mine. How would she have offered comfort to a child who could not understand why his friend had vanished from his life with no further explanation than he had died? Those words would mean nothing to a child Gil's age.

"The worst," Miss Hyacinth said, "is when a parent is transported."

"Sent away forever," added Miss Ivy.

"We know about such circumstances too well," Carrie said with a shudder as she recalled how that fate had nearly come to one of her sisters-in-law. "Sending parents to the far side of the world as a punishment for a crime and leaving their children here to try to survive alone solves nothing. The children often have no choice but to break the law themselves in order to get food and shelter."

Jacob spoke for the first time. "Is that what happened with the children's parents?"

"Possibly," Miss Hyacinth answered.

"We don't know for sure." Miss Ivy sighed. "The families who sought help could not care for six small children who had been left with them."

"We agreed to help, but found the children were too much for my sister and me to handle. That was when we decided to find them homes with people who would love them."

"Actually it was Peggy who had the idea of the boat."

"Peggy Smith from the village shop?" Carrie asked.

"A good girl," Miss Hyacinth said with a smile.

"An intelligent girl," Miss Ivy concurred.

"Very intelligent. She suggested we put the children in the boat, and she would push it out by the rocks. She released her hold on the boat only when she noticed Captain Nesbitt looking in its direction. If he had not come to get the children, she would have pulled the boat in and waited for someone else."

Carrie thought of how Susanna's husband and his first mate had rushed from their ship to bring the children to shore before the boat could capsize. Apparently the children had never been in any real danger. That thought soothed her, because she had been distressed at how the Winwood twins had imperiled the youngsters in their attempt to find them new homes.

"But why didn't you come to us?" she asked.

"We guessed you would want to find the children's families," Miss Hyacinth said. "They asked us to write the note we attached to the baby's shirt, because they hoped the children would escape from the horrible lives they had under the previous Lord Warrick."

"We mean no insult to your family, my lord," Miss Ivy hastily amended.

"You have made the miners' lives better."

"And safer. No one's died since you came to oversee the mines."

"And be a hero." Miss Ivy smiled as broadly as if she had suggested Jacob rescue the miners herself.

Jacob asked quietly, "Can you ladies get in touch with the families again?"

"If you wish us to." Miss Hyacinth glanced at her sister.

"Yes, if you wish, my lord, we can contact the families who put the children into our care," Miss Ivy said.

"Are you certain that is what you wish to do?" her sister asked. "Your family and the children have become very attached to each other."

"Very attached. The children have thrived with you and your siblings."

"Another separation will be painful for them."

"For them and for you."

"But their families must love them, too," Carrie jumped in when Miss Hyacinth drew in a deep breath to keep the conversation going with her sister, allowing no one else a chance to speak. Even though her heart longed to agree with the twins, she could not stop thinking about the desperation that had compelled families to seek help.

Miss Ivy rose and went into the bedroom. A few minutes later, she returned with a piece of paper. She gave it to Carrie.

Glancing at it, she handed the page to Jacob and watched his eyes widen. Like her, he must have recognized two of the names on the page as residents in the mining village.

"May we keep this?" she asked.

"Yes," said the twins at the same time, startling themselves as much as they did Carrie.

"Will you call the constable?" Miss Hyacinth asked in a choked whisper. For once, her sister remained mute.

"Why would we need to do that?" asked Carrie. "From what you have told us, the children never were in any real danger. You and Peggy were nearby until the children were brought ashore."

Thick tears rolled down Miss Ivy's face as her sister said, "All we wanted was for the children to be cared for and loved as part of a real family. We are too old to rear them, and Peggy is too young."

"Seeing you happy was additional blessing, my lady," Miss Ivy added.

"We saw how sad you looked around other families' babies."

"So sad, and you should be happy."

Carrie took each twin by the hand and squeezed their fingers gently. "I know your intentions were good. The happiness you have brought to my family—"

"We meant seeing *you* happy, Lady Caroline, was a special blessing. For almost six years now, you have thought only of doing your duty for others." Miss Hyacinth dabbed at her eyes with a handkerchief.

"Now you are smiling again." Miss Ivy took the handkerchief from her sister and wiped away her own tears.

"What will you do now?" asked Miss Hyacinth.

She stood. "First, I need to share this with my brothers and sister and their spouses, as well as with Father. Once we have contacted the people who brought you the children, we will arrange to meet with them."

"At Christmas?" asked Miss Ivy.

"Today, if possible." She looked at the list in her hand. "Their families will want them home for Christmas."

She thanked the sisters and said the Winwood twins would be the first to know what happened after the Trelawneys spoke with the children's families. She did not intend to bring the news herself, because even the thought of the children leaving with their families made her heart sore. She hoped she would be able to do what she must and give Gil and Joy back.

The Trelawney family had come together in the small parlor. The earl sat with his swollen foot propped on the settee where little hands could not touch it.

Jacob stood to one side not far from the doors opening into the garden. Cold crept through every crevice around the glass, but he did not move closer to the hearth. He was not quite sure if he should be part of the conversation with the distraught Trelawney family.

The parson's wife was sobbing softly as she cradled Toby against her, and Susanna had tears floating in her eyes. One escaped, and she wiped it away before it could drip on Lucy or Molly, who sat on either side of her. Maris's face was as pale as the snowflakes drifting by the window, and she had Bertie perched on her lap. Arthur, the parson, Susanna's husband, Captain Drake Nesbitt, and the earl wore identical, blank expressions.

And Carrie… His heart broke anew each time he looked in her direction. She pressed her cheek to Joy's soft hair as she let Gil stand on the chair beside her, his face against her shoulder. Carrie's pain was so searing, she was unable to cry. Every bit of her anguish filled him, as well. He longed to bring her into his arms and hold her until the grief was gone, no matter how many eternities it took.

"The answer is obvious," said the earl, shifting so he could look at each of his children. "The youngsters must be returned to their families as soon as possible."

Elisabeth wept harder, and Susanna could no longer restrain her tears. When one of the twins—he thought it was Lucy—reached up to brush away a single teardrop from Susanna's face, he felt as if someone had reached into his chest and ripped out his heart.

"Don't be sad, Susu," the other twin said. "No ouchie soon. Kiss and make it better?"

He saw tears rise in the other men's eyes as his own tears burned in his throat. Molly's innocent concern for Susanna almost undid him. The children had been torn away from their families once already. To do so a second time, when they loved this family so deeply, seemed beyond cruel.

"I will arrange the meeting," Arthur said quietly. "If the families are in the mining village, they should be able to come here and return home before dark."

Jacob shook his head and stepped out of the shadows. "Let me. They live on my estate, and I have come to know many of the miners and their families. I may be an outsider, but, forgive me for saying this, they are more likely to heed me than someone from beyond Warrick Hall." He looked toward Carrie.

For a moment, he thought she was going to keep hiding her face against Joy's hair; then she raised her head so her gaze met his. He wanted to look away from her pain, even as he ached to draw her into his arms and hold her, hoping his embrace would say what words could not. How could he explain he wished he could be as brave as she was, setting aside her own feelings to do what was best for the children?

"Thank you, Warrick." Arthur rubbed his hands together as if he did not know what to do with them. "I know it is Christmas Eve, but delaying will not ease what is to come. We can hold the meeting—"

"At the church." The parson looked around the room, catching each of his siblings' eyes before moving on to the next. "Meeting here or at Warrick Hall could make the children's families uneasy. Going to the village up by the mines will draw unwanted attention. God's house, where all are equal in His eyes, is the best place to meet. Agreed?"

Each family member nodded, and Jacob guessed their throats were as clogged as his.

As he was about to excuse himself to go to the mining village, the parson said, "Let us pray upon the words written in Psalms 62. 'In God is my salvation and my glory: the rock of my strength, and my refuge, is in God. Trust in Him at all times; ye people, pour out your heart before Him: God is a refuge for us.' He is here for us in the joy of having these children in our lives. He is here to hold us up when they return to their families."

"Amen," Jacob said, along with the others. When he turned to leave to contact the mining families, he glanced once more at Carrie and the children. He wanted the image of them together to last him for the rest of his life, because he knew how unlikely it would be that they would be together like that ever again.

"See Jacob?" asked Gil, rocking from one foot to the other in excitement.

"Yes." Carrie forced her smile to stay steady. Only now did she realize how she had hoped the meeting with the children's families would have to be postponed until after the holidays. Even though there was no good time for it, she wished she could have had one Yuletide with Gil and Joy. "And the other children will be at church, too. Lucy and Molly and Bertie and Toby."

"And Gil and Joy."

She nodded, bending to check Joy's bonnet once more, so Gil did not see the tears swarming in her eyes. Blinking rapidly to keep them from falling, she straightened and held her hand out to the little boy.

"Gil have chocolate today? No tea. Chocolate."

"Let's wait and see." She would not make promises she knew she would not be able to keep.

As she walked out of the house into the gray afternoon under the leaden sky, an unfamiliar carriage was parked in front of the house. She gasped when the door opened, and Jacob stepped out with only a hint of a limp. He must have stopped at Warrick Hall on his way back from the mines.

"May I escort you?" he asked as he pushed his spectacles up in the motion she found so endearing.

"In a carriage?"

"It is a beginning, because, as you can see, I am not driving it. I don't know how long it will take before I can do so, but I am going to try. Baby steps." He held out his hand. "May I, my lady?"

"Thank you." She took his hand and let him hand her in. When their eyes were level, she almost leaned in to kiss his cheek. She did not. She had been spared from discouraging his courtship once. She must not give him any suggestion now that she was interested in more than being friends.

As soon as the children sat beside her and Jacob across from her, the carriage lurched into motion. Gil kept up a steady chatter about having hot chocolate, so neither she nor Jacob had to make stilted conversation.

The trip to the church was too short. It seemed as if they had barely started when the carriage slowed in front of the lych-gate. After helping them all out into the snow which was beginning to fall, Jacob told the coachee to seek shelter in the church's porch, if he wished.

Jacob opened the gate and followed them into the churchyard. He offered her his arm, and she took it. She held Joy while Gil ran around to Jacob's other side and grasped his hand.

The little boy giggled. "Snow tickles."

"Try this." Jacob tilted his head back, opening his mouth. "See if you can catch a raspberry-flavored one on your tongue."

Gil ran around the churchyard with his mouth open.

"Should I have told him the truth?" Carrie asked.

Jacob put his hand over hers on his sleeve. Patting it, he asked, "What would you have told him?"

"That he is about to see his family."

"People he no longer even talks about." He ran his gloved fingers along her cheek. "Why not let him have these moments of happiness without having to worry about what his future holds?"

She looked through the church windows to see a handful of people gathered in one corner of the church while her family stood near the pulpit. She recognized a few of the people because they had attended services at the Porthlowen church. In fact, one had brought several youngsters to join the Christmas pageant choir. Now they had come to reclaim her sweet children.

"I don't know *if* I can do this," she whispered.

"You can." Jacob squeezed her hand again.

"You sound so sure."

"I am. Remember you are not alone."

She sighed. "I know. My brothers and sister and their spouses are here."

"And me, Carrie. Don't forget that."

"I haven't." She leaned her head against his shoulder. "Thank you, Jacob. I know you probably would prefer to be anywhere else on Christmas Eve."

"I wish I could spare you this pain."

"Thank you, but I took the children into my heart knowing full well this day was sure to come. I keep reminding myself next summer we will be welcoming Raymond and Elisabeth's baby into our family. God surely will bless my sister and Arthur with children of their own, as well." *But not me.*

No, she would not lament about things that could

not change. She would pray for things that might yet change. Like Gil and Joy being able to stay with her.

Holding her head high, she called to Gil. He ran to them, and together they walked into the church. She nodded to the families in the corner before joining her family.

Raymond said, "Now that everyone is here, shall we begin? Why doesn't everyone sit?"

As they obeyed, no one spoke. Not even the children, who must have sensed something extraordinary was happening.

Arthur stepped forward. He was no longer the naughty little brother who had once driven her to distraction. Now he was a married man and the heir to the family's title. As he stood there, his gaze moving from one person to the next, he looked every inch a future earl.

"It is good of you to come on such short notice," he said, "and on Christmas Eve, too. We are pleased to meet the families of these children, so they can be reunited with you. If we had known you were their families, we would have returned them to you long ago. As it is—"

A man stood. "Begging your pardon, my lord, but we want to make something clear right from the beginning. We are not the children's families."

Carrie glanced at Jacob, who was frowning as he said, "But your name was on the list we were given by the Winwood sisters."

"Aye. That is what you said when you called us to this meeting, my lord, but we had no idea you wanted to give the children back."

"You don't want them?" Carrie asked as she saw hope flare in her siblings' eyes.

"They aren't ours to begin with." The man motioned to another fellow sitting beside him. "Tell them, Ike."

The man named Ike stood, and Carrie gasped. He was one of the miners Jacob had rescued from the flooding shaft.

"Begging your pardon, my lords, but what he is saying is the truth. The children were left with us after their parents died. They are not our kin. We took care of them as we could, but extra mouths are hard to feed when food is so dear. You pay us fair for tutwork, Lord Warrick, but with both the crops and the fish failing, food has gotten very expensive. My wife does some cleaning for the Winwood twins, and she mentioned the children. They offered to help." He paused, then hurried on, "If they are a burden, we will take them, and make sure they don't starve."

"No!" cried Carrie, jumping to her feet. "I can speak for my brothers and sister and their spouses. They are no burden. We love the children."

As her siblings started to echo her assertion, Jacob raised his hands and called for silence. "Am I hearing what I think I am hearing?" he asked. "The children may stay with the Trelawneys?"

"If they will have them…"

"Yes!" came seven voices at once.

The man named Ike grinned. "Sounds like it is settled." He shook Jacob's hand. "Happy Christmas to you, my lord."

"You have made it a happy Christmas for us."

Carrie stepped to one side as Raymond went to thank the families who had come to the meeting and to invite them to return for the church service and pageant in the morning. Arthur spoke with Jacob while her sister and sisters-in-law hugged their children and each other.

She waited for Raymond to finish, then said to the man named Ike, "I have one question about Gil and the baby. Are they brother and sister?"

"We think so." He gave her a kind smile. "They were left together at my brother's house, and Gil always called the babe, 'My baby.'"

"He still does."

"If you don't mind me saying so, my lady, I don't think it matters if they were born brother and sister. It appears to me that in your eyes and in God's, they now are."

She smiled as tears swarmed into her eyes. What Ike said was true. She and the children had become a family, and it no longer mattered how that family had come together. If only she could count Jacob as part of her family, too...

"Chocolate for tea?" asked Gil as he grinned up at her.

"Yes," she said, bending to embrace him. "Yes, we will have hot chocolate for tea today, and we will celebrate how good God is."

The church emptied quickly because the mining families were eager to return to celebrate the Yule with their loved ones. Raymond and Elisabeth stayed behind to make sure the lamps were extinguished.

Carrie matched Jacob's steps. "You and Arthur seemed to be having a serious conversation."

"Ah, here comes your curiosity again." He chuckled. "We are hoping to arrange some sort of trading agreement to make sure the families in Porthlowen and on my estate have the food and other items they need. It will take some time to iron out the details, but we agree both estates and their inhabitants would benefit from such a plan."

"That is wonderful."

"Not as wonderful as you are." He paused and faced her, letting Joy lean forward to chew on his greatcoat's lapel. "Your courage at risking losing the children forever shows me that I have to be as brave if I dare hope you might someday fall in love with me."

"I won't fall in love with you someday, Jacob."

"You won't?" He stared at her in astonishment.

She smiled, pushing his spectacles up his nose. "You silly man, I can't fall in love with you someday, because I love you now. I will love you for every day of my life. I thought you knew that."

"I wanted to believe you did, but I have learned what I believe to be true may not be. I need proof."

"Will this do?" Putting her hand on his face, she brought his mouth to hers.

Even with Joy in her arms and Gil dancing around them, the kiss was sweet and warm and was everything she could have wanted. When he drew back, she murmured a protest. She did not want their kiss to end so quickly.

He dropped to one knee, then grimaced and switched from his right knee to his left. Taking her hands, he said, "Marry me."

She shook her head. "I can't."

"What do you mean? You said you love me."

"I do love you, but I cannot marry you. I cannot be the wife you need."

"Let me be the judge of that."

"You don't understand, Jacob."

He stood. "Then help me understand."

She stared at his lips as she recounted the pain which had troubled her for years. She left nothing out, not her disappointment, not her feeling of failure, not her grief when she had no part of her husband after he died so far away at sea. When she finished, she turned to walk away.

He grasped her by the shoulders. When she refused to face him, he released her and stepped in front of her. "I am sorry for what you have gone through, Carrie, and I am even more in awe of what you risked tonight, but nothing you said has changed my mind. I want to marry you."

"But I cannot give you a child."

"I know. Of course, it would be wonderful to have a child born of our love, but would it be any more wonderful than having Gil and Joy in our lives? I could not love any child more than I love them."

"But Gil cannot be your heir. You are Lord Warrick, and you need an heir."

"I have one. My brother." He sighed. "Emery has made poor decisions in the past, but he is beginning to take responsibility for his mistakes. He already has offered to help with the estate. When it is his turn to be Lord Warrick, he will be ready. I was a teacher, and I have been a student. I should be able to guide him as you guided me in my lessons." He gave her a lopsided smile. "Will you say yes to being my wife without me getting on my knee again?"

"Ouchie!" Gil announced.

"Yes, ouchie." She laced her fingers through his as

they stood face-to-face with the children who were now forever theirs. "And, yes, Jacob, I want to be your wife."

This time when he kissed her, there was nothing quick about it.

Epilogue

Carrie heard excited voices as she and Jacob approached the Trelawney family's favorite parlor at Cothaire. She paused in the doorway and drank in the wondrous sight.

The fire on the hearth flickered on the faces gathered there. In the very center of the family, Carrie's father sat with three children balanced on his two knees. The twins, Lucy and Molly, straddled one knee as if atop a pony. On the earl's other one, Toby perched proudly. Bertie sat on the floor at the foot of the man he called "Grandfather." He held a block out to Ada, who then offered it to her mother.

Elisabeth took it and smiled. "Very pretty." She handed it to her daughter who had inherited her ruddy hair color. "Like you, pumpkin." She was rewarded with a big grin.

Susanna sat with her husband, Drake, each of them trying to keep a naughty two-year-old boy from getting down and stealing the blocks. What a surprise it had been when the Nesbitt household was blessed with another set of twins! Tristan's and Marcus's big sisters helped them think of mischief, even though, as Carrie had seen, they did not need much assistance. Her brother stood behind his wife's chair. Maris was growing round with their child. Since the war with France had ended, both Arthur and his wife had seemed more at ease. The family understood why when he admitted that he had served as a courier for a spy network that stretched from the Continent to Whitehall. So many of Carrie's questions about the odd hours her brother had kept were answered with that explanation. His journeys now were solely for estate business.

A puff of cold air made the fire flicker when Carrie and Jacob entered the parlor, followed by Gil and Joy. Everyone greeted everyone else at once. Calls of "Happy Christmas" echoed through the room. Gil's voice rose over everyone else's as he bragged about having his first tooth loose.

"Let me tell you. We have learned it is much easier when those teeth are coming out than coming in," Jacob said as he patted his son on the head.

"Enough!" said the earl with mock sternness. "I have waited long enough." He held out his hands. "Where's my present?"

Carrie leaned forward and drew aside the blanket on the bundle she carried to reveal tiny lips tasting the air. While Jacob gave her the special smile he saved for her, she placed the baby in her father's arms.

"Here he is. Reginald Maurice Warrick." She let her family admire its newest addition. She remained in awe of the blessing she and Jacob had received. Both of them had been astonished when she discovered she was pregnant. Astonished and filled with elation.

"What a handsome lad," the earl said.

"He gets his good looks from his mother." Jacob winked at her, and she felt her heart melt as it had the very first time he had gazed into her eyes.

Gil sidled over to stand by her father's chair. Standing on tiptoe, he gazed with love at his brother's face. He raised his eyes, looked around at everyone there, and said in his most solemn tone, "My baby!"

Everyone laughed, and Carrie put her arms around Jacob as he held her close. He pulled her over to stand beneath some mistletoe by the garden doors. When he bent to give her a kiss, she halted him and slid his spectacles up his nose. Their laughter flowed together as their lips met in joy.

* * * * *

Dear Reader,

Thanks for selecting the final book in the Matchmaking Babies trilogy. I wanted to explore what happens when we try to be something or someone we aren't in the hopes of living up to others' expectations. Both Jacob and Caroline needed to learn that it's okay to be yourself and seek what makes you happy, but they stumbled along the way. They had to learn to depend on each other and trust themselves to be the people they were meant to be. Those struggles as they fell in love made the characters more interesting to me…and I hope to you.

As always, feel free to contact me by stopping in at www.joannbrownbooks.com. And look for my next book, *Amish Homecoming*, the first book in the Amish Hearts series, next month from Love Inspired.

Wishing you many blessings,
Jo Ann Brown

INSTANT FRONTIER FAMILY
Frontier Bachelors
by Regina Scott

Maddie O'Rourke is in for a surprise when handsome Michael Haggerty replaces the woman she hired to escort her orphaned siblings to Seattle—and insists on helping her care for the children he adores.

THE BOUNTY HUNTER'S REDEMPTION
by Janet Dean

When bounty hunter Nate Sergeant shows up and claims her shop belongs to his sister, widowed seamstress Carly Richards never expects a newfound love—or a father figure for her son.

THE TEXAS RANGER'S SECRET
by DeWanna Pace

Advice columnist Willow McMurtry needs to learn to shoot, ride and lasso for her fictional persona, and undercover Texas Ranger Gage Newcomb agrees to teach her. But as the cowboy lessons draw them closer, will they trust each other with their secrets?

THE BABY BARTER
by Patty Smith Hall

With their hearts set on adopting the same baby, can sheriff Mack Worthington and army nurse Thea Miller agree to a marriage of convenience to give the little girl both a mommy and a daddy?

LIHCNM1215

REQUEST YOUR FREE BOOKS!

2 FREE INSPIRATIONAL NOVELS
PLUS 2 FREE MYSTERY GIFTS

Love Inspired HISTORICAL

SPECIAL EXCERPT FROM

Love Inspired HISTORICAL

Maddie O'Rourke is in for a surprise when handsome Michael Haggerty replaces the woman she hired to escort her orphaned siblings to Seattle—and insists on helping her care for the children he adores.

Read on for a sneak preview of
INSTANT FRONTIER FAMILY by **Regina Scott**,
available in January 2016 from Love Inspired Historical!

The children streamed past her into the school.

Maddie heaved a sigh.

Michael put a hand on her shoulder. "They'll be fine."

"They will," she said with conviction. By the height of her head, Michael thought one part of her burden had lifted. For some reason, so did his.

Thank You, Lord. The Good Word says You've a soft spot for widows and orphans. I know You'll watch over Ciara and Aiden today, and Maddie, too. Show me how I fit into this new picture You're painting.

"I'll keep looking for employment today," he told Maddie as they walked back to the bakery. "And I'll be working at Kelloggs' tonight. With the robbery yesterday, I hate to ask you to leave the door unlocked."

"I'll likely be up anyway," she said.

Most likely she would, because he had come to Seattle instead of the woman who was to help her. He still wondered how she could keep up this pace.

You could stay here, work beside her.

As soon as the thought entered his mind he dismissed it. She'd made it plain she saw his help as interference. Besides, though his friend Patrick might tease him about being a laundress, Michael felt as if he was meant for something more than hard, unthinking work. Maddie baked; the results of her work fed people, satisfied a need. She made a difference in people's lives whether she knew it or not. That was what he wanted for himself. There had to be work in Seattle that applied.

Yet something told him he'd already found the work most important to him—making Maddie, Ciara and Aiden his family.

Don't miss
INSTANT FRONTIER FAMILY
by Regina Scott,
available January 2016 wherever
Love Inspired® Historical books and ebooks are sold.